The *Soprano*

Hazel Barker

The Soprano
© Hazel Barker 2023

Published by Armour Books
P. O. Box 492, Corinda QLD 4075, Australia

Front cover image: Dragos Cojocari | iStock
Back cover images: photocreo | Creative Fabrica;
        Anatoly Maslennikov | Creative Market
Opera glasses icon: microvectorone | Creative Fabrica

Cover, interior design, & typeset by Beckon Creative

ISBN: 978-1-925380-67-5

A catalogue record for this
book is available from the
National Library of Australia

Note: Australian spelling and grammatical conventions are used throughout this book.

∼ Also by Hazel Barker ∼

Heaven Tempers the Wind: Story of a War Child
Armour Books, 2016

The Sides of Heaven
Armour Books, 2018

Opera, Orchids and Oz
Armour Books, 2022

The Chocolate Story: The Story of a Conchie
Rhiza Press, 2016

Count Your Blessings: Colin's Story
Armour Books, 2020

~ *Acknowledgements* ~

Sincere thanks to members of my writing groups,
Especially Paul Garrety, author, who beta-read my manuscript.

My thanks also to Redland Libraries for launching my books.

My heartfelt gratitude to my husband Colin,
who suggested I write about the singer.
Who took me to workshops and writers' meetings.
Who encouraged my writing life.

Finally, I wish to thank my publisher, Armour Books,
who discovered me
when I first entered the world of writing.

Contents

I have written this story
for all those who love classical music.
For those who love opera.
For my former fellow patrons of Opera Queensland.
For my husband,
who suggested I write the story of
a soprano's love of singing
that endures even after so many obstacles and hardships
along her path to fame.

~ Chapter 1 ~

Voyage to Paris

Hobart, Regatta Day, 1910

AT SIXTEEN, MAGGIE'S DREAMS WERE full of promise, but there was a price to pay. No longer did the laughter of last month's fundraising gala concert ring in her ears. No longer did joy fill her heart. No longer could she suppress her tears. She had never been apart from her family. A lump rose to her throat. She swallowed hard.

Tethered to the pier, the ship groaned and strained at its hawsers. Maggie's family and friends gathered on the dock around her. The time of departure approached.

'You take care, Maggie.' Her mother smiled through her tears. 'Don't forget what I've told you.'

Maggie nodded. She would never forget all the sermonising of these past few weeks. She flung her arms around her mother, then turned towards her father.

'May the Lord bless you, lass.'

Maggie hugged him, standing on tiptoe even in her high heels. 'I can't go, Father. How can I leave you and Mother?'

'This is a chance of a *lifetime*.' He unlaced her arms from his shoulders. '*The Maggie Gard Society* has made all arrangements for your study and accommodation. Mrs Hempseed will prepare you for the audition with Madame Marchesi. You will be an opera star and sing in *La Scala*.' He wiped the tears from her cheeks. 'Write often.'

Mrs Hempseed frowned. 'Come along, child.'

Maggie dried her eyes, hugged her mother and each of her sisters again, then followed her chaperone. 'Bye,' she whispered.

The wind carried her voice away and sent her brown wavy hair into disarray as if in consort with her mixed emotions. As she stepped on the gangway, her heart thudded.

Mrs Hempseed strode to the ship's railing on the main deck and handed Maggie a red roll of paper. 'Hold one end and throw this down to your family.'

One end held tight in her fingers, Maggie flung the fragile strip towards her sisters, and watched a gust of wind tear the streamer asunder. The last link with her family and her country swooped up like a kite.

A wave of sorrow swept over her as she recalled the time she'd flown a kite to comfort her youngest sister, Josie, who was ill and had been watching the kite from her window. A tightness gripped her chest.

Long after the crowd had merged into a distant speck, she remained on deck, trying to see her family. In the distance, a ferry caught her eye, reminding her of the time her father had taken his family on a boat trip up the Clarence River and played his harmonica while they all sang. He had always encouraged her love of singing. Her chin trembled.

Her thoughts turned to Monsignor Gilleran. She had nearly squealed with delight when he'd said, 'Miss Gard, we are sending you to Paris to further your musical studies.'

But now an increasing expanse of water separated her family from her.

'Let's unpack before we're caught up in the social whirl.' Mrs Hempseed's voice broke into her reverie.

Maggie tore herself from the rails and followed her chaperone to their cabin.

'It's quite comfortable.' On the small bunk against the far wall, Mrs Hempseed opened her valise. 'There's ample room on deck for exercise and games. Also a well-stocked library and a music room with a piano.'

Maggie forced a smile and turned to the opposite bunk. *Everyone has done so much for me. I must live up to their expectations.* She flipped the switch on the reading lamp.

As the ship travelled towards Asia, Maggie followed a routine. Each morning, after breakfast, Mrs Hempseed played on the piano for at least half an hour, while Maggie went through her voice exercises. The day sped by with organised games like quoits. At night, dances or concerts in the saloon passed like a dream. Each new partner swept Maggie across the spacious ballroom floor. She loved the waltz and polka, but quickly picked up the more modern ones like the One Step, Foxtrot, Quickstep and Slow Waltz. The entertainment, her partners, the music and dance enchanted her. The longing for her family faded.

As the ship entered Singapore harbour, passengers flocked to the upper deck. Milling on the wharf were tides of hawkers, vying with each other to greet passengers with their wares. Maggie stifled her impatience as she waited for a signal from her chaperone to join the other passengers, lining up to step ashore.

Once ferried to the wharf, Maggie held a handkerchief to her nose to keep out the fetid odour of stale sweat and rotting refuse. Yet when she reached the food stalls and the fragrance of spices wafted through the air, a spirit of adventure seized her. Grabbing her chaperone's arm, she begged to try the exotic cuisine.

Mrs Hempseed bought her a plate of coconut rice and chicken curry. She took a spoonful, savouring the scrumptious flavour. *Nothing has never tasted like this.*

As they passed a fruit vendor, the odour of raw sewage assailed her nostrils. 'What a horrible smell.'

'That's durian,' Mrs Hempseed said. 'The natives love the fruit despite its smell. It is said to be an aphrodisiac.'

Back on board after a twelve-hour stopover in the Lion City, the ship steamed on, passing through the Straits of Malacca and the Andaman Sea before entering the Indian Ocean. The wind moaned, and large breakers dashed against the ship. At the sight of the churning cauldron in the inky waters, Maggie turned green and rushed to her cabin, hoping her stomach would settle down.

The turbulence had calmed by the time the ship docked at Colombo and, like a chameleon, the water changed colour. No longer seasick, Maggie gazed in wonder at the jade green sea.

From a distance the port looked peaceful with palm trees lining the shores. Cranes and gantries towered above the docks. *Travelling is such an eye-opener. There's so much to see. I can't imagine what Paris will be like.*

They wandered around, marvelling at the exotic wares. Shopkeepers shouted out, enticing them to enter.

All too soon, it was time to re-board.

Back at sea, the calmer weather restored the passengers' mood, but Maggie grew lethargic. By the time they reached the Mediterranean, she scarcely had enough energy to speak during the Captain's Ball.

The light from the chandeliers dazzled her. It required an effort even to keep her eyes open.

Mrs Hempseed tapped her shoulder. 'Are you ill, child? You look pale.'

'My body aches and my legs are as heavy as lead. I don't feel well—not well at all.'

'You need a good night's sleep. I'll take you back to the cabin.'

Maggie struggled to keep up with her chaperone's brisk pace and hung on the rails for support. When they reached their cabin, she staggered into the room and fell into her bunk. 'Good night, Madam.' Her voice was barely a whisper.

'Good night, child.'

Maggie lay shivering beneath the blankets. *What's happening? Have I caught malaria, or plague or smallpox? Will it affect my singing? My studies? Am I going to die?* Everything swam before her eyes. Lost and disorientated, she longed for her mother, her family. *If only I were back home now. Mother would know what to do…*

The following morning, the sun was streaming through their porthole when Maggie rose. The ship's rocking increased her dizziness, but she followed her chaperone to the dining room, even though she had no desire to eat. The aroma of burnt coffee reached her even before she entered. Maggie choked at the sight of bacon and eggs on the table.

Mrs Hempseed drew Maggie back outside. 'You look ghastly!' She retreated a step. 'I'll send for the ship's doctor.' She stopped a ship's steward as they headed for their cabin. 'Please fetch a physician as soon as possible.'

In a matter of minutes, a doctor hurried in and examined Maggie. He reached into his medical bag, and pulling out a small bottle of pills, handed them to Mrs Hempseed. 'It's probably a stomach infection. Singapore and Colombo are notorious for their nasty germs. Keep her warm. She should drink lots of water. Give her one tablet three times daily. She'll be fine in a couple of days.'

By the next morning, however, she was perspiring profusely. 'Everything's blurred. I feel so odd.' She felt a palm on her burning forehead, heard a sharp intake of breath, and lost consciousness.

A while later, she heard hushed voices discussing her condition.

The ship steamed up the Seine and docked at Rouen where the doctor assisted Maggie to the riverboat bound for Paris.

On their arrival, Mrs Hempseed hailed a cab and within fifteen minutes they were at their hostel. She assisted her frail charge into their room. Once there, Maggie teetered and collapsed to the floor. Mrs Hempseed threw a blanket over her, and rushed downstairs to the receptionist. 'I must get a doctor. My travelling companion has lost consciousness.' She spoke in perfect French. 'She needs help immediately.'

Maggie was vaguely conscious of Mrs Hempseed and a steward helping her to bed and later, after what seemed like hours, a physician arrived, clutching a black bag. He felt her pulse, took her temperature, prodded beneath her ribs, and lifted her eyelids.

His shadowy figure peered into her eyes. He shook his head. 'I don't want to alarm you, but I think she's suffering from typhoid fever.'

Mrs Hempseed's gasp horrified her, but the doctor's whisper was even more terrifying.

'Typhoid is known as the twenty-one-day fever and can be fatal. Perhaps her family should be informed.'

~ *Chapter 2* ~

Madame Marchesi

A SINGLE BED AND BEDSIDE TABLE dominated Maggie's room in the hospital. She lay in a semi-conscious state, her temperature raging for three weeks. On fire, she tossed and turned, tried to reach for the light that sometimes broke through her tangled thoughts, but she was unable to speak…

And then she was four again, skipping along the firebreak between the sugar cane fields at Harwood, singing an Irish ditty with her elder sister Polly. Like ballerinas in green tutus, the leafy tops waved their arms in time to her singing. The ground, scarred and serrated by fissures, crackled beneath their feet. The smell of molasses from the mills mingled with their song and rendered them ripe with promise. A slight breeze wafted the bitter-sweet aroma towards her, leaving the delicious taste of nectar on her lips.

On the side table, two candles emitted a waxy smell. Maggie sensed an oily substance on her forehead and, through half-opened eyes, glimpsed a shadowy form bending over her. The figure mumbled a prayer and placed a crucifix to her burning lips. The cold metal soothed her. *Am I receiving the Last Rites? Where's my family? Everyone has worked so hard to raise funds for my studies. I cannot let them down.*

The shadowy shape muttered something in Latin, and Maggie's lips formed the word, 'Amen.'

A sliver of golden sunlight shone between the slit in the curtains, and teased Maggie's eyelids. The pain in her head and the tortuous fire that had consumed her body was no more. Death had not claimed her. Her heart fluttered and a glow of warmth spread through her. She was alive. Alive and hungry. She longed to fall on her knees and thank God for sparing her. She attempted to roll on her side, her breathing accelerating with the effort. She tried again, braced her muscles, and used her arms as a lever.

The movement brought a nurse, who checked the girl's pulse. 'Thanks be to God; the crisis is over.'

When Maggie was well enough to leave the hospital, Mrs Hempseed took her to a hostel. Maggie's throat felt sore. *Will I ever be able to sing again? The Monsignor has raised funds to study voice, and now my voice is ruined.* Physically and emotionally drained after her discharge from hospital, she wept at her loss.

When the weather in Paris grew warmer, she lost much of the huskiness that had persisted since her illness. Her voice was still weak whenever she sang.

'Go through the scales each day for a few minutes at a time, but don't sing. It may cause permanent damage,' Mrs Hempseed advised her.

Maggie clasped her hands in a posture of gratitude. 'I can never thank you enough, Mrs Hempseed. You've been a mother to me.'

'You were no trouble at all. The nuns did everything for you, but you must work hard to regain your voice.'

Accompanied by her chaperone, Maggie ambled along the paths. Gently, Mrs Hempseed touched Maggie's arm and drew attention to the yellows and reds of the tulips blooming in the morning sun. The warmth of the springtime air kissed their faces as it drifted along the Champs-Elysees. Maggie opened her mouth to sing, as she always did when admiring the beauty of God's creation, but she sounded hoarse. More like a crow rather than a canary. Tears leapt to her eyes. She supressed a sob.

At Notre Dame with its superb Gothic architecture, the gloomy interior of the cathedral brought her dark fears to the surface. She clutched the pew, her eyes damp. Her breath came in short bursts.

Mrs Hempseed placed her hand on Maggie's shoulder. 'Have courage, child. You'll be better soon. Madame Marchesi will let us know if the typhoid has left your voice undamaged.'

Maggie now realised, in full force, the meaning of the words: *The Lord giveth and the Lord taketh away. Blessed is the name of the Lord.* Her voice was a gift from Heaven, but it was fragile and so easily lost. The future had looked rosy, but now, the canvas on which she painted her dreams remained uncertain. Maggie yearned to meet Madame Marchesi and hear her verdict.

At last, the day of the interview arrived. Maggie and Mrs Hempseed waited for a taxi beneath the shade of a linden tree. A slight breeze, carrying a faint perfume of wisterias and lilacs, ruffled Maggie's hair. She patted her tresses, tucking in the stray wisps that blew across her face.

Mrs Hempseed cleared her throat. 'Madame Marchesi is one of the finest singing teachers in Europe. She gave Dame Nellie Melba letters of introduction to friends in Europe and helped her throughout her career, and she has *not* forgotten her. You must never forget what your patrons have done for you, child.'

'I'll never forget my benefactors,' Maggie promised.

The taxi drove past boulevards and shops on its way to Rue Jouffroy.

'Paris is the world's fashion capital. Some of these couturiers promote Madeleine Vionet's latest designs in lingerie and dresses,' Mrs Hempseed said.

Maggie gasped. *With my voice in ruins, I'll never afford one of those lovely evening gowns.*

The taxi stopped in front of a stone house, north of the Arc de Triomphe. They stepped out of the taxi and Maggie gazed up at the famous Marchesi School. She had imagined the nursery of the stars to be a magnificent edifice and was disappointed to see a basic five-storied structure. *Disappointments occur in dozens. My greatest one is yet to come when Madame Marchesi tells me my voice will never recover.*

Mrs Hempseed knocked at the front door. A uniformed footman opened it and glanced at her card, before admitting them into the reception room. Mrs Hempseed slid her hand over the smooth surface of the classic French armchair and sank down with a contented sigh.

Crystal chandeliers reflected light on the white marble floor. Rich velvet curtains were fastened by gold sashes. *Such opulence!* Breathless, Maggie imagined herself in an opera house. *It will not do for me to look like a ghost.* She pinched her cheeks to bring some colour into them.

A maid ushered them through a large foyer, cool and dim after the temperature outside. They followed her down the great hall. A row of life-size portraits of former students decorated the walls. Maggie recognised Nellie Melba and let out a cry. *I know I'll never be rich and famous like her!*

The foyer opened to a studio. As Maggie entered, her feet sank into the thick red pile. Dressed in black, Madame Marchesi stood, barely five feet tall, beside a Steinway piano. Despite her small stature, she dominated the room. Little arrows of light were reflected from a diamond necklace around her throat, and a diamond-studded comb fastened her grey hair into a neat bun. Although stout, her rigid posture made her appear taller than she was. Three vertical lines between her eyes suggested a stern disposition.

She extended her hand. *'Bonjour.'*

Mrs Hempseed pressed forward with quick little steps and took Marchesi's hand. 'This is Marguerite,' she said, turning to Maggie.

Madame Marchesi nodded at Maggie. 'I see you've been admiring my students.' She pointed in the direction of Melba's portrait. 'You must know about your famous fellow compatriot. Perhaps you want to follow in her footsteps?'

Maggie coloured. *Is that so obvious?* She shuddered at the thought of returning home, unable to sing anymore. Returning to Australia and facing her benefactors. *What have I done to deserve this?*

'Melba is one in a million,' the prima donna continued, like a mother speaking of a cherished child. 'I discovered her, you know.' She waved Maggie to a platform not far from the Steinway. The tenderness in her tone vanished. 'Step on the dais.'

Still unsteady from her illness, Maggie stood on the podium with a thumping heart. She crossed herself. Madame Marchesi sat at the piano and let her fingers fly over the keys. She took her up the scale from middle C to high F. Maggie licked her lips and tried to sing, but no sound issued.

Marchesi frowned and replayed the scales.

A metallic taste coated the inside of Maggie's mouth. Fingering her collar, she swallowed, took a deep breath, and attempted again. This time, her voice, pure and powerful, rose and fell without a flaw.

At the end of the audition, Marchesi replaced the lid on her piano and, folding her arms across her chest, delivered her verdict. 'Fortunately, the illness has left the voice undamaged.'

Tears of thanksgiving dampened Maggie's eyes.

Marchesi made a complete circle around Maggie. 'Keep your legs bent while you inhale—like this.' She crooked her knees as if about to squat. 'Don't lock your knees as it makes your lower back rigid. You want your back open for inhalation. You may stand upright as you sing.'

Marchesi strode across to her writing desk, took a leather-bound volume from one of the pigeonholes and handed it to Maggie. 'This textbook contains elementary instructions for the development of voice. Use it as your Bible. Do them no more than three to four times a day and only five minutes each time.' She pointed out some vocal exercises in the book, then sat at her desk. 'Now for the paperwork.'

She passed an invoice to Maggie's chaperone.

Mrs Hempseed wrote out a cheque and handed it to the diva. 'Thank you, Madame. You don't know how worried I was over the girl.'

'You had reason to worry. Typhoid can leave one with a persistent cough and a sore throat. Marguerite has been most fortunate.'

With a surge of relief, Maggie crossed herself again, thanking God for sparing her voice as well as her life. *I will try my hardest to regain my voice.*

Marchesi waved a dismissal. 'Be here promptly at nine in the morning.'

The next day, excited at the thought of beginning a whole new chapter in her life, Maggie joined a group of ten girls of about her age and introduced herself to the student on her right.

The girl shrugged and replied in French. 'I'm Marie. Most of us are from France. There are also German and English students, but Madame insists that we converse only in French.'

Maggie silently thanked the Lord that she had studied French as a second language at college. She turned to the girl on her left. *'Bonjour. Je suis Marguerite.'*

'I'm Elizabeth,' the girl replied in English. 'But don't ever let the old girl hear you speak in English, or you'll never hear the end of it. She's a Tartar, so watch your step!'

Maggie gasped and turned to check whether Madame Marchesi had entered.

'Don't worry,' Elizabeth said. 'We all stand as soon as she enters the room. She's as regular as clockwork.'

At the stroke of nine, the babble of voices ceased, and the teacher entered. Like marionettes, the students rose from their seats, gathered at the piano, and did their warmups in unison.

Marchesi turned to Maggie. 'I've said this before, but I'll repeat myself for the benefit of our new student. There is a difference in timbre at different pitches. This is referred to as a register. It is the Alpha and Omega of the formation and development of voice, the touchstone of all singing methods.'

She explained things concisely, illustrating everything with hand or body movements. An indefatigable worker despite her seventy years, she drilled her pupils with the thoroughness of a Prussian sergeant.

Her strict discipline and stern manner kept Maggie in reverent awe. She tried to follow all the instructions, and, like a turtle, she withdrew into her protective shell whenever the diva frowned or stamped her foot. Did Marchesi expect them to click their heels when she barked orders?

'Beautiful singing is the primary goal of an opera singer,' Marchesi said. 'I teach the old *bel canto* style, which involves a precise use of muscles in the lower half of the torso, so I only permit my singers to raise their arms. Any movement like gesturing or even moving, could jeopardise the silky softness of your voice.'

Her glance swept over the girls. 'You must maintain an emotional reserve when singing, as an upsurge of emotion could disturb your tone.'

Maggie loved to express her emotions and was frustrated at having to hold her feelings in check. She realised this style was suitable for the older operas of Rossini, Bellini and Donizetti, but she found it difficult to control her natural instincts and restrain her emotions.

Marchesi reserved special attention for Maggie because of her recent illness. 'Remember, Marguerite. Always enter on the upstage leg. Start a move to the left on the left foot, and towards the right on the corresponding one. You should gesture with the upstage arm and from the centre out. Kneel on the downstage knee and never *ever* turn your back on the audience. Move just before you're about to sing. Don't forget these cardinal rules.'

Every day, Marchesi gave Maggie an individual lesson for a quarter of an hour. The strict discipline was intimidating, and she found the lessons daunting.

After lunch, all students attended lessons in opera and musical theory as well as drama and deportment. At lesson breaks, some of the French students gathered in a little group and whispered to each other.

One day, Maggie heard a student say, 'That Australian girl thinks she's a budding Melba. She tries to court Marchesi's favour.'

Maggie flushed. 'It's rather lonely to be thousands of miles from my family,' she said to the leader of the group. 'I wish I had friends here. You're fortunate your family and friends are close to you. It's true I long for Marchesi's patronage, but I want to be friends with everyone. Integrating into a new country and culture is difficult, but not having friends is even worse.' A cold shiver ran down her spine.

Her wistful attempt at friendship must have worked. From then on, the French students ceased their hostile behaviour, and Elizabeth, the English student, took her beneath her wings. Maggie began to enjoy life in the singing school.

'I'm satisfied with the state of your health, Maggie,' Mrs Hempseed said two weeks later. 'Now that you have settled in, my presence here is no longer necessary, so it's time I returned to Hobart.'

Maggie started. *Mrs Hempseed has helped me so much during my convalescence. She's been like a mother to me. How will I cope without her?*

'I've booked two seats for tonight's Stravinsky's ballet, *The Firebird,* at the Opera House. The performance is full of human interest. Unlike other ballet productions you've seen, the tale is told not just through dance alone but by the performers' facial expressions.'

Maggie grasped her chaperone's hands. *How thoughtful of Mrs Hempseed to soften the blow of her departure, by taking me to a ballet before she leaves.* 'Oh! Thank you ever so much, Mrs Hempseed. Should I wear my best dress?'

'Yes. Do that, child. It's your first evening out and you should go in style.'

When the taxi dropped them off, Maggie gaped at the neo-baroque decorative elements of the Palais Garnier, the Paris Opera House and its great dome. Once inside, she placed her hands on her heart, admiring the perpetual tremolo of the crystal chandeliers.

'Several years ago, part of the main chandelier collapsed and a member of the audience was killed,' Mrs Hempseed said. 'That may have sparked the author's imagination and inspired him to write his novel *Phantom of the Opera.*'

They climbed the red plush carpeted stairs. Maggie marvelled at the marble columns and the bronze sculpture of writhing snakes and all the life-like sculptures and paintings. 'To experience art in such a setting is something never to be forgotten,' Mrs Hempseed said, with a sweep of her hand. 'Music lifts us to a higher emotional plane—to sublime heights.'

That night, Maggie lay in bed, thinking of *The Firebird* and the superb Opera House before falling asleep. She floated on a cloud and the music resounded in her mind as she imagined herself on that stage someday.

Marchesi watched over her pupil's health. 'Remember not to overuse your voice,' she warned. 'You must learn from Emma Calvé. When she first came to me, her voice was so tired and overworked that I advised her to rest. Emma followed my advice and three years later, in 1885, she made her debut at the Opera Comique. She still writes affectionate letters to me.'

For months after her illness, Maggie tired easily, so she followed her instructor's method of short practice sessions and rested her voice between singing exercises. Her recovery from illness was like beginning to live all over again. She learned how to develop firm abdominal muscles and a soft, relaxed throat. However, she found the latter the most difficult task to master and tightened up when stressed.

Marchesi never permitted her students to shampoo their hair before a lesson, and whenever a student attended classes with damp tresses, she stormed at her. Maggie, thinking it was just a foible, asked, 'Why can't we wash our hair in the mornings, Madame?'

With her open palm, Marchesi hit the table twice. 'So that you will not catch a cold and get a sore throat. One *must* look after one's health.'

'Thank you, Madame. I did not doubt you.'

Marchesi appeared mollified. 'Your lovely personality reminds me of Adelina Patti, Marguerite.' She laughed. 'But I would not advise you to eat nightingales' tongues.' Admirers had compared the world-famous opera singer to a nightingale and word had spread that she had a sandwich containing twelve nightingales' tongues each day.

Maggie blushed. *I wish she would comment on my singing instead of my personality!*

'Few singers attain fame overnight. It took Calvé a decade to reach success. Aspiring singers have to work hard even when *Mon*

Dieu blesses them with a lovely voice.' Marchesi shrugged. 'But no matter how much some singers labour, they never gain recognition.' She scrutinised the girl's face as if trying to read it.

Maggie shuddered. 'The road to fame is difficult.'

Marchesi nodded. 'I told Emma she could not expect to become a good singer within two to three years. After the audience had booed her at *La Scala,* she was so discouraged she stopped performing for a while, but continued voice studies. You see, Marguerite, it is work, work, and more work all your life.'

'I'm not afraid of work, Madame.'

'No. You're a fine student. Don't ever give up.'

Intrigued by strange stories about Emma Calvé, Maggie often stood in the hallway, studying her photo. She admired the opera star for her beauty and talent and recalled reading that Marchesi had also helped shape Melba's career. 'Is it true that Calvé delves in the occult, Madame?' she asked one day after a session with her teacher.

Marchesi placed a finger on her lips before replying. 'In the early 1900s Calvé followed the philosophy of a famous Swami and joined him on a tour of Europe and Egypt.' She threw up her hands. 'But who cares?'

She brought the subject up again some days later. 'Emma has a Madonna-like face, but when she first came to me, she was too cold. I taught her how to enter her heroine's character. I told her, "Stir yourself, and you'll stir others." She and Melba are still grateful for my teaching. I gave a brilliant finish to their already well-trained voices. When showered with applause, most singers think they are geniuses. But Emma is the same loving person.'

Maggie remained silent, promising herself to always remember her benefactors. *Will I ever be as fortunate? Will the Maggie Gard Society be pleased with my progress? Will I be able to show them my gratitude in some way?*

Maggie spent her free time walking in the parks, often strolling on the gravelled alleyways of the Tuileries Garden, between the Louvre and the Concorde. Whenever she passed the sculptured horses, her mind would inevitably wing back to her home and family. Her chest tightened.

In the evenings, she attended Marchesi's musical soirees. Madame Marchesi chose her best students to perform along with famous singers. Maggie longed to sing with them, but her voice had still not yet fully recovered.

Spring passed swiftly. Maggie's voice grew stronger day by day and a wave of happiness carried her up on the sea of excitement each time she managed to extend her vocal range. By the end of six months, her voice had returned to what it had been before her illness, and from then on, it improved by leaps and bounds.

In winter, the sky was heavy with snow and the sculptured figures on the baroque façades of the Louvre stood out like sentinels. Christmas came and went. A new year dawned.

~ *Chapter 3* ~

Jean de Reszke

'I'LL INTRODUCE YOU TO ANOTHER TEACHER before you return to Australia,' Marchesi said. 'His name is Jean de Reszke. He is Polish. You'll like him.'

Maggie appreciated her training sessions with Madame Marchesi, but she eagerly anticipated studying with the famous tenor who had sung with Melba. *Fate is leading me in the star's footsteps. Perhaps he will not insist that I hold back my emotions when singing!*

Summer melted into autumn and the days started to shorten. Before another year had passed, Sir John McCall, Tasmania's agent-general, sent a letter informing Maggie that he would sponsor her studies at the London College of Music. Surprised, Maggie covered her smile with her fingers. This would give her time to complete her studies with Marchesi. *Thank you, God. Thank you. Now, perhaps I may have my debut at Covent Garden.* Her heart sang. In an ecstasy of joy, she strode to the Arc de Triomphe after dinner. Passers-by smiled at her, and she returned their smiles. It seemed that the whole of Paris rejoiced.

Maggie could hardly wait to tell Madame Marchesi about her windfall. The next day, during her individual lesson, she blurted out the news. 'Madame, Sir John McCall will be sponsoring my studies at the College of Music in London.'

'Good tidings, indeed. Just what you need.'

The diva appeared cold, but Maggie realised that Marchesi only showed her feelings when she spoke of her protégés, Melba and Calvé.

Three months before Maggie's departure for London, Marchesi introduced her to Jean de Reszke. The tenor's tall frame bent over her as he took her trembling hand in both of his and kissed it. His moustache brushed her skin, sending thrills of delight through her. She stood speechless before the man who had been the world's greatest tenor in his hey-day—adored for his voice, enunciation, charm, and striking presence. Now, although sixty-two and suffering from chronic bronchitis, he retained his ravishing good looks, but he was beginning to bald at the sides. Maggie wished she had met him as a young man with his long curly locks and dashing appearance.

'You remind me of my dear friend, Melba,' Reszke said. 'She too was from Australia. I used to call her Melbie. I taught her *Faust, Mireille*, and *Romeo and Juliet*, but as we have only a couple of months before you leave for London, I'll just concentrate on *Faust* with you.'

Hypnotised by his beautifully modulated tone, high forehead and long, slender fingers which he pressed together as he spoke, Maggie savoured every minute with him. 'Marguerite,' he would say, at the commencement of lessons, 'sing me an aria.'

He would then pick on the tiniest imperfection and work through it with her, until she could perform it faultlessly.

One day, in a light-hearted mood after a class, he imitated his adoring fans by mimicking them. Maggie collapsed into laughter. 'Melba was so fortunate to have sung with you.'

In the lightness of the moment, they remained in the studio while he talked about his days with Melba. 'We sang at Windsor

Castle, Covent Garden and the Metropolitan Opera House. We also played the star-crossed lovers.'

A pang of jealousy pierced her. 'Was she exceptionally beautiful?'

'Adorable. She always wore her jewels and never substituted imitations, but her voice was her greatest treasure. One night during a performance, a man climbed on stage and attempted to steal her necklace.' He threw back his head and laughed. 'I warded him off with my costume sword, and the audience hailed me as a hero.'

Maggie treasured every word that dropped from his lips.

'One day, hearing a *pinging* in Melbie's voice, I warned her not to hit the note too hard,' he continued in a more serious tone. 'She ignored my advice and her voice turned husky. A throat specialist advised complete rest after discovering a small nodule on her left vocal cord.'

Reszke placed both his hands on her shoulders. 'So, Marguerite, you must not strain your voice on any account.' He started to cough but stopped and took a sip of water.

Maggie wished she could alleviate his suffering, but there was nothing she could do. At the end of her final lesson, Reszke rose and kissed her hand. 'Farewell, Marguerite. You have talent and will go far. I wish you every success in your career.'

'Studying with you has been most enjoyable,' Maggie said. 'Thank you so much.'

Reszcke looked as if he wanted to say something further, but he broke into a fit of coughing. Flecks of blood stained his lips. He put a handkerchief to his mouth, rose to his feet and staggered out, his shoulders heaving. His strangled coughing reached her from the other end of his house.

He returned a few minutes later, holding on to the banisters as though for support, and breathing heavily. Then he sat down and wiped the perspiration from his brow.

Maggie balled her fists to stop herself from putting her arms around his shoulders in sympathy.

Conflicting feelings arose when Maggie's time to leave Paris arrived. She had spent the last two years in France, and both her singing and her French had improved beyond her expectations. She had been homesick for her family but had struggled hard to overcome the feelings of lethargy after her attack of typhoid. *All this time I've been without family and friends, and now I am going to another country, and won't be seeing my family for another three years.* Maggie fought back her tears. *But I am so fortunate to have been chosen to study at London's Royal College of Music.* Joy replaced her sagging spirits. *Thank you, Lord,* she prayed. *My accommodation has been arranged and my college fees paid.* Her pulse raced as she thought of her parents. *They will be so delighted with my good fortune.*

~ *Chapter 4* ~

London

September 1912

MAGGIE'S SOUL VIBRATED IN RHYTHM with the heartbeat of the ferry that kissed the shores of France before turning its bow towards England. Joy filled her heart. Joy at the prospect of studying at the Royal College of Music. Joy at knowing her friend would be joining her.

Her mother had written to tell her that Lisa Parsons, a friend from her days at Harwood Primary School, had also enrolled at the College. Maggie recalled Lisa's startling hazel eyes and chestnut ringlets. *Lisa had been so demure—never getting into trouble with the teacher. Not like me.*

The squawking gulls brought back memories of sitting together during lunch hour and watching birds squabbling over food scraps in the schoolyard. *We'd been great friends. It'll be exciting to catch up.*

As soon as Maggie disembarked from the ferry at Dover, her spirits plummeted at the grey skies. Then they rose at the sight of Dover Castle; the great fortress set high above the white cliffs. Promising herself a visit someday, Maggie smiled at the sound of English accents once again.

She bought a ticket to London and boarded the train to Victoria Station. The sidewalks were filled with stalls covered by canvas canopies to keep off the rain. People strolled by leisurely, crowding the sidewalks and spilling into the street. Horse-drawn vehicles drove past, splashing Maggie's dress. She tried to wave down a hansom cab, but she was on the wrong side. After several futile attempts to cross the street, she finally managed to get across and board a cab to Mr and Mrs Sutton's address at Fulham—where arrangements had been made for her to stay.

Once Maggie settled into her new home, she caught a bus to the College and formally enrolled. Most of the scholars were English, with a sprinkling of Scots and Irish. Some came from across Europe. Maggie and Lisa were the only Australians.

Maggie studied the art of gliding across a floor, practising all her movements until they were harmonious. Soon, she could sit on a chair, wave an arm, or rest her chin on her hand with grace. In her speech and diction lessons, her tutor placed some marbles into her mouth, making it difficult to speak without swallowing them, but knowing the importance of excelling in enunciation, she kept on trying.

'Marvellous! Marvellous!' her tutor said when she succeeded without choking.

Lisa studied pianoforte and, as many of their lectures coincided, the girls often spent time in each other's company.

Their first summer holiday together included sightseeing in London: Kew Gardens, Covent Garden, Hyde Park and the Tower of London. They never ceased feeling amazed at the sight of such beauty of nature and of man. The Tower of London intrigued them, and its history terrified them.

In the evenings, they attended operas, concerts, ballets and theatres, sitting up with the 'gods'—the cheapest seats in the house. They would climb the long set of stairs to their seats and look down from dizzying heights. The ornate decorations, the plush seats and the fragrance of perfume enraptured Maggie. Her heart pounded, and breathless with excitement, she would watch the pit-orchestra tune up. Then the first strains would stir from the orchestra. Maggie couldn't wait to attain that level of perfection and perform on stage.

Maggie wrapped her scarf more carefully around her neck. 'My attack of typhoid shows that even a common cold can ruin my voice.'

Lisa nodded. 'You wrap a scarf around your neck to protect your vocal cords and I always keep my fingers flexible and warm with gloves.'

On sunny days during lecture breaks, Maggie and Lisa would sit in the outdoor section of the College refectory and discuss current events and music. Their knowledge of worldly matters widened from idle gossip and blossomed like flowers in spring whenever they huddled together over a cup of tea. Summer in London was so much like winter in Australia, and they enjoyed the sunshine.

One day, while discussing professional jealousy, intemperate conductors and amorous advances, Maggie giggled. Then she dropped her voice. 'Before a performance, some singers stand on their heads, gargle their throats with champagne or drink an elixir of raw eggs and whiskey. I never imagined those handsome tenors stank of garlic when on stage.'

Lisa looked puzzled. 'What do you mean?'

'Most of them chew a cashew-sized sliver of garlic two hours before a performance to soothe their sore throats.'

'I thought all vocalists chewed a clove of garlic beforehand. Don't you?'

'Yes, but I nibble parsley afterwards.' Maggie leaned forward. 'Today, our lecturer warned us that performers get carried away, but we shouldn't miss a beat if a baritone singer fondles our breast, breathes garlic on our faces, nibbles our ears, or bites our lips on stage.'

Lisa's green eyes opened wide, reflecting the sunlight.

'Don't instrumentalists do anything extraordinary?' Maggie asked.

'You'd be surprised. Some conductors fly into a rage and fling their batons at us. Others sling insults. Our conductor shouts, "No. No. Make it sing. Now let's have it again." We're fortunate.'

'Wonder what we're in for,' Maggie said. 'Our lecturer even insinuated that divas did *it* before going on stage.'

Lisa went scarlet. Even at twenty, they were both still quite naïve. Simple country girls not daring to say the naughty word. Merely mentioning it was sufficient to make them blush.

Maggie had always listened to recordings of Melba's music. She admired the silvery brilliance of the diva's voice and her pure spring-like tone. She recalled trying to sing along with some of her records when she was only six.

One day a student muttered something about Nellie Melba's crude, colonial character. 'The media says she's a champagne guzzler, a drug-addict and a whore among French royalty,' another added.

'You've been listening to bigoted reports and malicious gossip,' Maggie retorted.

'Whatever her morals maybe like, no one can deny that her singing is unique.' She rose and swept out of the room with her chin tilted upwards, leaving the others stunned.

One day at college, while enjoying a hot brew of Earl Grey with Lisa, Maggie noticed an awkward-looking youth sitting at a corner table not far off. His long, slender hands moved delicately in time to some silent strains as he gazed in her direction. His thick horn-rimmed spectacles prevented Maggie from deciding whether he was looking at her, or reaching out to the space beyond the stars, in dreamy ecstasy.

'Don't look now, Lisa, but do you know anything of that tall mousy-haired student in the corner?'

Lisa's eyes twinkled. 'Oh yes. He's always around like a devoted sheep dog. He adores you.'

'I've never seen him before.'

'He tries to be as inconspicuous as possible.'

Maggie giggled. 'Let's have some fun. I'll drop my hanky and see what happens.'

Lisa laughed, almost spilling her cup of tea. 'Leave him alone. He's happy where he is.'

Maggie ignored her, and dabbed her face with her handkerchief, then let it flutter to the ground. She hesitated for a split second before bending to pick it up, but her watchful friend was instantly on his feet. Two lengthy strides brought him to her. He bent his right knee and picked up the embroidered handkerchief.

'I… t… th… think… this is yours, Miss,' he stammered, without rising.

'Thank you.'

The young man remained motionless, looking up at her. His shoulders were pulled forward and rounded. Maggie felt like Queen Elizabeth when Sir Walter Raleigh threw his cloak on the mud to protect her shoes. 'Pray, do get up, Sir.'

The dining room chatter ceased, and all eyes fastened on them.

His heavy spectacles had slipped forward when he had bent down. He pushed them into place with his index and middle finger. They sank within a deep indent on the base of his nose. He rose to his feet, bowed and commenced to back away.

'Do take a seat. I'm Maggie Gard and this is Lisa Parsons.'

He bowed. 'How do you do? I'm Albert Longbottom.'

She tried her best not to laugh. 'What instrument do you play?'

His hands shook as he removed his glasses and wiped them. 'I-I play the vi-vi-violin.'

Then as though her question had triggered something in his memory, he gasped. 'Oh dear, it's time for my class. Pl-Please excuse me. I--I must no- t be late.'

'No, indeed. Goodbye for now.'

'Th-thank you.' His body folded itself in two, at right angles to his legs as he bowed. He then turned, almost knocking over an empty chair at the table.

She watched his lanky figure until he disappeared around the corner. He had taken off his spectacles again and was giving them a final polish.

Lisa's body shook with silent laughter. 'You don't know what you've started. He'll be your shadow from now on.'

'*You* told me he had been following us.' Maggie's voice bubbled with merriment.

'Yes, but that was from afar.'

'A bit of fun won't hurt,' Maggie replied. 'We can't spend all our time studying.'

At times, Maggie sat in the library with her head in her hands, absorbed in thoughts. She wished she could contribute towards the cost of her studies. Melba had held concerts in Australia to raise money for her fare to Europe, but Maggie had to rely upon the citizens of Hobart to do that for her. She had sung at her farewell concert, but the society had organised everything.

One day, seeing an advertisement for a singing competition, she entered it and, in February, secured a prize of six hundred pounds as well as a Foundation Scholarship at the Royal College of Music, London. It took effect from the beginning of the summer term in May. The money paid for her living expenses for the next three years.

Harry Plunket Greene, a pianist and bass-baritone, gave her voice lessons at the college. She had pictured bass singers as big, beefy and barrel-chested, but her tutor didn't fit that image at all. Good-looking and over six feet tall with light brown eyes, he did not look his forty-nine years. His blond hair was grey at the temples and parted slightly off-centre. His foghorn pitch suggested heartaches, and like most of his other female pupils, she was mesmerised by him. When he sang, his voice dipped and soared to either end of his register, switching from sustained pianissimos to quaking explosions of wall-to-wall thunder. The brightly burnished timbre of his voice held a built-in caress to her melting heart.

Mr Greene's interests were wide. He passed this on to his students, insisting that training should stretch over all aspects of music as well as all branches of art. He was impressed by her musical ability, so his half-hour lesson extended to an hour when he had no other appointments.

At voice coaching sessions, Maggie sometimes forgot herself and raced ahead, singing in anticipation of what was yet to come. Then he would stop playing the piano and admonish her.

'Are you catching a train, Maggie? If you race through the countryside, you'll miss most of its beauty.'

During a lesson, Greene would say, 'When an opera is sung in a foreign language, you must try to understand the words you are singing.'

He stressed that vocalists should probe into the history and psychological motivation of each character. 'Most heroes and heroines, ample of brisket and bosom, thrash their arms and square off at high Cs.' He mimicked their movements. 'The composer Monteverdi, knowing the importance of drama in opera, created new methods of instrumental technique for singers to articulate a whole range of feelings such as anger and excitement. You must express yourselves. Hold nothing back. Nothing.'

Under his guidance, Maggie gave free rein to dramatic techniques hampered under Marchesi. At times when composing, he went through his work on the piano, and she listened in a trance, the notes falling like snowflakes, the hours gliding in enchantment.

Greene sometimes lapsed into Irish brogue and sang an Irish ditty; his fine fingers swept the keys; a far-away look in his eyes. Maggie knew he was thinking of his hometown of Dublin, where he often returned to visit his wife and children. He stood as a father-figure to Maggie, and she memorised every nuance of his voice.

When Maggie told Lisa of her admiration for Harry Plunkett Greene, Lisa laughed. 'He reminds me of our virtuoso trumpeter who puffs himself up as he prepares for a high staccato blast or a long, breath-defying legato lament. I've seen him swaying with dizziness from the effort.'

'I'm not amused.' Maggie pouted in mock anger. Then she burst out laughing.

A few weeks later, when the two friends were chatting over a cup of tea in the cafeteria, Lisa appeared more than usually silent. Talk from other tables drifted toward them and the aroma of coffee titillated their senses. 'My parents have asked me to return home.' Lisa placed her hand on Maggie's arm. 'I'm leaving soon after my exams. There are rumours of war in Europe. We'll be better off in Australia, away from the fighting. Do join me, Maggie. We could travel together.'

Maggie took a small intake of breath. 'Oh Lisa, I'll never get another chance to study overseas if I return now. There's so much more for me to learn. Besides, I've only done one year of my three-year scholarship.'

Lisa leaned forward. 'Why don't you write home and ask your parents for advice?'

'Letters take too long—sometimes up to six months.' Maggie shrugged. 'Besides, I'm sure Father won't want me to miss such a wonderful opportunity.'

Lisa shook Maggie's shoulder as if to re-inforce her words. 'Your life may be in danger, Maggie. Your parents will be so worried about you.'

'Everyone says it'll be over by Christmas, so don't worry about me, Lisa.'

As soon as Lisa completed her pianoforte exams, she sailed for Australia without even waiting to receive her certificate. The two friends flung their arms around each other and wept at their parting.

Lisa carried home letters for Maggie's family, a Nottingham lace doily for Maggie's mother and a musical score signed by Harry Plunket Greene for Maggie's father.

Maggie missed Lisa's companionship, but she devoted more time to her studies. *In two years, I will have completed college, and be ready for my debut at Covent Garden. My benefactor, Sir John McCall, will be present with his wife and their entourage. So too, will Harry Plunkett Greene and Albert Longbottom. It will be exhilarating.* She rubbed her hands together, imagining herself greeted by shouts, cheers, and much waving of handkerchiefs at the Opera House at Covent Garden. She could not wait.

~ *Chapter 5* ~

1914–1916

WAR BROKE OUT SIX MONTHS AFTER Lisa left for Australia. Students and staff of the Royal College of Music volunteered for military service, the college tottered, numbers dwindled. It struggled on.

Maggie spent time reading in the college library at South Kensington. Often her eyes would wander to George Butterworth, bent over a book, beetling his brows, and stroking his moustache. She longed to be introduced to the famous composer who had set the poem, *A Shropshire Lad*, to music, but it would be unthinkable for her to speak to him without an introduction.

In August 1914, when Butterworth enlisted in the Durham Light Infantry, Maggie hastened to the quay to watch his battalion board a ship for the battle zone. Crowds gathered—some cheering, others weeping. She participated in the war songs and joined in the rousing rendition of *Land of Hope and Glory*. A thrill shot through her at the thought of so many young men rallying to their country's call.

On 7 August 1914, Britain had begun a recruiting campaign, calling for men aged between 19 and 30 to join the army. Three weeks later the recruiting age was raised to 35. By the middle of September over 500,000 men had volunteered their services.

Albert Longbottom had often brought Maggie a bunch of forget-me-nots. He lived off her beauty and her voice, shadowing her on the fleeting wings of hope, as Lisa had predicted. One day, he came, eyes glistening through his thick glasses. 'I… I've come to wish you goodbye. I… I've volunteered for active service. I… I wanted to join the air force, but my eyesight is not strong enough. Joined the army instead.' He looked happy. Proud to serve his country. 'I… I would have liked to be here for your debut, Maggie.'

'That will not be until the war is over, Albert.'

'May I write to you?

'Yes, of course.' Maggie extended her hand and Albert clasped it. She had been happy enough to receive Albert's devotion. Now she was sorry to see him go. Only her voice teacher Harry remained in the College. *How long will hostilities last?*

In a sea of loneliness, Maggie wandered among the pink and white crocuses and yellow daffodils in Hyde Park or Kensington Gardens. At times, she stopped to listen to orators on their soap boxes, or hire a boat to row on the Serpentine. Then her mind would drift back to her trips to school by steamer. On weekends, she joined other singers and sang in Covent Garden for passers-by who stopped and tipped her a few coins.

Next year I'll graduate from London's College of Music. War will be over by then. I'll make my debut at the Covent Garden Opera House. Dame Nellie Melba made her debut there. I'd love to do the same.

As hostilities continued, more men enlisted in the armed forces. Women stepped in to fill their jobs. When the housemaid left for a factory job, Maggie cleaned her own room before leaving for lectures. From Fulham, she took the Tube from Parsons Green Station to South Kensington, frequently stopping to read posters urging men to join the army and encouraging women to seek employment in factories.

Men in black suits and bowler hats rushed by—newspapers under their arms. Women brushed by, their skin yellow from the sulphur in munitions factories. How different London was from

Hobart, where people were so friendly and always found time to stop for a chat.

During the festive season of 1914, Maggie made her way past the fog-shrouded stalls of fruit and vegetables in Covent Garden and gazed at the Christmas trees. Holly and ivy festooned the streets. Warmth radiated through her body at the sight of the decorations in the shops. Carollers stood singing at street corners, children held lighted candles, and hawkers roasted chestnuts on the pavement. Filled with wonder, she stopped and listened to the carol singers. When they burst into the hymn, *O Come all Ye Faithful*, she joined in, remembering the time she had sung it in Latin in the choir loft at the Hobart Cathedral.

A few weeks before Christmas Maggie asked her hostess whether she'd like some help in putting up the decorations.

'I'd love your help, Maggie,' Mrs Sutton said. 'I'm exhausted after the hustle and bustle at Oxford and Regent Streets.'

Maggie packed stockings with small gifts and wrapped the larger presents in coloured paper. She helped decorate the festive tree with gold and silver ornaments and placed parcels beneath its branches.

'Do you have any more shopping to do? I'll be happy to come along next time you go out.'

Mrs Sutton, who was about to put the star on top of their Christmas tree, paused, her hand poised above the tree. 'I have some last-minute shopping. It would be lovely if you'd help with that.'

On Christmas morning, Maggie's longing for her family tore at her heartstrings. They would be opening their presents and singing carols around the Christmas tree. She thought of her sister, Molly, who was four years older than her, and of Kitty, her junior by two years. Finally, her thoughts dwelt on her mother and little Josie who was now twelve. She wondered if her father still dressed up as Santa.

When Maggie joined the Sutton family for breakfast, the two children, Tommy and Mary, had already emptied their stockings and the room was strewn with paper wrappings. 'Look, Miss Maggie,' they said. 'Santa has brought us everything we asked for.'

Tommy blew his whistle and beat his drum. 'I'm going to be a soldier.'

Maggie ruffled his hair and gave him a hug, taking the chance to turn away and wipe the tears from her eyes.

'Do you have a cold, Miss?' Mary asked, seeing Maggie put a handkerchief to her face.

She flushed. 'No. I was thinking of my family back in Australia.'

The weather was cold, and snow had fallen, but inside they were safe and warm. The setting reminded her of a Dickensian novel. Maggie took a deep breath, inhaling the fragrance of pine from the Christmas tree.

At the Yuletide dinner, the Suttons enjoyed roast turkey followed by a glass of sherry, a slice of cake and mince pie. Maggie thought of her family back home, and a stab of pain plunged through her. A lump wedged in her throat during making it difficult to swallow.

After dinner, the children wanted to make a snowman. 'Ask Miss Maggie to help you,' Mrs Sutton said.

The first soft kiss of snow alighted on her cheek like a loving caress. A thrill of joy shot through her, despite the pain in her heart. Her heart ignited with warmth. Her face glowed, and she shut her eyes, imagining it was a kiss wafting across the seas from her family.

An eerie throbbing sound startled residents at Great Yarmouth on 19 January 1915, as a zeppelin appeared in the skies. Shortly afterwards, residents from surrounding areas heard explosions. A second zeppelin bombed East Lynn, some 44 miles north of London. Major zeppelin raids continued over the next few months…

Four months later, as Maggie settled down to sleep, a huge airship droned over London and dropped 90 incendiary bombs and 30 grenades on the helpless city.

Maggie pulled the blanket over her head and felt herself slowly folding up like a sheet of paper thrown upon the fire. She drew up her legs into a foetal position and a stifled groan escaped her lips. Silent tears rolled down her cheeks. *My parents will worry about me. Perhaps I should have returned to Australia with Lisa.*

The next morning, Maggie wrote home and assured her parents that bombs never fell anywhere near her. *Perhaps they'll feel better to know I'm in a danger-free zone!*

When dawn broke, newspapers reported that thousands of people had taken to the streets to watch incendiary bombs sizzling, crackling, spitting flames. Crowds watched the tarmac on the street bubble before a molten mass of black ignited. Nearby, a broken gas pipe spat tongues of yellow and blue into the air.

Unable to sleep, Maggie composed a letter to her parents in her head. Soon, the years melted away, and she was back in Hobart. *Maggie pictured her father putting a teaspoon of Bex powders in his glass of water. He reached out, gulped it down and smiled at her as though in some secret plot.*

The vision faded and she was back at Mrs Sutton's house in London. A suffocating sensation rose to her chest. 'O, how I miss my family,' she whispered.

After the initial strike on London in May 1915, zeppelins continued to hit the city. Londoners huddled in basements and sought shelter in the city's Tube stations to escape the terror from the skies. When Maggie went for walks in St James's Park during her leisure hours, the lake was no longer there. It had been drained to prevent its night-time glitter from directing zeppelins to nearby Buckingham Palace.

On 8 September 1915, the shadow of a sleek cigar-shaped zeppelin passed over the dome of St. Paul's Cathedral and unloaded a three-ton bomb on the city's financial hub, leaving behind burning buildings

British airplanes could not soar as high as a zeppelin, so it returned to its base unharmed. Life looked grim. By late 1916, however, Britain developed planes that reached higher altitudes, and their crew could fire explosive bullets that tore holes into the zeppelin's outer skin and ignite the volatile gaseous cocktail.

In retaliation, Germany launched its largest raid of the war in September 1916 and sent a fleet of 16 airships across the Channel to bomb London. However, anti-aircraft guns shot them down, and only one airship made it through to the capital. On its arrival, Royal Flying Corps pilot William Leefe Robinson raked it with new explosive bullets. The airship fell from the sky like a shooting star.

Londoners cheered and sang patriotic tunes as the incinerated zeppelin plummeted to earth.

Over the course of the war, German zeppelins staged more than 50 attacks on Britain, killing nearly 700 and seriously injuring almost 2000. Many young and talented musicians lost their lives both on the battlefield and in their homes. When radio announced Butterworth's death by a sniper's bullet at Pozières, the chill of war seeped into Maggie's veins, and shooting pains shot up her chest. War was heartless. War was cruel. War took the talented. Took the healthy. Took the youth.

Despite all this, Germany failed to break British morale.

On her way to classes, one morning, Maggie passed a noticeboard inviting Australian musicians and singers to join the *Australian Artistes*, so she volunteered her services. She felt at home among her easy-going and friendly fellow countrymen. Her sponsor, Sir John McCall, had been appointed medical officer in charge of the Australian Natives' Association in London. His wife, Lady McCall, invited the *Australian Artistes* to sing at the Anzac Buffet in London.

Maggie's silver dress shimmered as she glided among the guests, holding her chin up, her lips curved into a smile. A deep blood-red sash encircled her waist and matched the suede shoes and clutch-bag. A garnet necklace shot little red darts as it reflected the light from the chandeliers, rivalling the glow of pleasure in her eyes. Journalists interviewed performers and took photographs while visitors circled the room in black tie and evening gown.

Although Maggie had practised her scales and technical exercises repeatedly, her nerves were taut during the serving of cocktails and hors d'oeuvres. When she mounted the stage, her courage almost failed, but once the orchestra commenced, her voice never faltered. At the conclusion of the aria, a thunderous cheer went up from the audience. Maggie curtseyed and touched her fingertips to her lips.

As soon as the guests started to leave, she thanked the Major and his wife for all the help they had given her. Sir John congratulated her, and Lady McCall graciously shook hands with the tips of her fingers.

When everyone had departed and the echoes of voices had died down, a surge of homesickness swept over Maggie. *If only my family had been here. Will the time ever come when, like Nellie Melba, they'd be among the audience, and I could shower them with gifts?*

Maggie's mother, Catherine, sent her a cutting from a Hobart newspaper about the performance. 'Miss Gard has a beautiful voice; a voice of exquisite timbre and wonderful range.' She placed the report of her triumph in a folder, thinking of the day she would return and sing for her family, her friends, her benefactors.

The nuns had warned that the climb to fame would be strewn with criticisms and the journey could be long and laborious, but the flower of life was just beginning to unfold, and she strained to taste its nectar.

Maggie's debut had been delayed, but she did her bit by helping raise morale.

~ *Chapter 6* ~

War 1917–1918

BIRDS SANG, BEES HUMMED AND dragonflies flitted among the roses, but Maggie ignored the beautiful summer's day as she strode towards her voice teacher's office. The 1917 college term had ended, and Harry Plunkett Greene was about to leave for the summer vacation. He was at his desk, sorting papers as she entered. 'Well, Maggie, any plans for the future?'

'I'm at a loss what to do. The three years have flown so fast. I thought war would be over by the time my scholarship ran out.'

'It must end sooner or later. Both sides are running out of men and money.' He ran his hand through his neatly combed hair. 'Times are bad, Maggie.'

She sighed, realising she would be losing another friend.

He rubbed his chin. 'Practice as much as possible. Take every opportunity to sing in public.' His light brown eyes held hers. 'I'll give you a letter of introduction to the Royal Choral Society. Many singers have gone off to war and they will be glad to have you in the concerts at Albert Hall.'

'Oh, could you please?' Maggie clasped her hands.

He waved her towards a chair, and she sank into it. He puckered his brow and dipped his pen into the inkpot. Maggie watched the second-hand of the clock nibble away at the precious remaining moments with her voice instructor.

He wrote a note to Sir Thomas Beecham and, signing his name with a flourish, blotted it before placing it in an envelope. 'There now. It's done.'

Maggie took it, shook hands, and thanked him. Her friends had left London and now she would never again see Harry Plunkett Greene either.

Sir Thomas Beecham stroked his goatee beard as though milking a cow, while he read Harry's letter. He placed it in his work tray, then twirled his walrus moustache and moved his jaw as if chewing on his own thoughts.

Maggie sat watching him with an empty feeling in the pit of her stomach. *What if he is unable to help me? What will I do?* She curled and uncurled her fingers, and, in breathless anticipation, waited for his reply.

After a few minutes, he turned to her. 'You may sing with us during our Sunday afternoon concerts. I'm always looking for fresh talent.'

'Thank you, Sir Thomas.'

Beecham rested his chin on his hand. 'Why not attend our Wagner and Beethoven nights on Mondays and Fridays?'

Maggie took up his offer, thinking it would help to take her mind off her loneliness.

One Monday evening when she returned from a concert, her hostess, Mrs Sutton, met her at the door. 'Did you have a good time, Maggie?'

'Yes. I was at the Albert Hall. I love Beethoven.'

Drawing herself up to her full height, Mrs Sutton glared at Maggie. 'How can you tolerate music by enemy composers?'

Many Britons refused to listen to music composed by the enemy, but the lively German compositions had resonated within Maggie. 'Wood and Newman, who organise the German nights, say that music and art are world possessions and should not be suppressed.'

'Do as you like. It's a free country and I realise you go to enjoy the music, not to admire the composers. War will soon be over, and we'll put the Huns back in their place.' A frown darkened Mrs Sutton's brow as she shut the front door behind her guest.

Maggie shook her head. *If only people open themselves to music regardless of its country of origin!* She did not want to offend her hostess, but she continued to attend the concerts. Meanwhile, she needed to earn her living. She rejected the idea of joining a munitions factory for fear of her skin turning carrot-orange like the 'Canary Girls.' The Women's Land Army worked outdoors, so the cold and damp of England's winters could wreak havoc on her larynx. She needed to safeguard her voice—her sole asset—so she searched for employment that would not jeopardise it in any way.

Maggie's fear acted as a spur to search for a suitable job. She finally found one as a bus conductor and learned to collect fares into her leather pouch with jingling efficiency. As she shoved her way between the tightly packed passengers on London's buses, the odour of unwashed bodies nauseated her. Despite this, the East Londoners never failed to cheer her, and she enjoyed meeting the colourful Cockney characters with their delightful rhyming slang. She became familiar with their unique language. Phrases like, 'trouble and strife—wife,' 'bees and honey—money,' and 'plates of meat—feet,' fascinated her.

Maggie loved the way they called her 'love' or 'darling,' One Cockney, John, never failed to catch the bus on the East London run and always had something hilarious to say. One of his favourites was, 'Waterloo, please darling—the station—not the battle. I missed that, didn't I?'

Such simple exchanges gave a sparkle to her day. With Wagner and Beethoven Nights on Mondays and Fridays, and Sunday afternoons at Albert Hall, 1917 passed swiftly.

She loved Dickens and had often spent hours reading *David Copperfield*, laughing at Mr Micawber, always waiting for something to turn up. The scene of Betsy Trotwood and the donkeys kept her in peals of laughter.

One Tuesday after dinner, she picked up a copy of *Dombey and Son* from the bookshelf to keep her mind busy during the long summer evenings. *This book should really have been called Dombey and Daughter.* She read on until dark and switched on the light, intending to finish the chapter before retiring. Within a few minutes, hearing a gentle knock, she pulled on her dressing gown and opened the door.

Mrs Sutton peered in. 'Excuse me, Maggie. Lights must be out. There's a war on, you know.'

'Oh yes, of course,' Maggie answered. 'I'm so sorry.' She switched the light off, stumbled into bed and lay on her back with her hands tucked behind her neck. War was beginning to strain her nerves. *Will hostilities ever end?*

Early in 1918, Maggie's pulse quickened on hearing that Nellie Melba had been created Dame Commander of the British Empire for her fund-raising efforts. She pouted like a spoilt child. *Will I ever be rich and famous like her?*

When the Australian Prime Minister Hughes came to London in June 1918, Maggie was invited to sing at his reception. She was to partner Robert Cunningham, the famous Australian tenor. Maggie gave herself a self-satisfied hug, and worked hard, practising even on her busiest days. The move from the rehearsal room to the stage for technical and dress rehearsals was daunting, but the flood tide of her enthusiasm carried her along. *Thanks to benefactors like Sir John McCall, I'm gaining a reputation among the Australian community.*

Two thousand people were present at the Cecil Hotel for the Prime Minister's reception. The evening remained fine, and guests arrived, dressed in their best finery. The light from the chandeliers shone on Maggie's sleeveless, slinky black dress cut in the latest princess-line style. She wore a pearl necklace with silver accessories and floated around in a dream. The feeling of unreality continued as she went on stage. Beads of sweat broke out on her forehead. The hair on the back of her neck rose. When the orchestra commenced, Maggie joined in, her voice responding flawlessly as the music mounted towards the crescendo and the final chord.

Fortunately, no zeppelins flew over, no air raid alarms or blackouts occurred to shorten the show. At the end of the concert, Maggie made an elegant sweep and curtseyed. A sea of white handkerchiefs waved at her, and a deafening roar of applause swept through the theatre. She clasped her hands to her chest and glided off the stage to the cheers of the crowd.

Newspapers gave Maggie a tremendous write-up. 'Her friends have every justification for their belief that she will go far in the musical profession,' a reporter wrote.

Enveloped in happiness, Maggie strolled in Hyde Park and listened to the birds sing. At times, she passed a soldier walking arm-in-arm with his girl, and pangs of loneliness shot through her. She had dedicated her life to her career and relished in her triumph, but now she felt isolated.

In 1918, when April winds had subsided, daffodils withered and roses opened their petals to the hot summer sun, the *Australian Artistes Association of London* gave a free concert for army, navy, and air force casualties. Many had been brought home from the trenches of Europe, and suffered from shell shock, or burns, or the effects of poison gas.

A torrent of sympathy swept over Maggie like a gigantic wave, as she comforted the broken and maimed soldiers with her songs. Despite their infirmities, they cheered and clapped at the end of each song. The armless stomped their feet and smiled. Some trembled as they attempted to put their hands together to applaud or to wipe the perspiration from their brows. Others stared straight ahead with unseeing eyes, spittle dribbling from lips. Many wore masks to hide their scarred and disfigured faces.

At the end of the concert, a tall soldier on crutches, holding a bunch of marigolds, waited at the entrance. He wore a pair of heavy spectacles. Maggie nodded and was about to pass, but he held out the posy to her.

'P… please accept this from an ar… ardent a… admirer,' he stammered.

'Albert! She barely recognising the gaunt figure as her old friend. 'How are you? Why didn't you write? Are you gravely wounded?'

'A shell burst a few yards away from me and my leg was struck by shrapnel. Been taken off active service. Will be on desk duties.' His face crumpled and tears gathered, threatening to spill on his sallow cheeks.

Albert is wounded. Must comfort him. Maggie put her hand on his arm. 'I'm so sorry about your wound, but its lovely to see you. Do come again.'

Albert and Maggie met each Sunday. He would present her with a bunch of flowers after the concerts at Albert Hall. He still had his stammer and heavy spectacles and had now acquired a limp but, within a month, he recovered sufficiently to commence his duties at the War Office.

'Will you join me for a cup of coffee?' he asked Maggie one evening.

She did not have the heart to refuse him since he had suffered so much for his country. Still she winced when trying to match her pace to his faltering steps. Even though Maggie pitied him, she found herself grabbing the arms of her chair at the café, to control her impatience while he stuttered.

Despite her feelings, Maggie did not have dates with other men. She loved going to a dance or a cinema, but she recalled what the nuns had drummed into their students on Graduation Day. 'Be strong in resisting the snares waiting to entrap you when you leave the safety of the convent walls behind,' the Mother Superior had warned.

The subdued sound of Albert's sigh sank into Maggie's subconsciousness, and she awoke from a reverie with a start. Glancing towards him, she saw the longing in his eyes and a sense of guilt came over her.

'You... you seem pr... pre... occupied today, Ma... Ma... Maggie. Are you all right?'

'I'm so sorry, Albert. I was thinking of my folk back in Australia.' It was not true, but she could not hurt him. 'What were you saying?'

'I... I'm being sent off for... for therapy,' he answered. 'I'll be reporting for duty at Exeter ne... n... next week.'

'Oh Albert! I'll miss you.' She put her hand to her lips. This time she was not telling a lie. She *would* miss his companionship. 'When will you be back?'

'I don't know, but I... I'll be leaving my heart behind.' He dropped his eyes.

Maggie flushed. She knew she could never return his love, and her soul twisted in pain for him.

The trees shed their red and gold leaves, and winter cast a white blanket of snow over Europe. The numbers of dead escalated.

For more than a year, German submarines torpedoed supply ships, so prices shot up. Maggie's hostess now served smaller portions of bread but, to make up for it, she dished out an extra thinly sliced roast beef and a second helping of vegetables.

The poor, whose staple food was bread, stumbled on the streets with sallow faces and skinny bodies, searching for leftovers in garbage bins. Maggie's heart went out to them. One day, seeing a little boy scrounging for food, she hurried over and gave him her packed lunch. 'Here. Take this.'

The boy snatched it out of her hand and ran off without a word of thanks.

Towards the end of the day, she felt faint from hunger. In spite of that, before the week ended, she did the same for another child. With her low wages as a bus conductor, she was powerless to do more, but she continued to help the poor and suffering whenever possible.

~ *Chapter 7* ~

A New Beginning

ANOTHER WINTER DREW CLOSER, AND ON most days, a thin film of half-melted snow lay on the roads. Terror reigned in London during zeppelin raids. Searchlights scanned the sky, and anti-aircraft guns spat fire and death, but Maggie continued to entertain troops with her uplifting voice.

Aunt Polly, who lived in Harwood where Maggie had spent her childhood days, wrote about friends like the Darcy and Donnelly families, each of whom had lost three sons in the war. Maggie shuddered to think of them facing the horrors of cold and wet trenches.

Hostilities continued until 11:00 am on 11 November 1918, when an armistice was signed, and silence was observed at the first stroke of eleven. When Big Ben struck the hour, trams glided into stillness. Motor cars ceased to cough and fume. Men bowed bare heads and women wept.

After the hush, *Rule Britannia* and *Land of Hope and Glory* echoed through London's streets. Strangers hugged and kissed each other. People jostled around Maggie as she joined the crowds. A soldier, home on leave, grabbed her. 'Come here, lass,' he said, planting a kiss on her lips.

She caught the odour of tobacco and the whiff of alcohol on his breath, but her pulse raced as his firm, strong arms entwined her.

Her mind buzzing, Maggie returned to her room late that night, and lay in bed contemplating her future. She longed to make her debut in London, yet she yearned for her family. But she did not have sufficient funds for her passage home, so she wrote a letter to her father, asking for advice. 'My savings won't cover the fare home. Should I wait for Covent Garden to open its doors once again and make my debut in the Theatre Royal?'

Early the next morning, she stepped out into the cold drizzle and wended her way to the Post Office. Trash and cigarette butts lay strewn on the pavements. Garbage men were removing remnants of the night's celebrations. 'Morning, Miss,' they said, tipping their caps.

'Good morning.' Maggie picked her way among the heaps of rubbish and vomit from revellers. Quickening her steps, she placed her handkerchief to her nose to keep out the disgusting sour odour.

Soon, a gentle breeze blew, ushering in a new life. Now that the war was over, she could go ahead with her career which had been temporarily derailed.

In the following weeks, Maggie continued to sing with the Royal Choral Society. Robert Cunningham, with whom she had sung at the Prime Minister's reception, found her a place in the choir at the Savoy Theatre. She accepted it gratefully.

Slowly, men drifted home, but many, like the poets Rupert Brooke, Wilfred Owen, and Isaac Rosenberg, never returned. Brooke had composed the memorable words:

If I should die, think only this of me.
That there's some corner of a foreign field
That is forever England...

Maggie strolled to Hyde Park. Birds twittered and chirped. Bluebells carpeted the ground and azaleas and rhododendrons put on a bewitching display of vivid pinks, purples and reds. Inhaling the sweet perfume of the flowers, she chose a bench in a sunny spot. She recalled Owen's poem describing the horrors of gas warfare:

And watch the white eyes, writhing in his face, and
If you could hear, at every jolt,
The blood come gargling from the froth-corrupted lungs...

The poem conjured up images of suffering and soldiers. Her heart was torn to think of the casualties of war, and once again she recalled the wounded soldiers at her concerts. None of Maggie's relatives had died or been gassed, although her uncle Cornelius had been shot in his leg.

The poet Rosenberg had portrayed life in the trenches:

Strong eyes, fine limbs and haughty athletes
Sprawled in the bowels of the earth...

Maggie gazed at the bare branches of the oak trees. A cold wind blew. She wrapped her shawl around her more securely. *The trees have no leaves now, but soon they will be putting out new shoots. Like them, I too, will start again and resume my career.* She visualised herself decked in jewels—a diva's badge of office—and imagined her loved ones seated in the front row.

Her father sat up tall and straight, her mother wept for joy and Aunt Polly blew her nose in competition with the trumpeter. After the performance, a torrent of applause followed. A stream of admirers burst in to pay their homage, leaving behind bouquets of flowers and a sweet fragrance. The vision faded.

If only things work out. Maggie longed to be a dramatic soprano like Madame Calvé. When Calvé visited London during her English tour, Maggie received an invitation from her sponsor, Sir John McCall, to attend a reception in the diva's honour. She trembled with excitement, and recalling Madam Marchesi speaking of Emma Calvé she vowed to introduce herself to her.

At the reception, Maggie took deep breaths to quell a fluttery feeling in her stomach. She moved around the guests and gazed at Madame Calvé until the diva's eyes met hers. Unable to contain her feelings any longer, Maggie stepped forward and introduced herself. 'I have always longed to meet you, Madame. Could you please spare the time to give me your opinion of my singing?' Maggie held her breath, waiting for the diva's reply.

The prima donna reclined on a settee, her fingers forming a steeple. Her sapphire necklace sparkled in the lights as she looked into Maggie's eyes. 'Be at my place next Monday at three.'

In her mellifluous tones Maggie read a promise. *Has my luck turned?* In a daze, she practised her repertoire until the day of the interview. With trembling fingers, Maggie dressed in utmost care for the meeting. She wore her slinky red dress, to sing the famous aria, *L'amour est un oiseau rebelle.*

At 3 pm precisely, Maggie knocked on Madame Calvé's door and rubbed her hands together while waiting. Her palms were sweaty and her breathing fast. Her throat tightened.

A maid ushered her in. The spacious suite breathed opulence. Green and gold curtains hung from the ceiling to the carpeted floor. A bottle of *pinot noir* and two glasses stood on a table flanked by a pair of lush velvet-and-brocade cushioned settees and a matching chair. Beyond them was a leather-backed dining suite. Maggie's stomach muscles tightened into knots.

The diva received her with a smile. 'Would you like a glass of wine before you sing?'

'No, thank you, Madame.' Her words rushed out, her breathing fast and furious.

Calvé sank down on the settee and bade her begin. Shaking back her flowing dark wavy hair, she placed two fingers to her lips.

Forgetting the roar of the traffic that filtered through from the street below, Maggie visualised herself making her debut at Covent Garden. She had long practised for that event.

Calvé listened in rapt attention and clapped at the close of the aria.

Maggie's heart thudded. Had she made an impression on the diva, or did she clap simply as a reflex action? Nerves strung like a harp, she recalled Harry Plunkett telling his students, 'Applause means admiration for performing a difficult part, not a sign that the audience is inwardly moved.'

She struggled to control herself. So much depended on this meeting.

The prima donna said nothing at first. Then she stretched out her arm to take the girl's pulse. Maggie tried to calm her breathing, but her heart continued to race along. *Is the star testing my recovery rate?*

Calvé released Maggie's hand. 'You may stay with me at my castle in the Pyrenees to learn the part of Carmen.'

'*Live* with *you*, Madame?' Maggie's mouth slackened and her hands dropped to her sides. Had she heard correctly? Her knees weakened. She reached for the back of a chair, fighting to remain on her feet.

'Yes... study.' Calvé handed Maggie a card with gold lettering and bordered with red roses. 'Write to me. I'll be expecting you in February next year.'

'I cannot thank you enough, Madame.'

Madame Calvé waved her aside. 'My maid will show you out.'

In a state of mental intoxication, Maggie returned to her hostel, unable to sleep from sheer excitement. She lay awake, drifting, wondering, imagining. Then she threw off the bedcovers and paced the room. *Does the diva really mean I can live at her castle? Is it a cold and forbidding fortress? How can I afford to pay for lessons?*

The next morning, Maggie sent a wire, informing her father of this fortunate turn of events. She bit her lip until the salty taste of blood reminded her to stop.

The following day she received a reply. It read: 'Stay put. Letter follows.'

Maggie waited in breathless suspense, hoping and praying for her parents' approval.

White snow had turned to black mud and the violence of frost was beginning to thaw out, before mail from Australia arrived. Two envelopes lay on a silver platter beside Maggie's cup and saucer. She picked up the first envelope. It bore an Australian postage stamp, but failing to recognise the writing, she held it up to the light. Had her friend, Lisa Parsons, written from Harwood? She tore it open.

The letter was from the Mother Superior at Hobart, warning her of the ways of the world. Enclosed was a St Benedict's medal, asking her to wear it, to ward off evil. Sister Assumpta, her music teacher, had written a more explicit note.

It read:

Dear Maggie,

Emma Calvé has dealings with Satan and the occult. Had I known you were going to stay at her castle, I would have asked your parents to exert all their influence to prevent your young and innocent soul from falling prey to such evil. Do pray much and keep a constant vigil against the machinations of the devil.

Fondest love and prayers,
Yours in JMJ, Sister Assumpta.

Maggie's muscles grew rigid. She read both letters carefully and, once back in her room, she burned them in the fireplace. Flames curled around the epistles, turning them into black flakes. She stirred the remains until they were nothing but dust and ashes. *Much as I love the nuns, I've waited all my life for such an opportunity. How can I let it slip through my fingers? But what do my parents have to say?*

In a fever of excitement, she tore open the other envelope. Her father wrote saying that the *Maggie Gard Society* had approved of her studying with Madame Calvé and would help towards her expenses. She could go to Paris with her father's blessing. It meant so much to her. Besides, the Committee too, was going to help.

Maggie re-read her father's letter. The envelope contained letters from her mother and each of her sisters. Kitty's enclosed note told her that every time their father had read of zeppelin attacks on London, he had suffered from bouts of stomach-ache. She ended the letter, saying that her friend, Patrick Healy, was sweet on her, and they intended to marry in the near future.

Maggie tapped her fingers on the table in time to some internal musical strain until she realised she was humming the Irish lullaby she had sung to her sisters when they came to her in trouble. If only she could be there for Kitty's wedding!

The long months without music lessons, however, had sharpened Maggie's appetite for more serious voice work. Her pulse quickened as she thought of the diva. Madame Marchesi had spoken so much of Emma Calvé and Nellie Melba. She must put her career before anything else. Only then could she return to Australia, charm her audience, and see her family again.

In late January, Albert Longbottom accompanied Maggie to the ferry at Dover. He had completed his convalescence at Exeter and been discharged from the army. Now he was seeking employment as a violinist.

'Goodbye Albert,' Maggie said. 'I wish you the best of luck in your career.'

'When you re… re… return to London as a gr… gr… great opera star, may I… I visit you?' His love for her shone out from behind his thick-rimmed glasses.

Maggie kissed him lightly on his cheek. 'Do come, Albert.'

She waved goodbye to him as the ferry ploughed out of the harbour and he became a small black dot silhouetted against the white cliffs.

~ *Chapter 8* ~

Emma Calvé

WILD ROSEMARY AND EVERGREEN BOX gave way to pines as the limousine ascended the Pyrenees. Further up, heather and scrub pine covered vast stretches of land. A castle, grey and forbidding with its turrets and towers, perched at the edge of a cliff like a fortress dominating the countryside.

Calvé told her chauffeur to pull off the road and pointed. 'This is where you'll be staying.'

Maggie gasped at the sight of the great edifice with its castellated tower and flagstaff. She turned to Calvé, who smiled at her before nodding to the driver to move on.

The limousine wound its way up a hill to the top of a wide plateau. The chauffeur unlocked the cast-iron gates at the entrance of the estate, drove through an archway and parked the car in the cobbled courtyard. They entered the castle, their footsteps echoing on the paved surface of the hallway. Maggie followed in silence, scarcely able to believe she was to live here.

A maid answered the bell, curtseyed, and led them into a hall. The floor was tiled with black and white marble, and marble pillars supported an arched roof. 'You need to refresh yourself after your long trip.' Calvé nodded to her maid, who led Maggie up to her room.

Colourful paintings decorated the walls of a richly carpeted room. A wooden bedstead, encircled with thick curtains, stood in an alcove. A basin of water and a towel had been placed on one of carved side tables flanking the bed. A matching ornate dressing table faced it at the opposite end of the room.

Maggie had just finished freshening up, when Calvé sent word to meet her in the foyer. She wished to show Maggie the castle and its grounds. Slipping into a comfortable pair of shoes, Maggie hurried downstairs.

As they strolled through the vast expanse of the castle. Madame Calvé studied Maggie's face. 'Now tell me something about yourself. Is Maggie your real name?' She spoke in French, the only language common to both.

'I was baptised Marguerite.'

Calvé lay her hand upon Maggie's forearm. 'Then I shall call you Marguerite. Who were your teachers?'

'Madame Marchesi, Jean de Reszke and Harry Plunkett Greene.'

'Excellent. Excellent. They are all superior teachers.' Calvé clasped her hands. 'Although Madame Marchesi was like a mother to me, we did not always see eye-to-eye. She admonished me for attempting to get ahead too fast.' A faraway look came in her eyes. 'Jean de Reszke was the Romeo of every young girl's dream. The ideal Lohengrin, the perfect Siegfried. He's a master of singing. His style and finish have never been equalled. He used to sing with Melba. I think they loved each other... Did you fall in love with him, Marguerite?'

Maggie flushed and looked down. *How can she read my mind?*

'Everyone does, you know.' Calvé laughed her bell-like laugh and immediately put her guest at ease.

Surprises lay at every turn. Within the castle, marble nymphs embellished the halls and cupids frolicked in the centre of the baroque ceiling in the dining room. Tapestries depicting uninhibited ladies adorned each wall. Calvé gazed at the wall-hangings. 'This is where I'd like to retire and write my memoir. I teach in Paris for several months during the year. Russians, Italians, English, French and Americans attend my classes.' She let her words sink in before she continued. 'Father was a farmer and not wealthy enough to pay for a voice instructor, so Jules Puget, formerly of the Opera Comique, gave me lessons without any recompense. That's why I like to help others. I intend training young girls from every class of society here. The students will be beginners with untrained voices as well as those with years of experience. In summer, I'll share my comfortable country-life with them. The air is dry and bracing. Just right for a singer's throat and lungs.'

She lifted Maggie's chin with two fingers and searched her face. 'You're the first pupil I've invited here, and you'll spend more than *one* summer with me.'

'Oh, Madame Calvé, how can I ever thank you?'

'Be a model student and work hard. When you are rich and famous, remember to help others too. Music is sublime. It stirs the soul and leads to the divine. Just as the Creator is for all, so too is opera. Everyone should enjoy its beauty. Once we unlock the door of classical music, the multitude will demand more, until, like the waves of the sea, they are submerged by its spell.'

The words resonated within Maggie. She mulled over the phrase *when you are rich and famous*. Did Calvé have some way of looking into the future? Maggie promised the Lord that, like her patron, she too would help others.

Calvé's slim waistline accentuated her ample hips that moved seductively as she walked. She showed Maggie the Great Hall, the Minstrels' Gallery, the Throne Room and the Library. 'The Knights Templar still live here,' the diva said, her voice mysterious. 'They were brilliant scientists, builders and philosophers.'

In breathless admiration, Maggie took in a deep breath at the grandeur surrounding her.

Calvé moved to the ramparts and surveyed the castle gardens below. 'I arise at seven every morning and, if the weather is fine, I take a walk in the fresh air especially on opera nights. After lunch, I go outdoors again. It's a pleasure to be surrounded by flowers.' She turned her glance from the garden towards Maggie. 'I expect my students' every waking hour to be spent in activities that increase their capacity to study. Too much publicity at an early age is not good for a voice student. Great singers evolve ever so slowly.'

They descended from the battlements. Charged with excitement, Maggie held her hand against the walls to maintain her elegant deportment. Once they reached the gardens, she could not contain her emotions any longer. 'I love your lilacs and marigolds, sweet william and forget-me-nots...'

'And the fragrant blooms of the wall-flowers,' Calvé finished.

Maggie clasped her hands together in rapture. 'I used to wander in the countryside as a child.'

'Ah. You love nature and beauty. I studied at a convent and even longed to be a nun.'

'I too was educated by nuns,' Maggie replied, 'but I never wanted to be one.'

Calvé laughed. 'Once, when the nuns were taking us for a walk in the countryside, we came to a lovely castle and gazed at it in wonder and awe, admiring the towers and turrets silhouetted against the burning sky. I told them I'd possess it someday, and we all giggled at the absurdity of the idea.'

'Now you *own* one.'

Calvé swept her arm towards the stately structure. '*This* is the castle we had seen.'

Maggie placed her hand on her open mouth. 'How wonderful!'

'I must leave you,' Calvé said. 'I need to speak to my two farmers. Father supervised the farm until his death, but I do that now. You can wander around in the garden whenever the weather is clement. Dinner is at nine. Lessons commence tomorrow at ten.

Au revoir.' She hurried off, leaving Maggie to find her way back to her room.

At five minutes to nine, the maid knocked at Maggie's door and escorted her to the dining room. The odour of spices and roast meat drifted towards Maggie. They sat at one end of the huge oak table that could comfortably seat at least twenty guests. Maggie looked up at the large beams with their chandeliers sparkling and throwing patterns of light on the walls. The delicious meal of farm-fresh food spread warmth through her body.

After dinner, Calvé led her through the hallway. 'Come to the library and browse among my books, Marguerite.'

Shelves of books rose from floor to ceiling and red velvet curtains matched the armchairs surrounding the hearth. Small personal treasures covered the mantel piece—an ivory Madonna, a statue of St Joseph and miniatures of Madame Calvé and her mother. Volumes in soft leather covers lined the rosewood book cases. Among the vast array of books, a shelf had been devoted to mysticism. 'The spiritual life has interested me ever since childhood,' Calvé said. 'The Swami Vivi Kananda has influenced me. He's a Hindu monk. I'd been suffering from acute depression after the death of my daughter and tried to end my life. He advised me not to dwell upon sorrow, but to transmute it into external expression and live a happy life.'

Maggie gulped. *Even the great Calvé has her share of sorrows!*

Calvé picked a book from the shelf. 'Do choose whatever you like. I read in the evenings whenever time permits.'

While the diva settled down to enjoy herself, Maggie ran her index finger along a row of books, and immediately felt a sense of nostalgia. The odour of the paper, ink and glue conjured up memories of home when she had curled up on a settee, reading her favourite book. She missed the feel and smell of her books, and the longing for home grew acute.

Despite her loneliness, Maggie settled down with a book of poetry, focussing on the poem, *The Castle*, by Edwin Muir. Minutes later, she shut the book and studied the wall tapestries.

'Time for bed, Marguerite,' Calvé said at midnight, just before the stroke of twelve. 'Good night.'

'*Bonsoir*, Madame.' Maggie returned to her room, changed into a night dress, and switched off the light. Slipping into bed, she pulled up the eiderdown, thanking God for the wonderful turn of events.

As Maggie was about to drift off to sleep, Madame Calvé's powerful voice floated along the corridors, past her *boudoir*. Maggie noted that the diva's voice extended from F to above high Cs.

The next morning, the maid knocked at Maggie's door, entered the room and drew the curtains. Maggie rose, washed her face, and dressed for a breakfast of fresh eggs, butter and toast, followed by freshly picked fruit from the estate.

After breakfast, the maid led her to the classroom. A little baroque clock chimed out the hour and Calvé entered the room, her cheeks glowing from the fresh mountain air. She wore rough overalls and a sloppy hat, with a shabby shawl draped over her shoulders.

Maggie glanced at the diva's clothes in surprise.

'At my castle, I'm as free as the wind,' Calvé said. 'I wear what I want and do as I please, away from the conventions of the world. But come, let's enjoy the sunshine. Like a lizard, I love the sun. The beauty of nature is meant to be enjoyed. I follow a well-established routine, and so will you. Studying here will be a pleasure. Devote your attention to breath control, tone production and colouration of tones. Develop a well-informed mind.' She stopped, as though waiting for a response, but Maggie remained in silent adulation.

'We'll work until lunch,' she went on. 'Then I'll relax in my garden. You may join me, swim in the river, or ramble in the hills. Later, we'll have lessons in singing, stage craft and deportment.

Nothing is more expressive than a walk. We'll practise the swinging stride of Carmen, the modest steps of Marguerite in *Faust*, the hesitant stumbling of Ophelia in *Hamlet* and the mincing carriage of a coquette as she ruffles along in her flowing robes.' The cadence of her voice was hypnotic, her words magical. They intoxicated Maggie.

'Besides singing, study and exercise, I expect my pupils to appreciate literature and poetry. I'll take them to art galleries and museums to enjoy the marvels of the Italian Renaissance.' Calvé raised a finger. 'But first, you must understand Carmen's character thoroughly. Before taking the part of Carmen, I returned to Spain, where I had spent my early years. I watched the seductive way the dancers shook their shoulders, their graceful hip articulations, and torso undulations. They have a vigorous form of dancing.'

Maggie listened, lapping up everything like a cat licking every drop of milk from its saucer. She imagined the room filled with the odour of tobacco and the fumes of cigarettes. She saw the gypsies swirl their skirts; heard their hands clapping and their feet stamping.

'But that is not all,' Calvé continued. 'I also studied cigarette factory girls at their work and play.'

The lesson passed all too swiftly, and Maggie jumped when the lunch-bell intruded upon her allocated time. They had a meal of Spartan simplicity—freshly-picked lettuce, tomatoes, a slice of cheese and sticks of celery and carrots.

After lunch, Maggie asked, 'May I join you for a stroll in your garden, Madame?'

'Certainly, but you may call me Emma, in private.' She strolled towards the vegetable garden and glided her hand over the smooth contours of a cabbage. 'Fresh vegetables are served here at every meal.'

The fragrance of herbs like lavender and rosemary reminded Maggie of home. 'Father enjoys gardening too. He grows roses and has a vegetable plot.'

'You love your family, Marguerite. That's good. I, too, was devoted to my parents.'

They walked along in silence until they came to several wrought-iron benches. Emma sat on one and waved Maggie to sit beside her. She hummed a tune as the marigolds wafted back and forth in the breeze. Even the bees appeared to buzz in time to her refrain.

Maggie felt she was in a dream. Was she sitting beside the world's greatest diva?

'What are you thinking of Marguerite?'

'Of you… Is this true, or a dream?'

'Yes, it's true.' Emma laughed. It was a laugh with a brook tinkling through it. 'I'm not a spectre and the castle is real.'

'Is it haunted?'

'Oh, yes. Like every respectable castle, Cabrières possesses a ghost. The structure dates back to 1050, has witnessed the horrors of religious war and has been a refuge to the Knights Templar. One of the rooms is the Chamber of the Phantom. A former owner tried to build a bridge from one hill across to another, but never finished it. He still stalks around in his huge hat and long cloak.'

Maggie shuddered as she looked up at the turret. 'Ever seen him?'

Emma glanced sideways at Maggie, with a twinkle in her eyes. 'No. I've never met any ghost around here—*in a hat*, anyway.'

After dinner, they went to the library. Maggie sensed that her patron wished to be by herself, so she always left her company before the clock struck twelve. Once she heard Emma break into an aria, her voice rising and falling with all the strength and seductiveness of a prima donna at her peak. Listening to her patron's voice resonate with a ghostly orchestra in some submerged pit, her heart thumping, Maggie stood rooted to the spot, and recalled the supernatural stories Emma had mentioned. Was she entertaining the Templars who had lived here? A cold draft of air drifted through and sent a shiver down her spine. The hairs at the nape of her neck curled and quivered. Was she getting involved with spirits and the occult? Should she have heeded the nuns' advice?

The aria ended with a thunderous ovation.

Chapter 9

The Kama Sutra Room

A FEW DAYS LATER, THE DIVA CALLED Maggie to her. 'I will not be able to spend much time with you today, so wander about the castle but be careful not to get lost.' Her eyes twinkled as she added, 'We don't want you carried away by some knight with a long cloak.'

Emma's jest reminded Maggie of the areas within the castle she hadn't yet seen. The prima donna had already taken her to the main section, but she longed to go down the spiral steps and explore the narrow passages. Now was her opportunity to see the armoury, wardrobe, chapel and dungeon. To climb the complex of towers, bridges and barriers.

Intrigued, Maggie decided to investigate. Like most castles, the walls were of stone. The passages were narrow, and the silence told her that she was alone. She pushed open a large oaken door and entered a small room. Weapons were fastened on the wall— swords, spears, shields, bows and arrows and muskets. She slid her hand over a huge steel-tipped wooden lance, twice her height and as thick as her wrist.

A complete suit of armour wielding an axe stood, sentinel-like, in a corner. In her mind's eye, the noble knight who had worn it looked like Jean de Reszke in his prime.

Her eyes fell on the battle-axe he held. She visualised its crescent-shaped blade cutting into the skin and flesh, where a tiny chink in his armour left him vulnerable. The axe would split muscle and sinew; the head hitting the ground with a thump, and blood gushing out over the ground. Shuddering, she once again turned to look at the armour. Gauntlets protected the hands and yet allowed free movement of fingers. Maggie let her eyes rove over the metal piece covering the knight's entire chest. It would have been moulded to the wearer's contours. Stroking the breastplate and the pauldrons, she imagined the stalwart figure that once bore the weight of this protective gear. A thrill of excitement shot through her. What would it be like to be held in the arms of such a man?

Her thoughts turned to her patron. She was aware of her reputation for passionate and tumultuous relationships. Should she have heeded the nuns' warning? Too late now. She was already in the castle.

Maggie wandered back to the Hall of Fame, where paintings and photos in gilded frames portrayed the diva's acting days. Each picture displayed a different facet of Calvé. In one painting, a face of angelic sweetness beamed down, her silken hair caressing her shoulders like a mantle to protect them from the vulgar gaze. In yet another portrait, she looked like a queen in her flowing robes and stately mien as she stood before her adoring subjects.

Maggie stared, half-fascinated and half-scandalised, at the image. Her cheeks flushed. She noted the luscious curves of the breasts that had bewitched and beguiled innocent young men, and the long lashes that had enmeshed them.

Entering the next room, she drew back, startled. A row of ghostly figures lined up at each wall, so life-like that, at first glance, she thought she was in the Chamber of the Phantom. Then she realised they were wax figures adorned by the dresses her patron had worn over the years. The fragile relics of Emma's youth: costumes of Carmen, Marguerite, Juliet, Ophelia, Sapho and Santuzza. A faint fragrance still clung to the fading chiffons, velvets and tarnished cloths of threaded gold. Maggie pictured the wax figurines gliding across the room with mincing steps and swaying hips, their garments swirling as a gush of wind channelled through the open door. She visualised Madame Calvé as she stood on stage, the applause of the audience crashing upon her ears like a roar of thunder.

Maggie's insatiable curiosity drove her on. Shivering slightly from the cold, she drew her shawl more tightly around her shoulders. A long passage took her to a solitary room from which the smell of incense drifted. Like a genie newly released from her bottle, the scent swirled—sharpening her senses.

She opened the door. Gold and silver figures glittered in alcoves within the thick stone walls. Through the smoky haze, a statue with arms writhing like so many serpents hypnotised her. Incense sticks burned before the many-armed idol. To her left were two figures. Maggie's breath caught in her throat, her blood pumping faster. She glanced behind her. The door was still open, but she could not move. Her eyes were drawn back to the intimate pose before her.

Maggie felt the stirring of excitement rising from her nether regions and backed out of the room. *Someone must have lit the incense. What if they return? What if Emma's maid or even worse, a manservant, catches me alone in the presence of such objects? I've intruded on private ground—something unholy and profane.*

Maggie remained frozen; her eyes shut tight. A thrill of excitement ran through her. Never had she been aroused so much before. What did it mean? She closed the door, as if shutting it could prevent these scenes from haunting her. She recalled some English students she had met at the London College of Music. They lived in India but were studying in London. In hushed tones, the girls had spoken of the Kama Sutra room.

She paused. Then she recalled that Calvé had told her to feel free to wander around. Here was an opportunity to learn the facts of life. Ever since her days at the convent when she had referred to the sexual act as *it*, she had regarded intercourse as something dark and sinful. Now she could dispel the ignorance surrounding her mind. No one was around to embarrass her.

Maggie re-opened the door and shut it behind her. She turned from the first two figurines and gazed at the next couple. Her breathing became laboured, her cheeks hotter, but she did not stop. From one alcove to the next, Maggie's sexual knowledge expanded. By the time she had reached the last figurine, her senses reeled. She dashed from the room.

How she spent the remainder of the day Maggie could not remember. She remained in an extreme state of agitation. *The warnings from the nuns have come too late, but would I have heeded them? I love and admire Emma. I've only striven to strengthen the power of my voice and to emulate her seductive movements. I long to score success after success and draw millions of admiring worshippers like she has done. Is that wrong?*

That night Maggie dreamed of half-dressed sirens and terrible, terrible sights too dreadful to depict. Fortunately, as Madame had stayed closeted in her boudoir with her eminent guest, she did not see the diva until the next morning.

Maggie awoke to the singing of birds and lay in bed, listening to their chorus. Sunshine streamed through a space in the curtains. She rose in haste, knowing she had only a few minutes to wash and dress before breakfast. She raced down the stairs. Emma's guest had left. She was out for her morning walk, so Maggie had a hurried breakfast and hastened to join her.

In the September of 1919, when splashes of autumn colour suffused leaves, and a red and gold carpet covered the grounds, the diva took Maggie to her studio in Paris. There she instructed several pupils during the day and, in the evenings, she escorted them to soirées, balls and theatres. The taste of freedom and the savour of life in

Paris brought a rush of adrenaline to Maggie. How mature she felt at twenty-seven. She met other singers and learned more of the life of a *Prima Donna*. When an extraordinarily gifted singer occupies an eminent position in the world of opera and masters the high note, admirers unhitch the horses, step between the shafts, and draw her carriage. Calvé and Melba had experienced that. Would she, too, reach such heights?

Maggie knew about basic stage rules, but Emma summarised everything so simply and taught her pupils all the subtle ways of alluring an audience.

'You make it sound easy,' Maggie said.

Emma smiled. 'Vocal skills and technique can be taught, but talent, rhythm and imagination are entirely our own. It's God's gift.'

The diva had an inexhaustible fund of anecdotes. One day, seeing her holding a doll dressed as Carmen, Maggie asked, 'Is this a souvenir of your role in *Carmen*?'

Emma shook her head. 'I made it myself. Whenever I have a bit of bright ribbon or a scrap of lace, I sew a costume for a doll and give it to a friend. During the war, I sold dolls to raise money for our wounded soldiers. I sent one to the Lafayette Fund in New York for the war effort, and it raised $4000 in a raffle.'

Maggie spread out her arms 'You've done so much good. I'd love to model my life on yours, Emma.'

For three years of delightful bliss, Maggie came to Paris every autumn, but continued to study with her patron at her castle for the rest of the time. Emma's coaching—the spark that set her artistic fires burning—developed Maggie's voice in the direction of a dramatic soprano.

Her dreams came to fruition in 1921, when Emma bestowed on her the *nom de plume* of Djemma Velca, an anagram of Calvé, and made an appointment for the directors of the Opera-Comique to audition her.

On the day of the audition, Emma raised a warning finger. 'Singers are susceptible to emotional distress. Remember to always be relaxed. Learn to cope under the most taxing conditions. Otherwise, you will develop vocal disorders. Have confidence in your ability. Don't concern yourself about negative evaluations.'

At the audition, Maggie tried to relax. She rubbed the back of her neck and curled and uncurled her fingers in rapid succession, recalling Emma's words, 'Have confidence in your ability.'

She took a deep breath; her nervousness now tinged with confidence. *I'll do it. I'll show them what three years with Emma can do.* Holding her head high, she stepped forward, brimming with confidence. Her fingers unfurled. She spread her arms and threw back her head. Maggie's voice obeyed her every gesture, every command. Her aria rose and fell, filling the room. Her voice, subdued, searching, wistful, called to them like the haunting cry of a mother to her babes, captivating her audience

The executives were so pleased with her performance that they offered her a two-year contract to play leading roles. Maggie longed to throw her arms around Emma in gratitude, but she held back, knowing it was not correct to make a display of one's emotions in public.

M. Albert Carre, one of the directors who had been away during Maggie's audition, requested her to sing for him. On Madame Calvé's advice, she sang arias from *Carmen*; the *Habaner—love is like an elusive bird*—and the *Card* aria, a slow ominous melody concerning the futility of trying to avoid death. She also chanted the *Les Larmes* from Goethe's *Werther*.

Carre gave her a part that would do full justice to her voice. 'You'll sing in Goethe's *Werther* and play the heroines in *Carmen* and *La Tosca*. During the opera season, you'll perform in no more than five or six operas.'

The director of the Monte Carlo opera at Monaco, who was present at Maggie's audition, also offered her the lead role in Massenet's *Amadis*. Emma Calvé, confident of Maggie's success, requested the directors of the Opera-Comique to release her protégé until she had completed her season at Monte Carlo. They agreed, on condition she returned to Paris in three months to fulfil her contract. She did not hesitate.

Maggie commenced rehearsals, soon realising the absolute necessity of attracting the audience with her voice. The music of *Carmen,* with its turns of harmony and orchestration, was delightful. The vigorous tune at the beginning of the Prelude set the sunny scene of Spain for the tale of love and violence that was to follow. The martial music of the *Toreador Song* played *pianissimo* from the strings and repeated *fortissimo* by the orchestra, swept the audience off their feet.

Maggie thought of her family and friends who had encouraged her every step of the way. Eleven years had passed since she'd left them. Now she was about to make her debut. Her heart pounded. She placed her left hand on her chest to calm herself. She gave herself up to a delirium of delight and burst into peal after peal of laughter, then spun herself around the room like a dervish dancer. She collapsed into a chair and covered her face with her hands, dizzy with delight. *Please help me, God,* she prayed.

She wrote to her parents about her forthcoming debut.

Dearest Mother and Father,

How I wish you could be here for my debut. Without your encouragement, all this would only have remained a dream. It is so wonderful. I can hardly wait for Opening Night. Do pray for me.

Hope you are all well. Love to everyone, Your loving daughter, Maggie.

~ Chapter 10 ~

The Debut and Post-Opera Parties

EIGHT MONTHS AFTER HER AUDITION in Paris, Maggie checked in at a hotel in Monte Carlo. That night, she looked down at the terraced gardens from her room. Magnificent villas and luxurious hotels sprawled over this playground of the rich. The Mediterranean Sea was a ghostly grey.

Maggie could barely contain her excitement. She felt a lightness in her chest and burst into throaty laughter. In eleven years, she had risen from a timid student and was about to make her debut at the Monte Carlo Opera House. It was smaller than Paris, but its exclusive audience had the power to make or break her maiden effort. She recalled the time Emma had warned her she could be bruised. *If that's the price of fame, I can take it.*

She recalled asking Emma about the routine she had used while a diva. 'What routine should I follow when performing in the evenings?'

The diva had tapped Maggie's cheek before replying. 'I rise at seven and take a walk in the fresh air. Eat my main meal at three in the afternoon. If tired in the evening, I indulge in a small glass of port or a cup of coffee and have a biscuit. When the performance is over, I drink some milk or have a bowl of soup. I always avoid midnight suppers after a long and fatiguing evening's work.'

Maggie decided to follow Emma's advice. Now, after days of anxiety, the night of nights had finally arrived. Maggie waited

85

in the wings, her mouth parched and her breathing out of control. *Breathe deeply. Breathe deep.* She wiped her sweaty hands on her handkerchief, and stepped from behind the curtain, gliding to centre stage.

At first, everything was a blur so she focussed on the conductor. When he raised his baton, she forgot her fears and sang. *This is my debut. The audience expect something special. I will give it to them.*

Monte Carlo's elite sat forward, wreathed in smiles at Maggie's performance of Charlotte in Massenet's *Werther.* In Act I, when the strings vibrated and swelled through the entire orchestra, the elegant simplicity of the vocal line shone. Maggie trilled the *Clair de Lune* duet with the tenor and blushed when he embraced her. The thrill of being in his arms suffused her with joy.

At the end of Act One, Maggie received a long ovation. The cheers of the audience in the front rows, who had witnessed the modesty displayed by her blush, carried through to the rest of the spectators.

When she sang the Letter Aria in Act III, she fully immersed herself in the pain of being caught between duty and love. During her delivery, Maggie varied her range, surging first to a crescendo, then mellowing to merge with the receding tones of the orchestra. She also tuned in with the light, bright flourishes of happy memories, and concluded with the sobering mood of intense distress in the finale.

Acclamations rang out. A thunderous applause arose and lasted for several minutes. Swaying slightly, she stood enveloped in sheer joy. Heat radiated throughout her body. At the end of the applause, her triumph swept her, sylph-like, off the stage.

In her dressing-room, Maggie found a perfumed package among bouquets of flowers left by admiring fans. Heat rose to her cheeks as she gazed at the insignia imprinted on the wax sealing the parcel. *Oh! Who has given me this?* With trembling fingers, she opened the gift. Inside a green velvet case lay a turquoise bracelet.

She let out a gasp.

Maggie fastened it on her wrist and hurried out to meet her admirers. They thronged about, presenting her with flowers and ambushing her with praise.

A nobleman kissed her hand. '*Enchante.*' A ring on his finger bore the identical crest as the one on the parcel.

Her eyes sparkled. 'Thank you, *Monsieur.*' A ripple of excitement flowed through her, once again bringing a warmth to her cheeks. Entranced, she watched him leave, hoping to see him again. Admirers continued to crowd around her. Their adulation transported her back to London when Albert Longbottom had waited at the stage door of the Old Vic, grasping two-penny-worth of chrysanthemums for her. *What a long way I've come since then.* Maggie took deep satisfying breaths.

Thanks to her patron, after her performance in *Werther*, Maggie moved in an elite circle. Emma accompanied her on a round of social activities and parties. Young men surrounded her, elderly gentlemen ogled her. Dowagers, bedecked in jewels, presented their blushing daughters, eager to meet the rising star. Carried along by this enchanted season, she could be forgiven for spending nearly all her earnings on her attire.

Newspapers splashed her photograph across their pages. Captions spoke of her radiance and indescribable beauty. Phrases like, 'As if spring had taken human form,' and 'Exquisite in hand-sewn dresses of silk and lace,' dotted the pages.

After sending cuttings from the papers to her family in Australia, Maggie, thrilled by her newly found fame, gathered her treasured theatre programmes and newspaper cuttings in a small trunk.

Maggie's next opera was in Gounod's *Damnation of Faust*. Immersed in rehearsals, she noticed a chameleon-like change in her actions and feelings. At the opening night, Maggie created an evocative atmosphere, performing as Marguerite, an innocent young girl, charming but simple and naïve.

The applause reflected the excellence of her voice and acting ability. She had fulfilled all expectations. She enjoyed the adrenalin rush, and now that she had experienced the power of a dramatic soprano, she longed to continue holding audiences under her spell. Opera and the adulation of an audience meant more to her than anything else. At times, her humble beginnings came back in a rushing wave of happiness. She looked back to the time when, as a child, she had thrown the tablecloth across her shoulders and strutted about, singing. She reflected on all she had achieved since leaving home. *Thank you, Lord*, she whispered.

Months later, her face continued to grace the front pages of Europe's major newspapers. Captions spoke of her radiance and indescribable beauty. At *soirees*, she let herself be swept along in a flood of emotions.

One day, her patron Emma Calvé smiled at her with a twinkle in her eyes. 'We've been invited to a fancy-dress ball. A clandestine one. You'll go as Carmen.'

Outside, a half-moon glistened, and stars glittered. Emma's exotic perfume filled the limousine as she reclined on the leather-upholstered seat. Her clinging black dress moulded itself to her body and revealed her shapely form. The skirt was a flowing swirl of satin. She broke out into a trill of laughter and took out a silken scarf from a small gold-mesh bag. 'Our destination is secret. I must blind-fold you until we arrive.'

Maggie leaned forward, in happy anticipation of the evening. She wore a gown of red chiffon, aware that her bare shoulders would do full justice to her youthful figure and graceful curves.

The vehicle's wheels crunched on gravel as it made a sharp turn into the driveway. 'We've arrived,' Emma whispered. 'Now you may remove the scarf.' She placed a silver mask across her protégé's features and adjusted it to fit firmly. It had apertures for her eyes, covered her nose and her cheeks but left her luscious red lips exposed.

The chateau looked like a fairy-tale castle. A footman ushered them into an immense hall, and Maggie caught a glimpse of the plush carpets, the crystal chandeliers and the silk and velvet wall hangings.

No one announced their arrival, since everyone was in disguise. Some masks concealed the whole face—others merely hid the area around the eyes.

A tall gentleman dressed as a musketeer, bent over Emma's hand, and whispered to her. His velvet cloak of cerulean blue fell in graceful folds, revealing a baldric worked in gold. It supported a large sword. Emma waved him towards Maggie and floated away.

The musketeer bowed before Maggie and took her arm. Soon they were swept up in a wave of music. Before long, a tenor broke out into *Nessun dorma*, and one by one, the guests joined in—'My secret lies locked within me. No one shall ever know my name.' People toasted one another and champagne flowed. In vain, Maggie kept looking for the young nobleman who had given her the turquoise bracelet. She danced with partners disguised as pirates, highwaymen and knights, but none of them wore a ring with the nobleman's crest.

As the night wore on, the party grew wilder until it became a veritable orgy of abandon—all sense of decorum forgotten. Couples clung to each other like amorous leeches; bodies moving sensuously in time to the music.

The musketeer returned and claimed Maggie for a waltz. He held her in a firm grasp. 'Your time with Calvé is ending. Need a new patron?' His voice dropped low. 'I'll give you anything you like. I have influential friends. I will introduce you to composers and opera conductors. You'll be a second Emma Calvé.' He pressed himself closer.

Her pulse raced. She trembled with excitement at the smell of wine on his breath, the pressure of his right hand on her lower back, the silky softness of his glove as he stroked her bare shoulders with the fingers of his left. The thrill of pleasure overwhelmed her. Perhaps the champagne had aroused her. She recalled all the warnings given about men, but she pushed them aside together with all the gossip about Emma Calvé and Nellie Melba. *Is this how opera stars get famous? Maybe it is the only road to renown...*

Maggie's thoughts flew back to *The Damnation of Faust* when the tenor, Faust, sold his soul to Satan, and her strict upbringing finally rose to the fore. *Is this the price of being a celebrity? No. I will not sell myself to the devil.* She struggled to overcome her sensations and strained away from him; her throat constricted.

His lustful eyes swept over her.

Her voice rose. 'Stop! Please stop, *Monsieur.*' *Emma will soon be leaving on her world tour, and I'll need a new patron. I can't offend any prospective one.* She fanned herself. 'I need fresh air. It's stifling in here, Monsieur.'

'Of course, my dear.' With feigned gallantry, he gripped her hand and led her towards the shrubbery in the garden.

She stumbled after him. 'Thank you, Monsieur. Please leave me now and permit me to rest awhile.'

'But I cannot forsake you, my dear child. I am your protector now. You deserve the world. I want to give it to you.' He held her close, crushing her. Maggie felt the heat from his breath burning her soul. Drawing her to hell.

She struggled and beat her fists against his chest.

He loosened his grip. 'I'll let you go this time, but not before you give me a kiss.' When he lifted his mask, his fixed jaw revealed a determination to satisfy his desires. His eyes seemed to shoot flames of passion. His hot breath stifled her, and a wave of nausea swept over her as she was pinned against the shrubbery by her attacker. He reached down for her dress and drew it up.

Vice-like, her teeth clamped upon his tongue—no longer a venomous viper, but a quivering worm. She smelled blood. Its salty metallic taste forced her to relax her jaw.

He staggered back, his face red with pain and fury. 'You'll pay for this, you bitch. Leading me on…' He stumbled off; the rest of his words drowned by the sound of his steps.

Maggie spat and wiped her mouth with her handkerchief. Sounds of laughter awakened her from her close encounter. The guests were leaving. She tried to compose herself but could not stop trembling. Returning to the chateau, she staggered to the ladies' room.

Emma Calvé was putting the final touches to her toilette. 'Ah. There you are, Marguerite. Time to go now.' She slurred her words.

Yes. It's time to go. Time to leave my patron before I lose my soul. I love and admire her singing. I love the way she has trained my voice. I love her generosity, and I am grateful to her. But it is time to move on. I'll go to Italy and perhaps I shall fulfill my dream of singing at La Scala.

That night Maggie fell into a deep sleep and dreamed the figures in the Kama Sutra room came to life. A masked man stood before her and removed both their masks. His skin glowed. His full sensual lips met hers and lit a flame, sparking a spiralling pleasure that fluttered and quivered like a heartbeat. An exquisite sensation. Her breathing became fast and furious, and she let out a moan that awakened her.

Her dream had been so vivid. *Was the man in her dreams the young nobleman who had given her the bracelet? Would she ever meet him again?*

When all the glamour of post-opera parties and celebrations were over, they returned to Emma's castle in the Alps.

'People cannot imagine the work involved in going through an evening's performance,' Emma explained. 'You pour all your energy and emotion into the part, spend months in study and rehearsals; sing, walk, laugh and dance for hours. During intermissions and between acts, there's barely enough time to change costumes. The tension on the nerves, muscles and brain is extreme. What you need now is to recuperate.'

Maggie expected Emma to send her to bed and she was ready for it.

'We're going to the famous gorges of the Tarn. It's not far,' Emma said. 'Wear a pair of sensible shoes. We will have lots of exercise and fresh air.'

The weather was fine as they drove up the winding road, passing through pastures with rocky outcrops and herds of grazing sheep. A shepherd boy conducted them to a cave displaying coloured limestone formations. They followed their guide into the grotto of Dargilan, a cavern filled with stalactites and stalagmites. Passing through a labyrinth of halls and galleries, down flights of steps and along lamp-lit passages, they arrived at the 'Draperies' or frozen waterfall, where crystal lakes reflected fairy-like caves. In the 'Bell Tower'—the sixteen-metre-tall calcite columns—Emma commenced to sing, as she usually did when overcome by the beauty of nature.

At the end of the aria, the shepherd lad whistled at the magic of her music. 'The mistress will give you a job to sing for the tourists. You'd get a lot of money.'

'How much would she pay me?'

The boy screwed up his face. 'Hard to say… she might go up as high as five francs a day.'

Emma's eyes twinkled. 'I'll think it over.'

Maggie realised that her patron did not wish to embarrass the boy by letting him know he was speaking to *the* famous diva.

Towards the end of the year, Emma said, 'I'll be leaving on a musical tour shortly. I think it is time for you to make your name in Italy, Marguerite. I've written a referral for you to a vocal teacher, Giannina Russ, who lives in Milan.' She nodded graciously. 'Before I leave, let me warn you that our lives are not always a bed of roses. All is not gold and glitter in our profession, Marguerite. Once, I was so unhappy after the death of my child that I thought of taking my own life. I was in Venice at the time. I longed to release my anguish before eternal silence engulfed me, so I threw a cloak over my shoulders and hurried down the stone steps, untied a barque and floated on the still waters of the canal. My song poured out in a turbulent flood. I stopped only when my voice died, and my lips failed to emit any further sound. A profound silence prevailed, and I became conscious of a mass of small boats, each jostling for a position around me. In the barque closest to me, a young couple held hands and gazed at me. The next morning, I received a bouquet of flowers with a note signed Paul and Jeanne, thanking me for an unforgettable experience. This warning is my parting gift to you.'

Maggie's heart ached with sorrow, and her eyes filled with tears. *Am I to go through fire and brimstone before I can sing in La Scala?*

She smiled through her tears. 'Thank you, Emma. I shall never forget your kindness to me.'

~ *Chapter 11* ~

Milan

MAGGIE TOOK HER LAST LOOK AT the castle in the dim light of the early morning. It seemed cheerless now. No wind blew and the flag on the turret hung limp. In the Pyrenees, Maggie had witnessed the life of a diva with its whirlpool of social activities. Above all, she had made her debut at the Opera-Comique. Now, Emma was about to embark on a tour of the British Isles. Maggie longed to join her, but she realised the time had come for her to give way to other aspiring singers. She patted her letter of introduction to Giannina, tucked it safely in her handbag and lay back on the seat of Emma's limousine as it wended its way down the mountain.

At *Gare de Lyon*, Maggie boarded the Simplon Orient Express to Milan. Before settling down in the Second-Class compartment, she ordered a breakfast of coffee and croissants from the steward for the next morning. She dozed off to the murmur of voices and the sound of the train chugging along. Occasionally she woke and gazed at couples sitting close, their eyes for no one but each other. She longed for some romance. Though drawn to love, she had devoted her life to opera, and never considered marriage. Now at thirty, each time she saw happily married couples, she regretted that choice. Memories of times in England with her friend Lisa Parsons came flooding back. What was Lisa doing now? Devoting her life to a career or to children?

After a short sleep Maggie woke and watched the Alps draw nearer. In her imagination, she scaled their heights, not pausing to rest until she reached her goal—to sing at La Scala. The mountains drew her onwards and upwards until she stood at the summit, looking down at the world beneath her feet, singing to an audience who listened in rapture to her pure notes.

The snow-covered peaks reminded Maggie of her mother's icing-covered cakes. Her thoughts descended from dizzy heights to her home back in Hobart. She smelled the aroma of freshly baked cakes and heard the patter of Josie's feet as her little sister hurried in to get the first bite.

The thought of food aroused a pang of hunger, and she became aware of passengers chatting and laughing among themselves as the train pulled into Lausanne. Shimmering in the sun, the lake reflected the verdure of the countryside and a brilliant blue sky. Maggie gazed at the Arcadian scene. How she yearned to capture its beauty on canvas. It had been so long since she had painted anything.

As the engine whistled, she headed to the dining car for breakfast.

'*Bonjour, mademoiselle.*' The waiter bowed as she took a seat.

'*Bonjour,*' she answered.

Maggie watched the Swiss villages slide by while she enjoyed her coffee and croissants. They sped past meadows and castles. The Montreux Palace, a baroque-style building, stood against a background of mountain and mist. Time passed. Churches and houses appeared, and she was in Italy.

A sudden jolt brought the train to a stop amid cries of *Mama Mia.* Maggie had a window seat, so she opened the window. People crammed their heads out, crushing her with their bodies, almost suffocating her. The cacophony of voices left her bewildered, and her brain reeled with the sudden onslaught of words. After all her studies in Italian she only understood a few phrases—perhaps because they spoke too fast or used another dialect—not Milanese. *Why has the train stopped? Why is everyone so agitated? If people panic whenever a train makes an unscheduled stop, the situation here must be dangerous.* Doubts sprang to her mind, beating against her brain, clamouring for attention. She worried at her lower lip. Was she right to have come here? Why didn't she study the conditions before leaving Paris? Her triumph at Monte Carlo must have gone to her head. She should have sent a telegram home asking for advice. Father would have wanted her to follow her career. Her fingernails dug into her palms.

Will the Blackshirts drag off dissenters? She imagined the thud of jackboots as they boarded the train, and shuddered in fear.

But they can't touch me. I hold a British passport. She silently thanked her British ancestors for making this possible.

Several minutes later, passengers returned to their seats, their voices echoing through the train. Their words were meaningless, for she could only understand a phrase here or a word there.

The train moved forward with a jerk, and a man fell against her. Suffocated by the smell of sweat and garlic in the crowded compartment, she glared at him. Good-looking, with brown wavy hair and a straight Roman nose, he murmured an apology, smiled and departed.

Somehow his smile brought the sunshine back to her thoughts. She looked up at the mountains again. Their white caps glittered in the sun, waiting to be conquered. *Someone once said a Prima Donna died three deaths. When her beauty faded. When her voice failed and when she surrendered to the Silent Reaper. My beauty hasn't faded, my voice hasn't failed, and I'm alive. There's hope for me yet.* She squared her shoulders and took a deep breath. There was still time to prove herself. Nothing existed for her but opera. It was impossible to live without singing. Like Emma, she ached to be flushed with fame and decked in jewels. She longed to stand on a stage carpeted with flowers thrown by admirers. But the future was unforeseeable.

The conductor pushed his way down the corridor, checking that everyone was awake. Houses and factories flashed past, then the train passed the Milano sign, and pulled into the station an hour later than scheduled.

Passengers rushed to the windows, shouting greetings to friends on the platform. Maggie's heart lifted. She grabbed her portmanteau and followed the others. Swept along by the crowds towards the taxi rank, she entered a cab, gave the hostel address to the driver, then sank back in her seat with a sigh of relief.

No sooner had the driver started the car than he burst into one of Verdi's arias—the *Slave Chorus*, from *Nambucco*. The pathos of his voice moved her. Was he also an aspiring opera star? She shut her eyes and allowed her mind to drift back to Harwood, the Clarence River, and the *SS Woolwich* where her father had played on his harmonica. She, together with the Italians from New Italy, had sung that same aria, too—so long ago. If only her family were not so far away!

As the aria finished, she opened her eyes. The driver was speeding like a greyhound, weaving in and out of the traffic.

'*Lenta, lenta,*' she exclaimed, shrinking back in her seat.

He laughed, pressing his foot harder on the accelerator. Realising her pleadings were futile, Maggie remained quiet until the cab turned into Viale Salmoiraghi and stopped at the Ostello Piero Rotta where she had booked a room.

Charged with excitement, she got out of the taxi. A paved path through a small garden led to the reception desk. The driver carried her portmanteau into the hostel. After being paid, he broke into another familiar aria, *La Donna e mobile*, as he drove off.

So, this is Italy!

The hostel was respectable, clean, and inexpensive. A bowl of fresh flowers adorned the reception desk. Maggie checked in before strolling over to a café in the next street to buy a panino and a cup of coffee for lunch.

After a satisfying meal, she returned to the hostel for a siesta. Later, she phoned Giannina Russ and made an appointment to see her on the following day.

The next morning, the receptionist gave Maggie directions to the studio. 'It's within walking distance.'

Maggie stepped out, and in less than fifteen minutes she arrived at a grey stone structure. She knocked, using the brass knocker of a lion's face on the large wooden door. A maid opened it and invited her in.

Giannina's short-sleeved dress showed her dimpled arms and flaccid underarm muscles, but she still retained her good looks at forty-three. She drew Maggie to her buxom bosom. Amazed by her friendliness, Maggie returned the embrace, assured now of her welcome. She thought of her own loving family and their warm embraces.

'Where are you staying?' Giannina's dark curls bounced up and down at each word.

'At the Ostello Piero Rotta. It's not far from here.'

'Come and stay with me. Emma Calvé gave me a wonderful account of you. I'll coach you in singing and introduce you to all the right people.'

Maggie's mouth drooped as she shook her head. 'I must get a contract before I can afford fees for voice lessons.'

Giannina held up both her hands. '*Basta. Basta.* You stay here. Today we will visit the city. Tomorrow we will find you a new name. Afterwards we will meet celebrities and later, we'll go and see the great Toscanini.'

Maggie's hand flew to her chest. 'How will I ever be able to repay you for your kindness?'

With outstretched arms, Giannina smiled. 'Don't worry. Teach my family. Give them English lessons.'

Giannina Russ was all hustle and bustle. True to her word, she took Maggie to the Duomo as soon as she was free. 'The Duomo is the third largest Catholic Church in the world. You can see the Gothic style, yes?'

Maggie looked up in awe at the magnificent edifice with its beautifully sculptured statues and spires. Once inside, she prayed for the support she needed in her climb to stardom.

They returned home for a meal of *risotto alla Milanese*. Maggie delighted in the melding flavours of saffron and onions with its aromas. She sipped the sparkling white wine and, recalling the Spartan lunches at Calvé's castle, she realised she must watch her diet here and not put on weight. Giannina had obviously already given in to culinary temptations.

After lunch, they retired to their rooms for a siesta, a luxury Maggie soon found indispensable with warm days and late nights.

After their siesta, Giannina and Maggie went to Milan's famous Opera House, La Scala. Pedlars stood near the entrance with wheelbarrows, selling printed sheets of arias to the jostling crowds. Italians did not seem to shun body contact as the French did. Maggie recalled one occasion when she had accidently brushed past a lady in Paris who had exclaimed, 'Oh la la!'

The exterior of the building was plain and unexciting. This was the place she had so longed for! Maggie swallowed hard in disbelief.

As if reading her mind, Giannina shook a finger at her. 'You wait. The inside is lovely.'

Maggie gasped as she entered. Just as the diva had promised, the interior was ornate. Massive yet delicate, the crystal chandelier reflected light in the adjacent mirrors. Exquisite statues stood on both sides of the reception hall that led up the staircase into the main theatre. Red plush seats matched the velvet curtains. She was speechless. *This is where Verdi held audiences spellbound. Once an obscure composer, the maestro had risen to great heights. Can't I do the same? My goal has ever been to sing at La Scala.* Her pulse raced and she felt like shouting with happiness.

'Well,' Giannina said. 'You say nothing…'

'I'm at a loss for words. My father admired Verdi and encouraged me to sing. I used to listen to Verdi's arias on the gramophone and sing along with them when I was a little girl.'

'If you love Verdi, you'll love Italy. He stands for everything Italian. He inspires us and arouses our patriotic feelings with his melodies.' Giannina threw out her arms to show how much Verdi was adored.

Maggie hugged her. 'Oh, Giannina. I'm so glad Emma advised me to study with you.'

'Her letter of introduction for you is *molto bene.*'

'Emma's been exceedingly kind to me.'

'Yes, but Paris is all fashion and glamour. We Italians focus on family and friends, not fuss and feathers. Italy is the centre of civilisation, the home of opera. Here you'll find the finest culture.' She paused. 'Come. It's time to return home.'

It had been a long and exciting day. Too weary to say anything more, Maggie's mind drifted back to Emma's soirees and the fancy dress ball.

A leopard skin lay in the middle of the tiled floor of Giannina's lounge. In a corner was a chair covered with red velvet, its golden arms and legs ending in the shape of a claw. Giannina sank into it, her pose like some diva out of a Verdi tragedy. She beckoned

Maggie to the chair nearest her. Statues looked down at them from niches in the walls.

The maid fussed over them like a mother hen, making sure their cups of coffee were always full. '*Basta, basta,*' Giannina said, waving her away.

Between sips of coffee, the diva enthused about Italian opera. 'Do you know that opera was started in the seventeenth century by charitable institutions? Back then, nuns trained orphans and underprivileged children in vocal, choral and instrumental music. Composers offered them tuition too. Acrobatic vocalism demanded vocal skills like in the *Tempest* aria, *Amor di figlia*, when the singer's voice is like waves beating on rocks, symbolising a heart-beat.' Her robust voice boomed through the room.

Maggie listened, thankful her host spoke slowly, as she was not yet sufficiently fluent in Italian to follow everything. She had so much more to learn.

'Opera has flourished because of the rich,' Giannina explained. 'The nuns trained their students to sing, so they would not sell their souls for bread, and patrons paid to hear them.' She ran her middle finger around the rim of her cup, as though contemplating its delicate beauty. 'Opera is no longer the privilege of aristocrats. The rise of the mercantile class has produced a paying audience with public theatres.'

'England has some smaller ones like the Old Vic, where the not-so-rich also enjoy opera.' Maggie leaned forward. 'Was it during this period that composers introduced scenes from real-life situations and rural life?'

'*Si. Si.* That's when opera *buffa* came into being.' Giannina took a sip of coffee. 'Italy is the cradle of opera. In the seventeenth and eighteenth centuries, Italian singers, composers and instrumentalists taught in England, France, Spain and Russia, and Germans came here to study.'

'The French have their own style of opera, with emphasis on plot and scenery,' Maggie said.

Giannina's lips curled—half-smile, half-sneer. '*Si si,* but their musical forms are simple.' Her voice rose and she waved her arms. 'Italian-style is foremost everywhere in Europe.'

Not wishing to disagree and prolong the argument, Maggie did not respond. She was tired and found it difficult to keep alert despite the coffee. Glancing at herself in the mirror, she noticed dark rings beneath her eyes.

Giannina rang the handbell and told the maid to summon the chauffeur to take Maggie back to the hostel. 'And make sure he knows to pick her up the next morning.'

Maggie clasped Giannina's forearm, repeated her thanks and left, impatient for her bed.

Before dropping off to sleep, Maggie pondered what stage name she should choose for her Italian debut. The one Emma had given her in Paris wasn't likely to attract attention in Italy, and her own name was so uninteresting.

Mary Wilson, another opera singer, had chosen the name Florence Austral. Helen Porter Mitchell, a Melbournite, had used the stage name Nellie Melba. Maggie wanted her name to sound Italian yet remind the audience she was an Australian. 'Stralia' sounded Italian. Marguerite would become Maria.

She closed her eyes and dreamed of herself as Maria Stralia, the future diva, then she floated away in the haze of sleep.

~ *Chapter 12* ~

Giannina Russ

THE MORNING AFTER HER VISIT to Giannina, Maggie awoke early, with the thought of moving into her new home in the country. She packed her portmanteau, had breakfast and handed back her room keys.

'*Mi scusi, signorina.* Here's your mail,' the receptionist said. Posted to her last address in Paris, the letter had been re-addressed to her at the hostel.

Maggie sank down on the settee in the waiting room and tore open her mail—a long-awaited letter from her parents. She held it to her face and imagined she could distinguish the faint fragrance of her mother's *eau de cologne*. She caressed the letter, her sole link to her parents.

Her sister Kitty had enclosed a gossipy note. Maggie smiled, scanned it, folded the letter and tucked it into her handbag, intending to re-read it at her leisure. She paced up and down the lounge, waiting for Giannina's chauffeur.

On Maggie's arrival at the diva's studio, she breathed deeply before knocking. Would Giannina be just as welcoming as she had been the previous day?

The maid answered the door. *'Boun giorno.'* She relieved Maggie of her suitcase and led her upstairs to a small bedroom.

An opera score lay on a writing desk. Maggie opened her eyes wide. There were no plush carpets. No opulent fireplace. No works of art. Nothing one would expect to see in a diva's home. She unpacked her clothes then hurried downstairs.

Giannina kissed her on both cheeks like an old friend or relative. 'So, my dear, have you selected a stage name?'

'Yes. I've chosen Maria Stralia.'

'Bella. Everyone will know from where you come. Au – stra – lia.' Giannina smiled. 'We'll leave for the villa after our siesta. Bring all your things with you.'

Maggie felt foolish for having unpacked. She now realised the apartment was Giannina's residence when on business in Milan.

She returned to her room and started to re-pack. Aware that most Italians had an afternoon nap, she lay down for a rest, but the excitement kept her awake for a long time until she shut her eyes and slept from sheer exhaustion.

Refreshed from her siesta, Maggie dressed in readiness for the trip. She couldn't wait to see her new home. The maid tapped at her door and entered to take her case downstairs. Maggie followed, sliding her hand on the bannisters. Giannina looked bright and beautiful in a dark blue dress. Sapphires adorned her neck. 'Now let us go to my home.'

The diva stepped into the car and lounged back into the seat. With a conspiratorial air, she said, 'I've invited Claudia Muzio over. She arrives tomorrow. You have something in common with her. Like you, she studied voice in London.'

'I'd love to meet her,' Maggie said. Perhaps she would get to know what made her so famous.

Giannina glanced out of the window. 'I adore the countryside. It's good to be embraced by the warm air in the spring when the trees burst with buds and thaw the frozen corners of my brain.'

Maggie watched the country glide past. The road followed the River Adda. Groves of poplar patterned the green fields and water purled beneath bridges. They passed forests, isolated farmhouses and villages. Castles looked down at them from the hills, and an eagle circled overhead then swooped on its prey.

At Cassano d'Adda, a fortress high above the river, they stopped to enjoy the view. Maggie glimpsed sumptuous villas with expansive gardens in the valley below. Giannina spread out her arms as if to embrace the rustic scene. 'We're not far from my home now.'

Maggie had expected to live in a big and bustling city, not in such sublime surroundings. She clasped her hands to her chest in delight. Within half an hour, they turned off onto a rustic road and finally arrived at two massive stone pillars supporting wrought-iron entrance gates. The car's wheels crunched over the loose gravel path leading towards the villa. A maid opened the tall cedar door and took them through a long hallway tiled with white marble. The hall led to a flight of stairs. To their left was a dining room with walls tiled in hand-painted ceramic. Light from the windows above the stairs splayed geometric patterns on the floor, glittering and flickering as it danced on the floor tiles.

They ascended the spiral staircase. 'No one occupies the first floor at present,' Giannina said as they went on to the second floor. 'You'll be staying here. I'll be on the next level. Roam around as much as you like. *Mia casa tua casa.*' She left her guest to settle in. Her skirt swished as she proceeded upstairs to her own apartment.

Maggie found herself in a richly furnished living area leading to a bedroom. A fire crackled in the hearth. Scarcely had she taken her shoes off to warm her feet against the copper fender, when there was a knock at her door, and a maid entered.

'*Buona sera.* I'm Angela. Do you need anything, *Signorina*?'

'What's on the highest level? I'd like to look around the place, but don't wish to intrude.'

'The third floor has three bedrooms and a suite for intimate friends, *Signorina. Signora* Russ gives voice lessons in the tower. You may like to keep going up the stairs to it. You'll get a wonderful view of the countryside.'

'Thank you, Angela. *Buona notte.*'

The maid curtsied, and after turning down one corner of the eiderdown in a neat triangle, she left the room. Maggie unpacked her things and stored them in the ornately carved chest of drawers. Giannina had told her that dinner was at nine, so she had plenty of time. She slipped on her shoes and started exploring before darkness set in. Each level of the villa had its own covered terrace. In the tower, Maggie tried out her vocal registers before descending the spiral stairs to the dining room.

The aroma of garlic drifted up from the steaming lentil soup once the lid was removed. It was followed by roast pork seasoned with almonds, a dish of pasta, fresh green vegetables tossed in garlic sauce and a glass of chianti. How different from the bland dinners of roast beef, potatoes and peas at home, or those in London at Mrs Sutton's house. The delicious French meals too, differed from Giannina's. French dishes were rich in fat, but the presentation was almost sculpture-like when arranged on a serving plate. Italian cuisine, however, had more of the flavours of fresh food and less of the visual. Italy used olive oil in preference to butter and the fragrance of garlic and spices often rose from both French and Italian dishes.

When it came to dessert, Maggie missed the light French pastries. *I must get accustomed to this cuisine if I am to remain in Italy. How long will that be?*

~ After dinner, Giannina took Maggie up to the tower and asked her to sing while she listened and wrote down a few suggestions.

It had been a day bursting with happiness. Yesterday, La Scala had filled Maggie with amazement and awe, today the villa imparted peace and enchantment. Soon, she'd be singing in La Scala. She thanked the Lord for leading her to Milan.

The next morning Maggie met Claudia Muzio who had just returned to Italy after a season of opera in Chicago. Claudia was lovely, with an elfin face and full sensual lips. Maggie congratulated the star on her striking success and swift rise to stardom.

Claudia threw out her arms. 'I'm so glad I pleased the Chicago audience, but now I have a contract in South America. We'll see how the other hemisphere takes to me.'

'They won't be able to resist you.' Although Maggie had not heard her sing, she knew the audience would fall for her beauty alone. She suspected Giannina had invited the star over especially for her, and Claudia had accepted, despite her busy schedule.

'How did you like the English weather when you were there?' Claudia asked.

'That was the one thing about London I disliked,' Maggie replied. 'The cold and damp especially after the snow began to melt.'

'Oh. The slippery streets and the discoloured snow,' Claudia exclaimed, breaking into laughter. 'The weather here is much more pleasant.' Her face lit up and brought a sparkle to her large, alluring eyes. Her laughter sounded like the tinkling of bells.

She picked up a newspaper lying on a side table. 'If only the world concentrated on the arts, especially music. Italy is now a Fascist country. Mussolini is our Prime Minister. Is it a good or bad thing?' She gazed into the distance, as though searching for an answer, but Maggie knew she had asked a rhetorical question and wasn't expected to reply.

Claudia paused for a moment before continuing. 'When Mussolini commenced the march on Rome in October, I feared I was going to be caught in the middle of a civil war, but to save the situation, the king invited him to be Prime Minister.' She heaved a sigh. 'Italy is in a sorry state with bloody fighting between Fascists, Socialists and Communists. Because most of my countrymen think we've been cheated out of the fruits of victory, ill-feeling exists against the Allies, especially the French… But enough of politics. Tell me something of yourself.'

'Considering how unsettled the country is in, I'm beginning to wonder whether I should have stayed in Paris.'

The diva reached for her glass of wine and sipped slowly before replying. 'Being Australian won't help. Most Italians would regard you as an enemy.'

Maggie gasped and looked at her hostess for confirmation. Giannina nodded. 'Since the war, inflation and unemployment are rife. We had no coal and scarcely any grain left by the end of hostilities. It is difficult for demobilised soldiers to find employment and there is distrust against foreigners. That is why I told you to take an Italian name.'

Maggie flushed. She had nowhere to go. No funds left to return home. Soon, she would not have enough left for a ticket to London or Paris.

'I didn't realise things were so *bad*. Emma must have been unaware of the political situation, or she would not have advised me to come to Milan… Well, I'm here now, and there is nothing I can do about it. How long will I have to wait for an opening at *La Scala*? I need to get a contract soon. I don't wish to impose on Giannina who is already doing what she can by introducing me to influential people.'

'Italy is in turmoil. Let us hope Mussolini will do something good for our country,' Claudia said. 'He promised to restore Italian power and prestige, revive the economy and bring back law and order.' She took another sip of wine. It hid the sneer on her lips. Then she rose from her seat and took a turn around the room, appearing to glide rather than walk.

Claudia reminded Maggie of a butterfly sipping nectar from a flower. Her graceful movements and sublime beauty aroused a twinge of jealousy. Now a mature woman of thirty, she was impatient at her own slow progress. She supressed her feelings. 'I must not miss your next performance.'

'You're most welcome. My repertoire embraces all the leading Verdi and Puccini roles. As you know, Verdi had a keen eye for stage effect and wanted strong characters like Lady Macbeth or Rigoletto.'

'His music is soul-stirring. I'd love to star as one of his tragic-heroines, but that depends on Giannina.' Maggie looked questioningly at her coach.

'We'll see,' Giannina said. 'You may make a great Lady Macbeth.'

Claudia glanced at her hostess before proceeding. 'Giannina is famous for her Verdi dramatic-soprano roles. She'll know exactly what you're capable of.' She stopped pacing the room and selected a seat beside Maggie.

'I love Verdi, but I like to relax with Rossini.' Maggie tried her best to be cheerful. 'He has a genius for triviality. In *Barber of Seville*, his melodies sparkle with humour.'

Giannina nodded. 'Yes. Rossini's rhythmic energy depicts all the vitality and joy of living.' She stood up with an air of finality. 'Claudia has a contract to sing at the principal opera houses in South America. She must retire now as a heavy schedule lies ahead for her.'

Slowly, like a mermaid emerging from the water, Claudia rose. Her soft silken dress fell around her like waves in the sea. She extended her hand. 'Goodbye.'

Maggie stood, trying to imitate her style. 'Thank you for taking time to listen to my hopes and dreams.'

They shook hands in the formal English fashion rather than the more relaxed and friendly Italian custom of kissing on both cheeks.

That night, sleep was as remote as the stars, leaving Maggie tossing and turning in bed. Claudia's beauty, grace and charm had impressed her, but doubts and fears pounded their sledgehammer blows, bringing on a massive headache. She contemplated her circumstances. The political environment was unfavourable for her career, but she blamed no one. Her own relentless ambition had driven her to run with the wind like a ship without a rudder, heedless of consequences. She could not point an accusing finger at her patron Emma Calvé for advising her to study under Giannina Russ.

Her mind strayed to the past, probing the deepest recesses of her soul, her thoughts wandering in the garden of her memories. Should she have gone straight home from Paris? Were there any alternatives for her? Overcome by a desire to be with her loved ones, she longed to leap back into the innocence of childhood. To be a child with no responsibilities. To be guided by her parents.

Memories of long ago crowded in upon her. She thought of the time when her mother had enrolled her three daughters in Hobart at a school run by the Presentation nuns. She pictured her mother and young sisters in the waiting room with its overpowering perfume from the honeysuckle that wove it way up a trellis against the wall outside the convent.

She lay awake during the humid night, thinking of the possible repercussions against her. Slowly, her reflections turned from the past. *What should I do? How can I overcome the distrust Italians have for their former allies?* She gritted her teeth and choked back the sobs that tore at her throat. *I will have to master the language and assimilate with them. The alternative is to humble myself and return to Australia, England, or France.*

But despite all the teachings of the nuns, humility was not one of Maggie's virtues. It had never been in her disposition to admit defeat. She determined to chance her fate in Italy.

Early in the morning, she fell asleep as the first lark announced the beginning of another day.

She awoke heavy-eyed and dragged herself downstairs for breakfast. Her career remained marooned in a morass of isolation. Giannina was doing everything possible for her, but still she was unable to make headway. Neither was she getting any younger. Neither time nor tide would wait. What would the future bring?

~ *Chapter 13* ~

Depressing Thoughts

IN THE MONTHS THAT FOLLOWED Claudia's visit, Maggie continued to accompany Giannina to operas and concerts, but neither the sparkling lights nor ornate surrounds, scintillating atmosphere, exquisite fragrances nor verbal gymnastics of singers gave her pleasure. She watched opera with a critical eye, glowering at the performers; her hands tightening into fists. She could do better than any of them—if given the chance.

While wining and dining and breathing in arias, she was always mindful that preference was given to local talent. Despite Giannina's wide social sphere, Maggie's talents remained unknown and unwanted.

After a performance, Giannina would introduce Maggie to opera celebrities, but nothing came of it. It only made her more dissatisfied. At times, with hands immersed in flour and sleeves rolled up to her elbows, Maggie participated in her patron's cooking sessions, which took place for the greater part of the day. The fragrance of rosemary, marjoram and oregano filled the kitchen. Cooking was an art, just as nearly everything in Italy—like dressing oneself and decorating one's home.

Giannina did not confine her cooking to dishes of the Lombardy region. She made desserts like cannoli with a crunchy crust, covered with chocolate and separated by layers of vanilla cake. At times she made brioche, a yeast bread, rich and golden with butter and eggs. In summer, her speciality was a mulberry granita—a semi-frozen dessert topped with whipped cream.

These sessions only served to stimulate Maggie's longing for her home—for her family. The days dragged by. She wrote to her parents, telling them of her social contacts and the theatre, but evading the truth about her career. She realised they were caught up with their growing number of grandchildren and so responding less frequently. Aunt Polly, however, an inveterate letter writer, passed on all the gossip. During the Great War, she had written of visits by the destroyers *Yarra, Warrego* and *Parramatta*. At the conclusion of hostilities, she sent photos of the Victory March at Harwood and passed on the sad news of friends who had lost their lives.

Maggie's mind drifted back to the wounded and maimed soldiers she had sung for in London. Sorrow laid its hand on her heart, squeezing it until she cried out in despair. Her stomach churned to think of her lost opportunities. Should she try her luck in London now? A tiny voice warned her to hold back. *London must wait. I'll sing at La Scala first. But will I ever get there? Trapped, I can neither go forward nor back. The fare home is beyond my means. I have no savings and am not earning anything in Milan.*

Summer passed. Still no interviews with prospective employers or contracts to sing. One evening after dinner, Maggie decided to broach the subject to Giannina. Her breathing grew faster, and her voice trembled. 'Toscanini is always so busy. Do you think I'll ever get a chance to see him?'

'Everything will be all right soon. Be patient, my child. Do not worry.'

If only she could open her heart to Giannina. Maggie bit her lip. But how could she unburden herself to her dear hostess who was doing so much for her already? No matter how much she tried, Maggie failed to throw off the blanket of depression enveloping her. Would she ever be discovered?

The tapping of raindrops on the tiled pathways created a pleasant symphony of sound. The soft hushing sound filled the room. As if unwilling to disturb the distant patter, she contemplated the ceiling before giving a long-drawn-out sigh. The rain poured down, sounding like a Wagnerian outburst of drums and trumpets. Thunder roared. A howling wind shook the trees.

The air had grown cooler even as the storm had ceased. The rain, now reduced to a spasmodic patter, was in rhythm with her thoughts—a meaningless smattering of sounds strung together like a child learning to utter its first words. Trying to voice random utterances.

Maggie's irritation at being overlooked grew daily. Unable to subdue the haunting fear of failure, she lay awake at nights. At dinner, she drank more wine than normal. Headaches hounded her. She blamed herself for coming to Milan. Nothing cheered her.

She thought of writing to Emma Calvé. Having been through a period of depression also, *she* would understand her state of mind. But the diva was touring the British countryside, and Maggie did not wish to trouble her. She gazed out from her balcony. *I'm a failure in Italy. What will Mother and Father think? What will the Maggie Gard Society say? And Monsignor Gilleran? She looked down. It would be easier to jump off from this balcony than face them!*

Maggie recalled Emma's dark despair in Venice—that city of delight with its canals and gondolas curving around corners. Emma had told her she had contemplated taking her own life when the shadow of sorrow darkened her days. If the world's greatest Carmen suffered from depression at times, surely it was not unusual for other singers to be dejected too, Maggie thought. She tried to conquer her feelings, but the black dog continued to maul her. Day by day, she watched the red and gold leaves fall, and her heart plummeted. *How different life was in Paris with Emma Calvé.*

The fire crackled, sending sparks upward. Maggie warmed her hands and fixed her eyes on an envelope postmarked from Australia. It was winter in Milan and dark clouds hung overhead, but back home the sun was probably shining in all its brilliance. She slit open the cover and unfolded the letter.

Aunt Polly had written, telling her that Kitty had married. Maggie visualised her young sister radiant with happiness—the church decked with roses—Kitty's favourite flower. Tears spilled over her cheeks and splashed on the letter. She dabbed the letter with her handkerchief.

Her thoughts swung around to herself—alone in a foreign land. *I've missed out on my sister's wedding and am still far from achieving my dreams. The people of Hobart have raised money for my studies, and they expect me to return as an opera star.*

In an attempt to shake off the mantle of gloom, Maggie threw a cashmere shawl over her shoulders and slipped outdoors into the cold. She shivered and drew her wrap tighter, rambling aimlessly until she came to a church hidden among a grove of trees. Entering the sacred precincts, she blessed herself with holy water and genuflected before the altar. The clouds had cleared, and the late evening light slanted through the tall windows, making golden ribbons across the marble floor. She knelt on the soft, cushioned pews and burst into tears. Her body shaken by sobs, she prayed for Kitty's happiness and for her parents, before storming heaven for herself.

Dear God, please, please tell me what to do, she implored. As she begged God for guidance, a wave of peace engulfed her. She believed in the power of prayer, but in her dark moments she had forgotten the solace it brought.

How long she remained in the church she did not know, but hearing footsteps, Maggie turned. An old man shuffled up. Smiling, he jangled his keys and looked toward the exit. '*Buona notte.*'

'*Buona notte.*' Using the top of the pew for support, Maggie rose and genuflected.

'*Basta. Basta.*' A priest stepped forward, placed a restraining hand upon the janitor's shoulder and turned to Maggie. 'Can I help you, *senorita*?' he asked in Italian.

'I was passing by and came in to pray,' Maggie said. 'I'm staying with Giannina Russ.'

'Senora Russ is my parishioner. I don't see her often, but she sends a generous cheque every month… Where are you from?'

'Australia. I love Italy and Giannina is very kind to me, but it worries me that she rarely attends church. At home, my family attend Mass every Sunday.'

'This is a problem here,' the priest said. 'Although Catholics all over the world have the same belief, some countries are more rigid in observing one aspect of canon law than others.'

'In Australia, the Irish priests are very strict about their parishioners attending Sunday Mass,' Maggie said. 'It seems different here.'

'*Si. Si,*' the priest answered. 'In Italy people are unstinting in the upkeep of the church and towards helping others. You know the saying; *charity covers a multitude of sins.*'

Maggie nodded. 'Yes, Father.'

'My child, *to understand is to forgive*. In countries like France or Spain, things are different. There, people believe in prayer and penance. But of course, not everyone follows this too rigidly.'

'Thank you for enlightening me, Father. I've always known that people with different backgrounds were different even though they had the same religion but could never understand their ideologies.'

The padre smiled. 'You're always welcome at church. I understand you like to do what your hostess does but remember that God is forever waiting for you. You can pray anywhere.'

'Thank you, Father. It's been lovely speaking to you. A load off my conscience.' She hesitated. Should she confide her fears to the priest? She opened her mouth to say something, but the words choked in her throat.

The priest raised his hand in blessing and placed it upon Maggie's head.

Before turning to leave, Maggie nodded at the janitor who followed her and swung the heavy door, which squeaked on its hinges before shutting her out. With a lighter step and a clearer mind, she traced her way back, using a tall building as a landmark. Fortunately, it remained visible in spite of the darkness of the night.

Fifteen minutes later, Maggie was back at Giannina's home. The housemaid opened the door in answer to her knocking. If she was surprised to see Maggie come in by herself at such a late hour, she did not show it. Giannina had already retired.

Glad to be alone, Maggie retreated to her room and sat by the fire to write a letter home. She thanked the Lord for the peace that now flooded her soul. In a happier vein, she wrote to her parents, reiterating that her goal was to sing at the La Scala Opera House.

Six weeks passed before Maggie received a reply from her mother, who wrote that the Australian singer Gladys Moncrieff was now married to Thomas Henry Gard, a distant cousin of hers. Maggie had never encouraged her prospective suitors, thinking that life as a single woman could bring her dreams to fruition much faster. Now she began to regret her actions.

Months went by and Maggie's Italian improved. She met famous prima donnas and, at times, she sang in a choir at concerts.

Claudia's words, 'Being Australian, most Italian singers would regard you as an enemy,' held her back even as she sang. Her face tightened. Had she been asked to sing merely to please Giannina and not because they wanted to see her perform? Did the audience simply tolerate her presence?

That winter, worry lodged within her, teasing the corners of her mind. If only she could have that interview with Toscanini! She knew he would help her just as Sir Thomas Beecham had done in London, during the war.

$$\sim \text{\textit{Chapter 14}} \sim$$

Arturo Toscanini

ONE SPRING MORNING IN 1924, Maggie awoke to the warbling of wrens. She faced another weary day of disappointment. Reluctant to get up from bed, her good manners forced her to rise. She slipped on a dressing gown and looked down from the balcony. Bluebells flanked the path running up to the front door, their brilliant colour heightened by an azure sky.

At breakfast, Giannina beamed and rubbed her hands together. 'You've been granted an audition with Toscanini. He's been extremely busy since returning from a tour with the La Scala orchestra, but he has agreed to fit you in at short notice.'

Maggie hugged Gianninia. *Is this my make-or-break moment? I'd almost given up hope of ever having an audition with him.* Her grip around Giannina's shoulders tightened and she stuttered, 'Th-Thank you. Oh, thank you, so much.'

After breakfast, she hurried to her room and sorted through her wardrobe for some time, before deciding to wear her gown of black chiffon with its cloud of white lace framing the shoulders. The dress exposed her cleavage, and her mind flew back to one Sunday Mass when the Mother Superior had scolded her for her low-cut dress. She shook with laughter at the thought of what the nun would think of her now.

Maggie fastened a turquoise bracelet and hummed to herself as she climbed up to the tower. Once there, she went through her vocal registers in preparation for her meeting.

Next morning, on the way to meet Toscanini, Maggie bit her lip and gazed out of the taxi with unseeing eyes. A chill rolled down her back. 'What if Toscanini loves my voice but fails to find me a position because I'm not Italian?'

Giannina placed her hand over Maggie's clenched fist. 'Don't worry, my dear. He'll like you. In the old days, composers ruled the opera world, but now *musical conductors* possess that power.'

'Do you think he'll be able to help me with my career?'

'Of course, my dear. Your looks and singing will charm him. Relax. You worry too much.'

Maggie shut her eyes and took a deep breath before she stepped out of the taxi.

They entered Toscanini's studio, where several musical scores lay on his desk. The maestro stood before a raised podium and music stand. Snowy white hair grew at the sides and back of his bald pate, and a steely grey moustache adorned his firm, sensual lips.

Giannina introduced her. 'My protégé, Marguerite.'

He appraised Maggie. 'Well, show me what you can do.'

Her pulse quickened. *This the magic moment—the moment I've worked for, waited for*. Her mouth was dry, but she had come prepared. Without hesitation, Maggie commenced on a selection from her repertoire—the *Habaner—Love is like an Elusive Bird,* from *Carmen.* A thousand recollections of all she had learned from her voice teachers merged in her mind.

Toscanini listened, resting his right cheek in the palm of his hand, his deep-set eyes appearing to undress her as she sang. After a few minutes, he cut her short. 'That will do.' He took her hand and planted a kiss on it. 'Charming.'

He turned to Giannina, 'A position in the *La Scala* choir is hers as soon as a vacancy occurs.'

Maggie took a step back, feeling as exposed as a newly shorn lamb. Her spirits plummeted. *Why has he not allowed me to complete the aria? What have I done wrong?*

Giannina thanked Toscanini as he steered her towards the door.

Maggie stumbled after them. *What was charming? Me, or my singing? Why hasn't he commented on my voice? All he has offered me is a position in his choir.*

The taxi awaited them. Giannina stepped in and Maggie followed, her shoulders drooping. She swallowed hard and covered her face with her hands. *Is Italy to be a land of disappointments? Here, I'm simply a pebble among a million other stones on the seashore.* She stifled a sob.

Giannina leaned towards her and placed an arm around her shoulder. 'I'll get a friend of the maestro to talk to you about Arturo Toscanini and her performances at *La Scala*.'

Maggie made a vain attempt to smile. 'Thank you so much. I'd love to know what the maestro thinks of my singing.'

Mist was gathering among the buildings by the time they arrived home. Even the trees, already decked in light green, the colour of hope, failed to instil a spark of confidence in Maggie. Unshed tears accumulated and, like dark clouds swollen with water, threatened to fall.

They entered the house, and Maggie excused herself. She slunk back to her room, sinking even lower into the mire of despair. Waves of sadness engulfed her. Her pride had been deeply hurt. She thought of the deafening ovations she had received in Paris. *What should I do now? Should I just sit back and wait for an opening in the* La Scala *choir?*

Maggie raised her tear-filled eyes to heaven.

At lunch, her eyes were red from weeping. Giannina patted her shoulder. 'Don't worry. Everything will soon be fine.'

Maggie forced a smile. 'Thank you for arranging the interview. You've helped me so much.'

With tireless energy, Giannina continued to coach Maggie. 'I'll be having Rosina Storchio over for a few days,' she said, after a session in the tower. 'She is only forty-nine, but she retired from opera last year. She will share the secrets of the stage with you. Talk to her. Ask anything you like.'

Since the audition with Toscanini, however, Maggie found it hard to reach for the lifeline of hope thrown to her. Her feelings had sunk to their lowest depths, so she could only respond with a softly spoken, 'Thank you, Giannina.'

Rosina arrived late that evening, and the maid ushered her upstairs to the seclusion of the third floor. Maggie caught a glimpse of a full figure and a surprisingly small waistline as the star swept up the stairs.

Maggie met the diva at breakfast the next morning. She had a charming smile and a youthful appearance. *I hope I'll look just as lovely at that age.*

'We must catch up on all the gossip,' Giannina said, after breakfast. 'Please excuse us.'

They remained closeted in the parlour while Maggie sat on a garden seat, flicking through the pages of a book, unable to concentrate. After a solitary lunch, she retired to her room for the usual siesta, wondering what the two ex-divas were talking about. What could Rosina teach her that she did not already know? She thought of Emma's fancy dress ball and shuddered.

A few hours later she rose and scoured the paper for the day's news. Hearing a knock, she rose to answer the door. It was Giannina and Rosina. She stepped aside to allow them to enter. 'Rosina says that the maestro was pleased with your singing. I'll leave the two of you to have a chat.' She looked meaningfully at her before she left.

Rosina floated in and dropped into the nearest chair. 'What did Toscanini say after your audition?'

'He promised me a place in his choir, but I don't know how long it'll take before a vacancy turns up.' Maggie suppressed a sob.

'Things have not been pleasant here since the Blackshirts murdered the socialist politician, Giacomo Mattioli,' Rosina said. 'Toscanini does not approve of Fascism and is thinking of leaving for America before he meets the same fate as Mattioli. You may have to wait a long time.'

Maggie shifted uncomfortably in her seat. *My dreams have shattered into fragments, and I can never piece them together.*

'Italy has many theatres,' Rosina continued. '*La Scala* is not the only opera house. Try elsewhere too.'

Maggie gazed at her hands, not daring to look up.

'It has not always been easy for me as well,' Rosina said. 'During my title role in the premier of *Madama Butterfly* at *La Scala* when I was just a few years younger than you are now, the audience were cruel and derisive. I swore I'd never sing in Italy again.'

'But you've performed in opera houses all over the world,' Maggie replied, forgetting her own misery.

'Oh yes, I did, but I only returned to sing in Rome after sixteen years. It takes a long time to get over such an insult.'

Maggie relaxed as the evening progressed, realising that Rosina was telling her not to be too disappointed by her lack of success in Italy. *Perhaps she's right. Could I survive the jeers and boos of an audience?* 'I admire you, Rosina. If they treated you like that, what chance do I have? Even now, I suffer from performance anxiety.'

'The audience did not jeer at my *singing*,' Rosina murmured. 'People were scandalised because I was pregnant with Toscanini's child at the time.' She held a hand against her jaw as though to hide her trembling chin.

Maggie's eyes widened. *Rosina had been booed at* La Scala *because she'd been pregnant.* She pressed the palm of her hand against her lips. Coldness crept up from her belly. Never had anyone been so frank with her.

'Toscanini loved me and would have married me, but he already had a wife,' Rosina continued. 'He was passionate, especially after a musical performance. He made love with such passion… But our baby was still-born.'

Maggie's face burned. *What is she saying?*

Rosina went on—face flushed and eyes flashing. There was no stopping her. 'He had affairs with the wives of musicians too. Society does not mind if a married woman falls pregnant to another man, but I was unmarried *and* carried his child. *That's* why the *La Scala* audience took it out on me. Toscanini had showed his love for me openly and everyone knew the baby was his.' She adjusted the folds of her dress and gazed at the carpet with a faint smile as she re-lived the love she felt for Toscanini.

Shocked, Maggie remained in a daze, unable to speak. Rosina's words echoed in her ears. She stared ahead with parted lips. *Giannina has probably asked her to tell me this.*

Rosina glanced at the clock on the mantelpiece. 'We must not keep Giannina waiting. Must hurry back to my room and dress for dinner.'

Maggie rose like a robot and opened the door for Rosina, her voice quivered. 'Thank you, Rosina.'

Within an hour, they met in the dining room. Rosina wore a low-cut red dress and a ruby necklace that contrasted with Maggie's bare neckline. Divas usually sported their jewels and Maggie longed for the day when she too, could arch her neck gracefully like a swan and display the finest gems.

Talk ebbed and flowed at dinner, but Giannina and Rosina spoke animatedly and too fast for Maggie to understand. Unable to focus on their conversation and too exhausted to throw herself across the chasm of understanding, her thoughts wandered off. *What will it be like to perform on stage, with your beloved's child in your womb?*

She pondered on the emptiness of her present life. In this country of opera, she, Maggie Gard, selected to study in Europe with all expenses paid, had not yet sung in Milan. She had only sung at few recitals here or a concert there; or at local halls or weddings. Occasionally at celebrity dinners. She had sacrificed love for this. It was not what she had come to Milan for. Not what her family and friends expected of her.

That night, Maggie lay awake, staring at the ceiling. *What will the future bring?* She gnawed at her lower lip. *I must swallow my pride and take any position that comes up.*

The next morning at breakfast, Maggie decided to tell her host of her decision to take on whatever job turned up.

Giannina reached out and touched her shoulder even before she began to speak. 'Would you like me to introduce you to Dino Grandi? He is Mussolini's right-hand man and selects good-looking young singers to entertain Il Duce and his Blackshirts.'

Maggie sputtered over her cup of coffee. Taking on whatever turns up did not mean sleeping with anyone. She had to draw the line somewhere. 'No, Madam. That might cost me my career and result in the end of my dreams, but my voice is to comfort others and heal sorrows, not to satisfy anyone's lust. I'll do *any* job that *does not* compromise my morals.'

Giannina nodded. 'I didn't think you'd like my suggestion, but many singers have chosen that way as a shortcut to fame. Don't be offended, Maggie. It may be the only road open to you.'

Maggie realised that, under the circumstances, she would never make it to *La Scala. I'll earn enough money for my return passage home or get to London. I'll sing my way to stardom there before old age claims me.* Her chin trembled and her legs felt weak. She made a vain attempt to square her shoulders. In her heart, she knew she had no alternative but to accept the fact that she was a foreigner in a foreign land. Currently, she had neither the heart to hope nor the energy to do anything.

Maggie was undergoing the enervating lassitude that comes with hopelessness. She was weary. Weary to death.

~ *Chapter 15* ~

The Tide Turns

MAGGIE FLUNG OPEN THE WINDOW and inhaled deeply. The sheltered corner of the garden, so innocuous during the winter, had begun to bloom. Snowdrops peeked through the debris of the previous year and the swelling tips of daffodils rose to greet the spring of 1925. She thought of Wordsworth and his poem, *Daffodils*, and recited the words. When she came to the third verse she paused.

A poet could not but be gay,
In such jocund company...

Soon I too will look on a field of golden daffodils. How can I be anything but joyful? She humm ed a tune as she floated down the stairs for breakfast.

Giannina greeted her, arms outstretched. 'You've been invited to sing at a wedding. World-renowned celebrities will be present. You'll have the opportunity of a lifetime. The reception is to be held outdoors at Lake Garda. It will be magnificent.'

Maggie grasped Giannina's hands and thanked her, but the unsuccessful interview with Toscanini had tempered her expectations so she held her feelings in check.

'Believe me,' Giannina continued. 'It will be a day to remember. Mussolini himself won't be attending, but his right-hand man Dino Grandi and his men are coming.'

Maggie's breathing quickened. Maybe she would impress a celebrity at the reception. Her feet danced with eagerness even while they ate, and Giannina chattered happily about the feast.

Each morning, Maggie struck a day off from her calendar with a firm stroke of her pen. On the day of the wedding, sun shone brightly in a cloudless sky, trees wore a mantle of green and the scent of blossoms filled the air. The limousine stopped before a church and the chauffeur hurried around to open the door. Maggie followed Giannina out of the car. A buzz of excitement hung in the air. The groom stood at the entrance, holding a bouquet of flowers and shifting his weight from one foot to the other, as he waited for his bride.

'We don't think she'll come,' a friend teased him.

'Did you tell her the wedding was today?' another joked.

Maggie joined in the laughter. By now she had imbibed almost everything about Italian customs, and knew the groom carried a piece of iron in his pocket to ward off the evil eye.

Giannina and Maggie took their seats. Soon the organ played the Wedding March. A sense of melancholy took hold of Maggie as she wondered if she would ever walk up the aisle on a lover's arm. Time was passing, but it was not too late for cupid's arrow to strike her heart.

After the ceremony, when the bride and groom went to sign the register, the chauffeur drove Giannina and Maggie to the reception at Lake Garda, where Maggie was to sing. Along the way, they passed lemon and olive groves interspersed by farms and forests of pine and cypress. Colourful lanterns illuminated the reception area which was festooned by flowers. The best man greeted the guests while waiters stood by with trays of cocktails and canapés. Each guest received a little mesh bag of *bomboniera*—sugar-coated almonds—signifying the union of bitter and sweet. Uniformed waiters bustled about, leading guests to tables covered with embroidered white tablecloths. White damask fastened by large pink ribbons enveloped the chairs, and vases of pink and white roses decorated the tables.

Everyone kissed the bride. Ladies, adorned with choker pearls and diamond tiaras or jewelled combs in their hair, held tiny satin bags and sashayed in their chiffon gowns. Maggie's sequined gold lace and chiffon gown hugged her curves, then flared out to a full flowing skirt. Its cutaway style bodice, and pearl bead encrusted-neckline, needed no jewellery to enhance her beauty. Opera length pale gold gloves covered her arms and peep-toe platform-heels gave her extra height.

The exotic perfume of the ladies and scintillating atmosphere sent Maggie's senses reeling. Waiters jostled, serving sole topped with sweet pepper cream or cream of carrots and mint. The main course featured crumbed veal fillet and truffle sauce, potato tartlets sprinkled with thyme, and spinach flavoured with garlic. Dumplings in clam dressing followed. Maggie attempted a few mouthfuls, but she was nervous and had no inclination to eat.

When everyone else had done justice to the repast, waiters cleared the dishes and brought in dessert—slices of wedding cake garnished with ice cream mignon. Between mouthfuls, Giannina said, 'There's Count Dino Grandi.'

The Count carried himself with dignity. The thin line of hair that connected his moustache to his beard created a stern image. His hair was combed back, his bearded chin jutted forward. It would not be pleasant for the person who dared to cross him, Maggie reflected.

The Master of Ceremonies called upon each speaker. Toasts were made and the wine drunk amid bursts of laughter. Maggie trembled in anticipation. Soon it would be her turn.

The Master of Ceremonies beckoned Maggie to the podium and announced her. She glided forward and curtseyed, then caught and held the gaze of a gentleman sitting next to the Count. Clean-shaven and good-looking, he held his head high, but appeared more relaxed than his friend. She took in the powerful set of his shoulders and swallowed hard. Many admirers had stared at her. She had seen their admiring looks, but this time something moved within her. Heat rose to her face, burning her cheeks and shortening her breath. She glanced away, feeling unsteady but warm. *I'm allowing myself to be carried away by the lovely spring weather, the stirring music and the exhilarating atmosphere. Take care, Maggie!*

She stepped onto the platform, still transfixed by him. *Will this be my only chance to sing before such a large audience in post-war Italy?*

Her aria, full of exacting runs and high notes, soared upwards one dizzy moment then cascaded down, captivating her listeners. She had eagerly anticipated this celebration; now she glowed from the lengthy applause.

Later, she mingled among the guests, nodding at all those who caught her eye. Divas and dowagers smiled at her with approval, and guests stopped to ask questions or pay a compliment.

A good-looking man in his thirties strode towards her, making his way through the crowd that parted like chaff before a wind. Immaculately dressed, his well-tailored suit showed his athletic figure to advantage. 'You have a most beautiful voice. Why haven't I met you before?'

Maggie realised he was the gentleman who had been gazing at her during her performance. She blushed.

'You're lovely… But pardon me. I haven't introduced myself. Giovanni Grandi, stage designer at *La Scala*.'

'Marguerite Gard—Giannina Russ's guest. She's coaching me.' *How fortunate to meet someone of importance from* La Scala!

'Will you be singing at any of our theatres?'

Maggie drew herself up to her full height. 'No. But I'm waiting for a vacancy at *La Scala*. Arturo Toscanini has auditioned me.'

Giovanni shook his head. 'He may take too long. Don't hide yourself. Have you tried Bologna, Florence, Venice or Rome? You should climb the ladder from the bottom, not the top.'

'I've sung at Paris, London and Monte Carlo.' Maggie matched his haughty manner; not too sure she liked his tone.

'Do you wish to be by-passed by others on the road to fame?' His voice rose and his dark eyes glowed as he spread out his hands. 'Don't be a violet. Expose yourself to the light and grow to be a world-famous singer. You're too lovely to be lost.'

Mollified, her eyes shifted from his well-manicured nails to his face. 'Thank you. Perhaps I've been aiming too high.'

'No, you must reach for the pinnacle.' He placed his hand upon her arm just below her shoulder in a possessive gesture. The swift movement of his arm released a pleasing, masculine smell, impossible to describe. A flame of desire leapt within her. 'But do not remain idle in the meantime. When the opera season in Milan is over, I'll take you to Bologna for an audition.'

His manner magnetised Maggie, and she burst out, 'I'd love that.'

Giovanni broke into a smile. His teeth, even and white, contrasted with his olive skin. 'We'll take the train to Bologna. Count Dino resides there, and you'll be most welcome. I'll arrange something for you at the Theatre Comunale.'

Maggie's sense of propriety prevailed, and she turned away from him. 'I must speak to Giannina first.'

'Don't worry. She's a good friend. I'll mention it to her before I leave.' He leaned forward and took her hand, holding it a little longer than necessary. A thrill of pleasure shot through her as he bent over to kiss it. His dark hair gleamed in the light. Raising his head, his gaze lingered on her face before he turned and strode off, leaving a warm empty space where his touch had been.

Blood rose to her cheeks as she watched him depart. His lengthy strides displayed confidence and vitality. Something melted within her body. *Don't go*, her heart cried. *Stay a little longer... I wonder why Giannina has not introduced him to me before.*

One of the guests, who had been waiting to approach her, stepped forward, and she turned to speak to him.

No sooner had the Milan opera season closed than Giovanni arranged for Maggie's audition at the Theatre Comunale in Bologna and accompanied her by train. Giovanni sat next to her, their shoulders touching. The train sped along, the constant swaying of the carriage throwing them closer to each other, sending thrills of excitement within her. The trip was no more than a few hours, and Maggie longed for them to stretch out for eternity. She enjoyed the sense of freedom.

Giovanni's presence removed all traces of her nervous tension and she looked forward to her audition with confidence.

After her audition, the manager said, 'Sorry, but I can only offer you a minor part as we have already filled all vacancies for the following year.'

She gratefully accepted the offer.

Giovanni proved to be more than a useful contact. When he took her for auditions to Rome, Florence and Venice, opera houses opened their doors to her.

In public, Giovanni and Maggie conversed in Italian, but they spoke in English when alone. She no longer found him over-bearing. One evening at dinner she asked, 'Would you mind if I called you Joe? It's easier on my tongue.'

'If I may call you Margherita.' He raised his glass and appeared to be contemplating the colour of the contents. Curly hairs covered his muscular forearm. He tasted the wine and placed it down, all the while stroking her hand and playing with her fingers. His light touch sent little shivers of excitement throughout her body. 'Giannina told me about you. I am surprised no nobleman has carried you off to his castle. I, too, have never married although I'm only a few years older than you.'

'Why are you still a bachelor? Are you too attached to your family?'

'I'm the only child and I am everything to my widowed mother—but that's not the reason why I've never married. My work entails moving around. I started as a portrait and landscape artist, went to St Petersburg and worked as an opera designer, returned to Milan in 1922 and obtained a position at *La Scala*.'

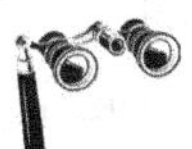

The months flew by. At Rome, Giovanni took her to the Sistine Chapel, where the paintings on the walls and ceiling rendered the truths of Scripture easier to understand. They sat in silence, listening to what sounded like a choir of angels. Maggie's heart soared heavenwards and hovered among the clouds until the singing ended.

Giovanni serenaded her in the beautiful Roman gardens. The clear resonance of his tone, his high cheekbones, his eyes, almost black, his firm and sensual lips rendered her inarticulate. He possessed a rich baritone voice that won her over. His steady arm never failed to support her when she tripped on piles of rubble while wandering around ruins at the Forum. He exuded something that aroused a fire in her—a fire dormant for years. His hands with their strong and solid fingers thrilled her, and the ripple of his muscles shot little arrows of excitement into her heart. Warmth flowed from his body. She quivered and pulsated with life. A flame shot up, burning and consuming her.

They wandered through narrow streets where the aroma of garlic hung beneath the eaves and down stairways. Devoid of paint, dilapidated shutters creaked upon rusty hinges. Laughter of children and the shrill voices of housewives floated across to them. He escorted her to restaurants with low-raftered rooms. Strings of garlic dangled from the ceiling and the appetising odour of herbs drifted to them as they entered. Music played in the background. Just the right atmosphere—cosy and warm. 'You see, *cara mia*,' he explained. 'Italy is a land of contrasts. I take you to restaurants no tourists frequent because I want you to see my country through the eyes of a native. Only then will you understand our mentality.'

Maggie savoured the food and revelled in Giovanni's undivided attention. Absorbed in all he said, she remained silent, listening to every word. One evening, as they stood drinking in the magical scene at the Trevi Fountain, each made a wish to return and threw coins in. The sound of water tinkling down imparted an ethereal atmosphere. Maggie held her breath, aware of her own heartbeat. She ached with longing. Would he ever hold her close?

Giovanni ran his fingers up and down her spine. Then, as if reading her thoughts, he took her in his arms. 'I love you.' He covered her mouth with his.

The tingle beneath his touch was electric. The sweep of his tongue sent shock waves vibrating within her. They swept over and engulfed her. Maggie had known passion through music and singing. Now, a new longing rose in her. At Giovanni's merest touch, her heart fluttered like a bird. She walked with light steps and smiled at nothing and everything. *What had she been missing all these years?*

~ *Chapter 16* ~

Milan to San Francisco

A WOOD-FIRE BLAZED IN THE HEARTH, sending the smell of burning pine logs drifting towards Maggie. The sound of couples laughing and the clinking of cutlery mingled with the soft background music. The plush seats, cherry-wood panelling and flickering candles cast a romantic mood in the restaurant. Caught up with the amorous aura, Maggie watched clouds covering the panoramic view of the Eternal City, then turned to Giovanni. He drummed his fingers on the table and appeared to be deep in thought, examining the floor. Maggie wondered what was on his mind. 'Are you all right, Joe?'

'Amando Agmini, the Artistic Director of the San Francisco Opera has offered me a position I cannot refuse. I *must* go, but it is heart-breaking for me to leave you.'

The music faded and the lights appeared to dim. Sounds drifted through the windows—the roar of traffic, footsteps on the cobblestones and discordant voices.

'How long will you be away?' Her voice sounded hollow in her own ears.

'It's difficult to say. I will be making my debut as a set designer at the United States premiere of *Giovanni Gallurese*, under the baton of Tullio Serafin in February. We will have five performances during the season.' He kissed her hand. 'Will you come with me, Margherita? This may be your big opportunity.'

Her pulse quickened. *Is he going to propose to me?*

'To prevent a scandal, you should travel as my wife. I'll introduce you as Mrs Grandi.'

She gasped. *His wife! I'm going to be his wife!* She replayed the words in her mind. *Wait… He said, 'Travel as my wife.' He's not proposing. Does he want me as his mistress? I will never stoop to that. But I cannot part from him, and I can't miss such an opportunity for my career.*

'What about Giannina? What will she think?'

'Let me sort that out. Don't worry. I love you and want to marry you, but our wedding must be a grand one. No Grandi ever had a small wedding.'

She knew Giovanni had descended from a long line of famous ancestors. She recalled him telling her of Giuseppe Grandi, the renowned artist, and Alessandro Grandi, one of the most progressive composers of the early seventeenth century. She knew that family pride would not permit him to have a hurried marriage.

'Trust me, *cara mia*,' he reassured her. 'I will not harm you in any way. Travel is so much fun. You will *love* America. You'll get a singing part too. Believe me.'

She remained silent, her thoughts in a whirl. 'Do you intend to marry me, Joe?'

'Of course. You know I don't break my word. Have I not always treated you like a queen?' He put his arm around her shoulder, whispering, 'Come with me, Margherita. I'll give you a new name, a new life. We'll see the world together. Come.'

Her heart beat wildly. *I cannot refuse him. But what would he expect of me if I go?* 'Couldn't we marry before we go? It would mean so much to me.'

'I can arrange it, but the marriage must remain a secret. We'll have a grand wedding after I tell my mother. She wants me to marry an *Italian*.'

She struggled from his embrace. 'You've never mentioned that to me before!' Heat rose on her face. Her voice shook. She heard pounding in her ears and her vision clouded. *Is he leading me on to the point of no return?* She stepped back from him, grabbed her shawl from the chair and turned to leave.

He took the wrap and draped it across her shoulders. A snap of his fingers drew the attention of a passing waiter. Giovanni paid the bill and led her out of the restaurant.

Outside, he slid his arm around her waist and swung her around to face him. 'You know I'd never deceive you, Margherita. Have faith in me. I will tell my mother about us when she's ready to receive the news. She's quite ill. In fact, she's dying of cancer. You wouldn't want me to hasten her death, would you?'

Maggie scanned his face and attempted a smile, but her lips were trembling. 'Of course, I don't want you to do that, but you never even *hinted* about her illness before.'

He dropped his eyes. 'It is a painful subject to speak of... I thought if I held back long enough…'

Maggie finished the sentence for him. 'She'd be dead, and you wouldn't have to tell her!' She crossed her arms, her mouth twisted with sarcasm, wanting to hurt him and put him in his place. Show him he was not indispensable. He had led her to believe he really loved her, and she had given her heart to him.

He frowned and tugged at his lower lip. 'Well, I'll speak to her if you promise to come with me.' He searched her face and rubbed his chin as if waiting for her response.

The restaurant door opened and the light from within dazzled Maggie's eyes. She raised a hand to brush away the tell-tale tears, but tightness restricted her breathing as though a rope was strangling her.

Giovanni sprang towards her. 'Is there something wrong, Margherita? Perhaps you should sit for a while.' He led her to a garden seat in the shrubbery.

His lips strayed softly on her neck, and his breath in her ear stirred a longing to return his embrace. *But can I trust him?* She turned her face away. 'Please take me back to Milan. I can't think clearly now. I need to return to Milan.'

Giovanni hailed a passing taxi, and they went to the station to get their tickets for Milan before returning to their hotel in Rome.

Disappointed he had kept things from her, Maggie packed her clothes, and when it neared time for their departure, another taxi drove them to the station.

Maggie shut her eyes and reclined on her seat in the train, making sure she sat as far as possible from Giovanni. Angry and hurt, a lump rose to her throat.

He tried to initiate a conversation. 'I apologise if I have hurt your feelings, Margherita, but I assure you I had no intention of deceiving you. If you come with me, we will marry in secret. The Opera House has paid my fare to San Francisco, and I will buy your ticket. We would be together all the time. Wouldn't that be wonderful?'

'I need to think things over. I'm not in a mood to talk now.' She folded her arms, turned her head away, and pretended to sleep through the eight-hour journey to Milan.

Giovanni dropped her at Giannina's place and knocked at the door. 'May I see you tomorrow to continue our discussion?' He kissed her lightly.

She nodded. 'Good night.'

'*Bona sera, cara mia.*'

When the maid answered the door and let her in, Maggie dragged herself up the stairs, hoping Giannina had retired for the night. *What should I do? I will never compromise my morals for the sake of my career.*

She prayed, asking the Lord for guidance.

The next morning, she told Giannina everything. 'What should I do? Will it cause a scandal if I accompany Giovanni to San Francisco?'

The diva clucked her tongue, set down her glass and cupped Maggie's chin in her palm. 'Don't let life pass you by, dear.' She kissed her on both cheeks and crushed her against her ample bosom. 'Enjoy yourself.'

Maggie sighed with relief, deciding to join Giovanni, on condition they married before leaving for the United States.

'We will marry in San Francisco,' he said. 'I'm too well known in Italy.'

Maggie, deeply in love, reluctantly acquiesced.

The time for their departure drew near, but Giovanni's visits grew less frequent. Once again, Maggie's fears rose to the surface. *Does he mean to slip off to San Francisco by himself? Have I been jilted?*

A few days before they were due to leave, Giovanni came to see her. 'I've been very busy organising things for the next opera season here. I haven't spoken to my mother yet, but we'll marry in San Francisco. Here in Italy, there are unwritten laws and a strict code of conduct. If I don't follow them, we'll be treated as outcasts, and I don't wish you to go through that, *cara mia.*'

They both travelled in upper class berths, indulging in dances, with drinks and games on deck. Maggie followed the principles laid down by her rigid upbringing, delighted in Giovanni's companionship and love, but she was determined to remain a virgin until her wedding night. They shared a cabin, but he slept in the reclining chair.

'Don't forget your name is now Margherita Grandi,' he would remind her each morning.

Most evenings, they walked arm in arm on the deck. On warm sunny days, they swam and frolicked in the heated swimming pool, splashing and showering diamond droplets around them, like a pair of dolphins. When he stroked her bare arm, she would reach out, lacing his fingers with her own. She felt safe, thinking she could curb her desire for him.

The penitentiary of Alcatraz loomed out of the mist, enveloping the dock at San Francisco, and gulls screamed a shrill greeting. Maggie leaned forward, trying to discern the dark outline of the grim prison.

'We've arrived,' Giovanni said.

Maggie's mind wended its way back to her first sea trip to Paris in her teens. She had fallen ill then. Now, at thirty-three, she felt like a filly frisking in the fields and basking in its freedom.

Before she had time to catch her breath, Giovanni had rented an apartment for them and, within a few days, obtained a place for her in the San Francisco Opera choir. His work kept him busy, and singing practice occupied most of her evenings, so the months flew by in a blur. 'Somehow,' she said wistfully one night, 'we never seem to have enough time to make the arrangements for our marriage.'

He yawned. 'Soon… we must do it soon, but tonight, my mind isn't on it, *cara mia*.'

They smiled at each other and headed off to sleep—Maggie loath to leave him.

Like most theatre artists, they arose long after daybreak. Maggie had her shower before Giovanni awoke, and feeling domesticated, prepared their breakfast. She sang as she worked. Sometimes he would join in, though he often listened silently, clapping when she completed the aria. Keeping up the Italian tradition of a light breakfast, a hearty lunch, and a heavy dinner with wine, they breakfasted on coffee, toast and jam. Submerged in a wave of domestic bliss, she dreamed of the grand wedding they were to have when they returned to Italy.

After each performance, they would join a group of friends for dinner.

Giovanni was popular among his male friends, who slapped his back and called him buddy. The women ogled him.

Maggie's new importance elated her.

Towards the end of the season their contracts with San Francisco opera were about to expire, so Giovanni booked their passage home. Their ship was to touch in at Sydney and South Africa on its way to Europe. 'Will we be able to visit my parents in Hobart, even if the time is short?' Maggie asked.

'That will depend on how long the liner docks at Sydney and whether there's a vessel that can get to Hobart and back before the ship departs.'

Maggie's heart sang, and she prayed everything would work out so she could see her family again. 'How do you think my parents will react to all this? Should I tell them about our engagement?'

'You must say nothing until I have informed my mother. I'll have to break it to her gently.'

Her heart melted as his eyes begged for understanding, and she realised that the shock of hearing he intended to marry a non-Italian could kill his mother.

A few days before they left California, Giovanni brought her a copy of *The Oakland Tribune* dated Thursday, 1 October 1925. He held it aloft, shouting, 'Look, Margherita, our names are in the papers.'

She snatched it from him. 'Don't tease.'

He released the paper and pointed to the news. The article stated that Giovanni Grandi, the grand opera scenic artist who had come from La Scala for the opera season in San Francisco, would be sailing for Sydney *en route* to South Africa and Europe, accompanied by his wife.

She stared at it, aghast, her hands turning cold. 'What if my parents should see this? What will they think?'

'Neither your parents nor my mother will know unless *you* tell them, *cara mia*. They have no knowledge of your new name, anyway.'

Reassured, she said, 'Let me keep the paper, Joe. I'll always treasure it as a memento of our trip together.'

He kissed her. 'The first of many, I hope.'

Yet doubts drifted like dark clouds across Maggie's mind. *Will Giovanni marry me? Am I just a secret liaison? All those nights living in the apartment together, he never attempted to force himself upon me. Yet he must have made love to other women. Does he really mean to marry me? How can I face my parents? He must wed me before he takes me home to them.*

Sleep was a long time coming, and when it did come, it was full of confused dreams, punctuated by sharp jerks back to reality. At two the next morning, Maggie awoke with a raging headache. A thin pencil of light from his room shone in her eyes. She sat up, and slipped out of bed. Staggering to the kitchen, she filled a glass of water from the jug, stirred in a teaspoon of Bex powders, and gulped it down before she returned to bed.

She recalled her mother saying, 'A cup of tea, a Bex and a good lie down will soon fix it.' *If only Mum was here now.*

~ *Chapter 17* ~

Marriage

'YOU HAVEN'T BEEN SINGING. Do I no longer make you happy?' Giovanni asked the day before their departure from San Francisco.

'Of course, you do,' Maggie replied, 'but I'm worried.'

'That I won't marry you?' His voice sounded hoarse.

Tears stung her eyes as she nodded.

'Margherita, the timbre of your voice mesmerises me. I love to wake up in the mornings to your singing. You stimulate my senses. What do you think I've been doing recently?' His throaty baritone was now high and tight.

Maggie noticed his lips pressing together and the muscles of his neck cording like a rope. *Is he hiding something from me?* He had always appeared calm and relaxed. She had never seen him agitated before. Her chest tightened.

After a few seconds, he appeared to unwind. 'Wear your most beautiful frock and meet me at this address at eleven this morning.' He handed her a slip of paper.

She read the address. 'Where's this?'

He gripped her shoulder. 'Don't ask. You'll know soon enough.'

'Am I to have an audition?' Her tone teasing, she tilted her head to one side.

Giovanni raised his eyebrows and folded his arms. 'Just do as I say.'

'But why this secrecy?' The tears were back, ready to spill over.

'*Ma Ma mia.*' He kissed her, letting out a heavy sigh as if the answer should be obvious, and left.

His words had sounded like a rebuke. They whirled around in her mind, raising questions. She took the dish cloth, dried the breakfast dishes several times and emptied the sink. Then picking up the feather duster, she dusted the rooms with more vigour than usual. She glanced at the clock. Barely half past nine. Another hour before she had to leave. She paced up and down the room. Half-filling the bath, she stepped in. The warmth of the water and the perfumes of the bath salts infiltrated her senses.

Fifteen minutes later, her body eased, she dried herself. Her skin glowed after a brisk rub with the towel. She dabbed on her favourite perfume, slipped into her royal blue dress, and gazed into the full-length mirror. The reflection was not displeasing. Her features softened. *Is he taking me for an audition? Surely, he'd tell me days before, as I would need to practise my repertoire. He loves to spring surprises on me. I'll just have to wait and see what he has up his sleeve.* She slipped on her blue shoes, grabbed a matching handbag, rushed out and hailed a cab.

'Where to?' the cabbie asked.

She handed him the address, too full of excitement to speak. Each time the taxi stopped at a red light, Maggie thumped her fisted hands on her thighs at the delay.

Finally, they halted in front of the Law Courts. Giovanni stood outside, holding a bouquet of flowers. Adrenalin surged through her veins. Her heart pummelled her chest. *How blind I've been. I'm to be married. He wanted to surprise me and was angry because I had tried to winkle out his plans.*

The cabdriver held the door open. She paid him and nearly tripped on the pavement as she ran towards Giovanni. He kissed her and presented the bouquet. Without a word, he took her arm and led her indoors. At last, she was to be married! A burst of happiness elevated her. She linked her other arm over his and gazed into his eyes as he stroked her hand. The warmth of his touch and the sensation of his closeness overwhelmed her.

A man in a dark suit met them. 'I'm the officiating magistrate. Two gentlemen will act as your witnesses. Hold on a minute.' He stepped out into the corridor and beckoned to the men, who joined them.

They proceeded in silence to a chapel. A photographer sat at the back; camera poised. Beams of light streamed in from the high stained-glass windows. She dropped to her knees on the cushioned pew. The smell of incense mingled with the perfume from a bowl of red roses. The flowers reminded Maggie of her father, who grew them back home. *If only my family was here now.*

Giovanni held out his hand and led Maggie up to the magistrate. Her pulse raced.

They were married with no sound except the clicking of the camera, the words of the celebrant and their voices exchanging vows. Maggie regretted the absence of family and friends, altar and priest. No organ echoed in the chapel, but such was the music within her soul, that in her mind's eye, a full orchestra played in C Major. She could hold her head up and meet her parents now.

The ceremony ended and the magistrate congratulated them.

Outside in the gardens, Maggie beamed at Giovanni in a delirium of joy. Her hand shook with excitement as he fastened a diamond-studded choker around her throat and stepped back with a satisfied look. 'More gold is in your voice than in that necklace.' Pride shone in his eyes.

He brushed his lips against hers. 'Wear it tonight. We've been invited to Miss Martin's farewell dinner. You'll outshine all the other ladies.'

Maggie had met Miss Martin, a high society belle. 'I'll imagine we're celebrating our marriage.' Her legs grew weak. She clung to him. *With Giovanni at the helm, my ship will brave the stormiest seas.*

At dinner, the Master of Ceremonies requested her to sing. Warmth radiated from her chest, spreading upwards to her neck. To her cheeks. She pulsated with sheer joy. Her elation carried her to the topmost cloud, and she sailed in a deep blue sky. The evening passed like a dream.

After a few hours' sleep, they took a taxi and boarded the ship for their voyage. The skies over the sea were blue by day, and the stars twinkled down on them at nights, setting the scene for a perfect honeymoon and a delightful homecoming. Hand in hand, they strolled on deck or relaxed on deck chairs beside the pool. When not embracing each other, Maggie laced her fingers behind her head and Giovanni looped his thumbs in his front pockets. Always solicitous of her welfare, he never failed to show his affection in the most endearing ways. At times, he left little notes declaring his undying love; on other occasions, he would return to the cabin with a bouquet of flowers or a box of chocolates.

The ship docked at Sydney for a few days to take on bales of wool. Maggie's face flushed as the breeze played on her hair. Soon she would be seeing her family. Her hands tingled. Her feet floated two inches above the ground. She clutched Giovanni's hand and leaned over the handrail. He kissed her and left to verify that the ship had not missed the connection to Hobart.

Please God, let everything work out well, she prayed.

After what seemed like ages, Giovanni returned. 'The *S.S. Ruahine* is to leave Sydney for Hobart tomorrow morning. I've bought a ticket for you. I'll have a tour of the city while you're away.'

'Aren't you coming too, Joe?' The question trembled on her lips. She stepped back, searching his face for an answer.

'No, *cara mia*. I want our marriage to remain a secret. If I come with you, your parents will ask too many questions. If my mother gets to hear of this, it will send her to the grave before her time. I must be the one to break the news to her. But you go and meet them. Remember to keep our secret for the present.'

Her heart dropped. She clutched the handrail for support. She had never lied to her parents. Now, she would have to keep mum about so many things. Perhaps tell untruths. She swallowed hard, trying to console herself that she needn't say she had married in a law-court—not in a church.

Although disappointed Giovanni was not with her, Maggie could see his point. She knew he had not told her earlier in order not to dampen her joy. She dropped her ticket into her bag with a trembling hand and slipped her wedding ring in the innermost pocket of her handbag.

Giovanni escorted her to the *SS Ruahine*, a 10,000-ton vessel on the UK-NZ route via Sydney and South America. He left without once turning to wave. Maggie knew he was not one to show his feelings. Her muscles felt weak. A void replaced the joy that had filled her only minutes ago. Perhaps he, too, had tears in his eyes? How she had anticipated introducing him to her family.

Alone at the handrail, she watched Sydney disappear in the sea mist. The howling of the storm and the shriek of gulls accompanied the ship across Bass Strait. Maggie's strong emotions and the rocking of the vessel were more than she could bear. She leaned over the rails and threw up her last meal. Embarrassed, she staggered to her cabin, wanting to be left alone with her spinning world. She ventured out only when the vessel had docked at Hobart. It seemed a lifetime since her voyage from Harwood to Hobart as a child. Her mother, who had been seasick, had already raised a family of four girls by then. How many children would she have? A boy and a girl, perhaps? Giovanni would love a son and she longed for a daughter.

Was she doing the right thing to turn up without any warning? Should she have sent a telegram? She must keep a low profile until she could return like Melba, who had come on a grand tour of Australia. Jean de Reszke had been among her entourage.

Maggie recalled de Reszke, who had given her voice lessons just before her departure for London. He had still been handsome then, and she'd been enchanted by him. She pictured herself in Melba's place, welcomed by thousands. Then stark reality set in and she bit her lip. Fifteen years had passed since she left home, and here she was with a sinking feeling in the pit of her stomach, slinking back with no laurels on her brow.

The bitter taste of defeat arose. The bitterness of shattered hopes. Yet like a bird with wet wings, Maggie shook off her despondent thoughts. *I'll be landing in about an hour. In place of fame, I've found love. I'll soon be meeting my beloved family again.*

Warmth spread over her, and she moved away from the rails, her inner being vibrating. Vibrating with joy. Vibrating like the ship's engines. Vibrating like the thrilling tones of a lover.

~ *Chapter 18* ~

Hobart

HOBART HAD GROWN. MAGGIE GAZED at the changes in her hometown until the taxi finally turned into her old street. The house appeared the same. Flowering bougainvillea added a blaze of blood-red, bright yellow and purple hues to the front yard. The queen-of-the night shed its perfume. Maggie breathed in its fragrance and strode up the gravelled path leading to the front entrance. Her heart pounded as she raised her hand and knocked—timidly at first, then more loudly. Spring had commenced a month ago but the evenings were still cool. She had dressed casually and had wrapped a scarf around her face and neck to keep off the night air.

The sun left long shadows on the lawn. Molly opened the door and peered into the darkness. Maggie recalled the time they had wandered in the cane fields at Harwood Island, singing at the top of their voices. Like her mother, Molly had a roundish face and attractive features, but now she had lost her youthful charm. Maggie cast her mind back two decades to when her sister's golden curls and innocent blue eyes had given her a fairy-like appearance.

She wanted Molly to think she was a stranger, and not rob her parents of the element of surprise, so she stood in the shadow and spoke in subdued tones. 'Are Mr and Mrs Gard at home?'

'Do come in. I'll get them,' Molly said.

Maggie stepped inside and kept away from the light. Above the recess in the wall, a vase of roses sat at the foot of St Patrick's statue. The red cedar sideboard stood, polished and shining like a mirror. The wallpaper with red and yellow blossoms was faded and greying. Cockroaches had gnawed through some of the corners. The paper had peeled in places and damp had set in, staining the wall.

Her father hurried into the sitting room. He had put on weight, and time had not been kind to him. His worried glance added even more lines on his furrowed brow and his tall frame bent with age. Bernard Gard was now in his early sixties, but Maggie had not expected him to look so careworn. She always thought of him as she had last seen him—strong and handsome.

She rose and stood framed by the window. A sob escaped her lips. 'Father.'

He stood still, placing his left hand on his heart before stepping forward. 'My Maggie. My girl. I knew you'd return.' He enveloped her in his arms, before scrutinising her face. 'How you've changed, lass!'

Her mother entered, her hair slightly dishevelled. Wet smudges at the sides of her dress showed she had absent-mindedly wiped her hands after removing her apron. Maggie guessed she had come straight from washing dishes in the kitchen. A limp, dank lock of grey hair hung loosely on Catherine's forehead. She had gained weight, especially around her middle, but time had been less unkind to her.

'Our Maggie has come home,' Bernard announced.

Catherine threw her arms around Maggie. 'Why didn't you tell us you were coming?' She held her closely for a long time. Then she reached for a handkerchief and wiped her tear-filled eyes.

It pained Maggie that she could not speak to her parents about her marriage. She had never kept secrets from them. 'I've been auditioned by Toscanini. I also have met a diva who tutors me in return for English lessons.'

Bernard rubbed his beardless chin. 'That's great. Always remember to keep up your voice practice.'

'Don't fail to attend Mass on Sundays, Maggie,' Catherine added.

Molly was in a fluster. 'If I knew you were coming, I'd have baked a cake, and invited our friends and family.'

'Do settle down, Molly.' Maggie spoke as though *she* was the elder sister. She turned to her mother. 'I can only stay a short time, Mother.' She had rehearsed the words many times and they poured out without a pause. 'My ship has docked at Sydney, and I can only manage a flying visit. I have to leave tomorrow morning. I'd rather remain incognito until I obtain a contract to tour Australia like Melba did.'

'Our Maggie's right. She ought to be welcomed with fanfare,' Bernard said. 'She'll return as a famous star. Then the whole of Hobart will be out to greet her.'

She blushed. Her father's praise always brought the colour to her cheeks.

'Tell me about Kitty and Josie. How are they? Aunt Polly writes often and gives me all the gossip, but I'd love to see their photos.'

Molly rushed out of the room and came back with some snapshots. Maggie grabbed them, devoured the photographs, put them to her lips and hugged Molly. 'I wish I could get to see them too, but the ship has docked in Sydney, and I must be back before it leaves.'

Catherine and Molly wanted to get in touch with the two absent sisters, but finally agreed to keep the visit a secret, as Kitty and Josie lived too far off to come at such short notice. Bernard put his arm around his daughter. 'That's all right, lass. We'll keep mum about your visit, but I'll accompany you to Sydney.'

Maggie feared he would meet Giovanni and realise she'd kept something back from him. Besides, Giovanni would think she had not kept her promise to him. He would never trust her again. 'You're not to take time off on my account, Father.'

Bernard nodded. 'You've always been the sensible one of the family.'

'Put the kettle on, Molly,' Catherine fussed.

Maggie bent over and kissed her mother, who had settled down in her old spot opposite her father. Catherine raised a finger in admonition. 'You didn't write often from Paris, and you hardly ever wrote from Milan.'

'Sorry, Mother. I've been working hard to get a contract in Italy first. No point in getting you worried, you know.' Her conscience gave a twinge and she tried to justify herself. *True, I didn't write, but I couldn't burden them with my suicidal thoughts. It would have grieved them.*

'You made us all anxious,' Molly chimed in.

Bernard smiled. 'But our Maggie is here now.' He turned to her. 'How did you manage to visit us, lass?'

'You did receive my letter from San Francisco saying I'd joined the Metropolitan Opera Chorus, didn't you, Father?' She paused. 'The ship docked at Sydney on my return voyage to Milan and I just couldn't miss the chance of seeing you all again.'

He nodded. 'But what happened to La Scala?'

'Americans pay good money, Father. Besides, I was tired of always speaking in Italian.' *That isn't a lie either. Why make my parents worry?*

'Did you meet many Irish folk in America?' Molly asked.

'A few,' Maggie said, glad she had escaped having to tell a falsehood so far.

Catherine placed an arm around her daughter. 'What about some songs for us?'

'*Arias*,' Bernard corrected. His eyes twinkled and he straightened himself like old times.

'Please play the accordion for me, Father.'

'That can wait. We must hear you sing when you've finished your cup of tea.'

'I'm sure the tea's cold by now,' Catherine said.

'Don't worry, Mother. It's all right.' Maggie gulped her lukewarm drink down. She did not want anyone to leave the room and make fresh tea. Every minute with her family was precious. She burst into her favourite arias. They sat in rapt attention, even forgetting to applaud. Her father blew his nose and her mother had tears in her eyes.

Molly fired more questions. 'Did you meet any nice men, Maggie? What's it like singing with a handsome tenor? Did you fall in love? How many admirers do you have?'

Maggie told them about Albert Longbottom, and they laughed at his odd name and queer ways. Finally, after much persuasion, Bernard played his harmonica and they sang *When Irish Eyes are Smiling*. No one retired until the wee hours of the morning. Maggie wanted to stay up the whole night, but realised her father had to report for work early.

'Perhaps it would be a good thing if we did sleep in and you missed the boat,' he teased, staring down at his hands.

Maggie kissed him goodnight.

'Just one question before you go to bed, lass.' His eyes bored into hers. 'You seldom wrote from France when you were at the castle. Why's that?'

'Oh, Father. You know how it is. Always such a lot to do.'

'The nuns were worried,' Catherine said. 'Was Madame Calvé good to you?'

'Wonderful, Mum. So full of fun and ever so generous. She took me everywhere and taught me everything.' It would not do to tell her of the Fancy Dress Ball and the Kama Sutra Room.

'She didn't get you involved in Satan worship or anything of that sort, did she?' Bernard persisted.

'No, Father,' Maggie said, mentally crossing her fingers. 'I was not aware of any such rituals. The nuns wrote to warn me about it, but they needn't have worried.'

Catherine laid her hand upon her daughter's shoulder, turning her around to look into her face. 'Sister said she gave you a St Benedict's medal. Do you still have it?'

St. Benedict was reputed to ward off evil, so Maggie realised they had been worrying about her. 'I can't always wear the medal, Mother, but I carry it in my purse at all times.' She touched her purse to indicate it was even now with her.

After a few hours of sleep, Maggie awoke. A storm of emotions arose within her. The emotions she had held in so tightly. She longed to tell her parents of her marriage. Only the fact she had not had a church wedding kept her from breaking her word to Giovanni. Tears hung on her lashes as she hugged each of them in turn. She left part of herself at Hobart as the child in her wrenched itself from her body like a baby leaving its mother's womb.

Bernard drove Maggie down to the jetty. In a daze, she walked up the gangway. *Will I ever see Father again?* She turned to wave. Sick with nausea, she stumbled, but regained her balance and held onto the rope to steady herself. She staggered on, carried by the tide of people behind her. *Can they hear the pounding of my heart? Will my parents tell Kitty and Josie I've been home? They'll never forgive me for not staying to meet them.*

The early morning fog matched her sombre mood.

The vessel drew closer to the Sydney docks. Gulls squawked and circled above. Maggie leaned against the handrail and searched for her husband. She spotted him scanning the passengers. When his eyes alighted upon her, he broke into a smile. It never failed to uplift her.

As soon as the ship docked, Giovanni pushed his way through the crowd until he reached Maggie and locked her in an embrace. 'I was afraid you wouldn't return.'

'You know I'd never be able to live without you.'

That night they lay in bed for hours and talked of the future. Her time with her family now but a dim and nostalgic memory. Maggie's guilt and inhibitions fell away like a saddle off a weary horse. Giovanni stroked her back. He was wonderful—the way he spoke, his muscular body and the power he possessed. Lovelier than any dream she had. Their bodies meshed. Never had she experienced anything like this.

The journey from Sydney to South Africa and then on to Europe was a continuous ecstatic time. Maggie sang to Giovanni as they stood on deck beneath the stars with the wind whipping her tresses over her face and into her eyes. He brushed back her unruly curls, applauded when she finished, and handed her a glass of champagne after each aria.

Back in their cabin, Maggie whispered, 'My happiness will be unending. Like the waves of the ocean, it'll never cease.' She laid her head on his chest within the circle of his arms.

'Yes. They'll only carry us higher and higher,' he agreed, stroking her hair.

She had never seen him as happy and relaxed as he was on the last leg of their journey. The memory of that magical trip would live with her forever. The elation she had felt after her debut in Paris was nothing in comparison to the joy she had on their voyage back to Europe. Maggie saw their road strewn with roses as they went forth to forge their names in history. *No longer will I have to walk the path alone. No longer will I have to fend for myself. Home will be where my husband is. Italy will be my home from now on. I'll face the world hand in hand with Joe. We love each other. adore music and opera. What more can a woman want?*

$$\sim \textit{Chapter 19} \sim$$

Bergamo

PROFUSE WITH APOLOGIES, THE SHIP'S STEWARD, so typical of the easy-going Italians, told Giovanni they would not be in time to catch the Milan Express from Genoa. His words galvanised Giovanni into action, and a generous tip to the taxi driver got them to the station in record time. He grasped Maggie's hand and hurried forward, led her into a carriage and sank down in the first-class compartment.

The engine gathered speed and raced northwards. Maggie clutched her hands together and kept glancing out of the window, eager to see her new home. Her stomach fluttered as she rose to leave when they pulled into Milan, but Giovanni remained seated and held her hand. Chin raised and eyes wide open, she shrugged—a habit she had picked up from Calvé. *I thought we were going to Milan, where Giovanni's mother lived.*

He smiled and patted the seat she had just vacated. She snuggled up to him but could not fathom his mysterious ways. The train chugged on. Thirty-one miles northwest of Milan, they disembarked at Bergamo. A liveried chauffeur met them at the station. He conducted them towards a limousine, so well-polished that the paintwork reflected their images.

'Will we be meeting your mother now, Joe?'

'Not yet, *cara mia*, but we're going to her country estate. I'm taking you to a villa which has been in my family for generations.'

She took his arm, enfolding it in both of hers. 'Do tell me something of the place, darling.'

'Mother lets me live on her estate. She's too ill to travel.' A cloud crossed over his features. Maggie, reluctant to delve any further, remained silent.

They passed olive groves and scattered stands of cypress and cherry laurel. Cows grazed on the lush grass, giving an Arcadian atmosphere. The fragrance of pine grew intense as they drove through undulating hills where beech, larch and spruce dominated the view. Birds tilted their throats to heaven and sang, and Maggie joined in, humming softly, watching a stream cascade down the hill and meander its way through the meadows.

'The streams flow south to join the River Po,' Giovanni said. 'I'd like to take you sailing in one of the lakes around here.'

'I'll love that.' She leaned her head upon his shoulder.

He brushed his cheek gently against hers. 'But we'll wait for warmer weather.'

'Is the villa far?'

'No, *cara mia*. It's right here in the centre of all this beauty.'

The car crunched to a halt on the gravelled road before a massive gate. A gnarled jasmine creeper covered a pergola, and the Alps towered in the background. A driveway lined with cypress led to the entrance of a two-storied villa nestled in a valley. On either side of the driveway, the lawns were dotted with beds of violets, roses and asters. The chauffeur stopped the car at the main entrance of the house.

'How charming,' Maggie exclaimed.

Giovanni pointed to one of the paths. 'Mario, and his wife, Anna, live in a cottage at the back. Mario manages the few acres… We have some cows. Anna cooks sand keeps the place clean.'

The cottage was not visible from where they stood, but Maggie guessed it would be delightful. *How wonderful to have domestic staff who live on the premises. A life of luxury lies ahead.* She gazed at the rustic paradise stretching before them and could hardly wait to explore the estate.

Giovanni swept her off her feet and carried her across the threshold. It left her mind spinning and her heart beating in sheer delight. Her whole body quivered with the intensity of her feelings. The large oak beams and an arched ceiling gave the impression of a castle, reminding Maggie of her stay with Emma Calvé. Sunlight reflected a reddish tinge from the wooden floor. Ancestral portraits decorated the walls.

'It's all so delightful, darling.'

Giovanni smiled. 'The furniture and photo frames are made of larch from the surrounding forests. On warm days you can get the faint fragrance of the timber... Do you like the house?'

'Love it.'

His raised his shoulders slightly. 'My hideaway. I come here when I want peace.'

They climbed the sturdy staircase to their bedroom on the top floor. It was heavily carpeted and had a huge fireplace.

'You'll get used to the split levels,' he said. 'We have two bedrooms upstairs. The kitchen, dining room and other bedrooms are below. You'll have heaps of time to explore later. The main entrance, as you've seen already, leads to the single-storey parlour... I'd like to show you the garden before it gets dark. We'll go for a walk to the village later.'

He held out his hand and led her downstairs. At the back of the house, a path took them to the cow shed—a solid stone barn. A calf nuzzled up to them. Bees buzzed around. Maggie waved them away.

'Don't wave. They'll get angry and sting if you do that. Let them land on you.'

He paused and swung his arms in a wide sweep. 'This area is famous for its honey and goat's cheese.'

'I've never tasted goat's cheese.'

'It's so fresh and melts in your mouth.'

'Like your kisses.' She laughed and placed her hand in his as they strolled along, oblivious of time. 'I love the rustic atmosphere. As a child I used to wander in the scrub around Harwood Island. This is so different. An entire new world.'

'It's your home now, Margherita. When I'm at work I'll remain at my studio in Milan but will be here as often as possible. You won't be lonely. You can go for a walk or sing as much as you like. Anna and Mario will be in the cottage.'

The thought he would not always be with her had never occurred to Maggie. 'I'll miss you, but you'll come often, won't you?'

'My duties as a scenery director are demanding. I'm responsible for the smooth running of an opera.' He frowned. 'To delegate anything to another can be disastrous. I have to live up to my name, my reputation.'

'Of course, work must come first, dearest.' She remembered how opera was always foremost in her life. She told herself this parting would only be temporary. Giovanni would soon get her a contract to sing at *La Scala.* Then she would be with him in Milan throughout the opera season. 'When will I meet your mother?' The thought of the meeting had been niggling her for a while.

'Not until I've spoken to her about us, *cara mia*. I'll visit her before the opera season commences, but now I'll show you around. We'll have dinner at a place close by.'

After a siesta and a shower, they strolled to the restaurant. The path took them through a meadow and wound its way to the village. Fragrant flowers cascaded down from window boxes and balconies. Everyone knew Giovanni. The men doffed their caps and women dropped a curtsey. No one seemed surprised he had a lady with him. It crossed Maggie's mind that they did not seem curious about her, but she supposed he cultivated privacy over the years.

The moon had already risen by the time they returned.

'I used to live here as a child,' Giovanni said. 'I know this area like the back of my hand. Ask Anna to show you the best way up the mountains but stay away from them in winter. The snow and ice can make them dangerous. Thick fog rolls down from the summit and reduces visibility. You could get lost or fall and hurt yourself. It's beautiful in the spring with blue gentian and patches of delicate red primrose. I'll take you to my favourite places before I leave.'

The next day the weather remained fine, and after lunch Giovanni drove her to the city, just a few miles away. 'I'd love to know the history of these old cities,' Maggie said.

Giovanni parked his car at the first available spot and headed for the funicular railway. She hung on to him as the train ratcheted noisily, pulling them up the side of the mountain. On the hilltop, they passed churches and cobbled lanes of the old city, entered the *citta alta* or uptown through the massive gates, and strode along winding, narrow pathways.

Giovanni took Maggie to the Basilica of Santa Maria Maggiore where they blessed themselves with holy water at the entrance. Maggie marvelled at the lifelike figures in Giotto's *Tree of Life* and Gaetano Donizetti's great Crucifix portraying the *Painful Christ*. She knelt before the Blessed Sacrament. The glory of the art and the spiritual message of the artists filled her with repentance for neglecting her religious duties.

By the time Giovanni had finished showing Maggie the sights, the sun was already low on the horizon. In the purple twilight, he directed their steps towards a tavern with crisp white tablecloths and an old-world atmosphere. Weary after their sight-seeing of the city, Maggie collapsed into a chair. Giovanni glanced at the menu with its assortment of promising dishes, his face lit up with pleasure in the candlelight. They enjoyed marinated salmon on greens and pasta of dumplings with stewed tomatoes and taleggio cheese, washed down by a carafe of red wine. Maggie recalled her mother's words: *The way to a man's heart is through his stomach.* She resolved to increase her culinary skills.

Giovanni left a tip for the waiter, and they ambled along window-shopping, caught the final train back down the mountain, picked up their car from the parking lot and returned home. Overcome by happiness, Maggie fell asleep within minutes.

The next morning, they awoke to the chimes of the singing belfries. Maggie stretched in luxuriant abandon and threw her arms around her husband.

'I love listening to the carillon in the mornings,' he murmured.

The days sped past, and soon it was time for Giovanni's return to Milan. 'I must visit my mother,' he said, on the day of his departure. 'Take care of yourself, *cara mia*, and be good.'

She sensed something pre-occupied him. 'Are you worried about your mother?'

He nodded. 'I don't wish to cause her any distress. But don't worry. Everything will be all right.'

After breakfast the chauffeur drove the vehicle to the door and Giovanni left without looking back. He had told Maggie he never liked to prolong a farewell.

She watched the car drive off until it rounded the bend then slowly, she mounted the stairs and slumped down in the lounge, recalling the words he had spoken, the sound of his voice, his soft touch. Did she have to wait the whole opera season until he returned? She thought of Madame Butterfly, who had waited for her husband, the naval officer, Lieutenant Pinkerton. Who had waited for the swallows to usher in the spring. Who had waited in vain. Her shoulders slumped, but soon she straightened them and broke into the famous aria, *One Fine Day*.

~ *Chapter 20* ~

A Solitary Christmas

MAGGIE RECEIVED ENDEARING NOTES FROM GIOVANNI, but when the wind, with a growl of winter, rattled the windows, his letters grew fewer, and finally stopped. Christmas drew near. Still, he did not return. *Why is he procrastinating? Does he mean to keep our marriage a secret forever?* As the sun rose, snowflakes on the old fir trees in front of the house melted and shone like teardrops. Trees sighed with the wind. Sighed like wind through a haunted forest. Eerie. Heavy. Dreadful.

Maggie shuddered, ordered a taxi, and visited the shops in Bergamo, hoping the Christmas spirit would uplift her. The sun shone on ripening oranges and terraces of grey olives as they ascended the hill. In the city, shopfronts sparkled with tinsel. Maggie wandered along, as lonely as Tennyson's proverbial cloud.

Stalls, displaying tiny bells, silver balls, lovely dolls and toys, stretched on both sides of the paved streets. With cries of joy, children skipped along, holding balloons. The gaiety made Maggie's longing for Giovanni even more intense. *If only he were here.*

On Christmas Eve, village children sang carols, and Maggie rallied to the sentiments of the songs, distributing cakes and sweets among the carollers, but when they moved on, the last vestige of cheer vanished.

The chauffeur had driven Giovanni to Milan and remained there, so on Christmas Eve, Mario used their horse and buggy and drove Maggie and Anna to church. The bells attached to the cart jingled merrily all the way through the snow. Sounds of carols and laughter drifted from the houses, despite the windows shut to keep out the cold, but Maggie's heart was leaden.

After the service, Mario and Anna left to celebrate with their family. Maggie thought of her first Christmas away from home. She had been with an English family then. Now she was all alone. *If only Giovanni were here.*

Waves of sorrow swelled and crashed on her lonely shore. She gazed out of the window, scanning the horizon, starting at the least sound, imagining his car on the driveway. Giovanni's presence would be the greatest Christmas gift she could receive. *O God, do bring him to me*, she prayed.

Time dragged on. The wind sobbed its way down the hills and wandered around the house.

Maggie brought in the New Year, sitting before a crackling fire, roasting chestnuts, and reading *A Christmas Carol*. Tears dimmed her eyes and blurred the words. *Perhaps Giovanni regards me as his kept mistress because a priest has not blessed our union. We are legally married, but not in the eyes of the church. What if his mother forces him to marry the girl of her choice? What if, like Madame Butterfly's Pinkerton, he returns with an Italian wife?*

Doubts stormed her mind, leaving her agitated. She could not remove the hairshirt of her thoughts and wondered if her marriage had been a hoax. Still in her nightclothes, she threw a wrap over her shoulders and hurried over to the drawer where she stored her letters. There they lay, neatly tied in a white ribbon. She opened the envelope containing their marriage certificate and perused it. The document appeared authentic. Maggie crawled back into bed and pulled the eiderdown over her, trying to shut out her fears. *Am I the first woman he has entertained in this villa? If work is keeping Giovanni away, he should write and let me know. To whom can I turn?* The wind howled and rain beat against the tightly shut windows. The floorboards creaked. *Has he returned and is even now creeping in to surprise me?* She waited breathlessly…

Alone in bed during the long and lonely nights, Maggie stretched out her hand to touch Giovanni, but he was not there. She sobbed herself to sleep, her pillow wet with tears. The days lingered on. Maggie read the foreign papers, which arrived daily at her door. In England, the unions called for a General Strike, and French newspapers foretold a revolution in England. She imagined a red flag on the Post Office, overturned trams, gaols broken open and dozens of released criminals prowling the streets. *Is Italy any better off with Mussolini's thugs beating up people?*

Grief washed over her, swept her up—tossed and slammed her against the rocks of anguish. Restless, she longed to wander outdoors, but the temperature had dropped to below zero. Giovanni had warned her not to venture out alone in winter as the paths were covered in snow and the landscape with its familiar landmarks would be eradicated. She gazed out of the window at the mountains. Everything was stark white—deadly white—like her own face, now devoid of colour. Ever since meeting Giovanni, he had been the compass she steered by, but now in a storm of anxiety, she remained a rudderless ship without him.

She considered taking the train to Milan and going straight to Giannina Russ who would know what to do. She resolved to ask Mario to take her to the station but kept delaying her departure for Milan, in case Giovanni was on his way back and their paths crossed.

The first week of 1926 brought sunny skies, but no news from Giovanni. Maggie gnawed her lower lip. She decided to tell Mario she needed to get to Milan without delay. By mid-morning, before she had the chance to speak to him, the postman called. Anna brought her a letter written in a familiar hand. Maggie tore open the envelope, not even waiting to use the paper knife on her desk.

Giovanni informed her his mother had been ailing from cancer, and he had stayed at her bedside until the end. Too distraught to think of anything else, he had remained on to settle her affairs. He promised to return as soon as the funeral was over.

Like fire licking up hay, Maggie devoured the information. She guessed that remorse at deceiving his mother consumed him. At the same time, she sensed a relief at not having to meet her. Maggie had always feared she would not be accepted—that her mother-in-law would have been offended by his secret marriage. The thought of seeing Giovanni cheered her, but the opera season continued in full swing, and she saw nothing of him. The honeymoon was over. *What has become of my life? My blighted career? Am I to stagnate here, no closer to my goal than I'd been in Australia? I've let down my friends, my family, my patrons. I've betrayed them all.*

Deep down Maggie knew she was thinking illogically but, lonely and depressed, dark thoughts saturated her, dragging her mind into a morass of despair. *Why didn't I write to my parents informing them of my marriage? Was it because I didn't want to hurt them, or was it due to my pride in wanting a lavish celebrity wedding?*

Maggie wished to be a child once more. She visualised her mother crooning her to sleep with a lilting Irish lullaby, and her father singing in his tenor voice… The image faded. She imagined herself at Grandpa Ryan's farm, gathering eggs from the hen yard, and feeding the hens. Once she had tripped and smashed all but one of them. She had been inconsolable until Grandpa had wiped the tears from her eyes and the grime from her knees…

Overcome by worries, Maggie neglected her singing during the cold, weary days of winter. Her only exercise was to walk in the garden. Spring brought new hope. Snowdrops began to peep out from nooks and crannies, and fir trees shook off their burden of snow. *Like them, I should shake off my load of sorrow. I must do something about my career.* Maggie used the stable as her studio and sang to the horses that neighed in reply. She sang for two hours in the morning and again in the late afternoon before dinner, if her voice felt strong. Warmth radiated throughout her body. How could she have forgotten the joy of singing?

One day after a session, Maggie returned to find a delivery van at the gates. Anna brought her a docket to sign. A grand piano. Mario, along with three others, carried it to the drawing room and placed it beneath the window over-looking the olive orchard and herb garden. The mahogany surface of the Steinbeck shone like burnished copper. Maggie lifted the cover and ran her fingers along the keys. They needed some fine tuning. *Soon Giovanni will be back. He will know who to send for.* Her heart pounded.

A few hours later, the piano-tuner arrived. Giovanni had thought of everything even in a time of mourning. Maggie knew he drowned his grief in work, but she eagerly anticipated the end of Milan's opera season, knowing she would have him back soon. At nights and during inclement weather, she practised on the piano and went through her repertoire, keeping an eye on the road to the villa while she played, hoping she would see his car appear from the mist.

The trees still stood bare, but the snowfalls were lighter, except for the Alps to the north. With Anna as a guide, Maggie took walks on the mountains, as they turned green again. Wildflowers, like gentian and primrose, bloomed in little patches of colour, and masses of red and pink rhododendrons tumbled down the slopes. She delighted in the scents rising from the newly awakened earth. The exercise and invigorating air did her good and brought a glow to her cheeks. Her appetite, lost through worrying over her husband's long absence, returned, and she throbbed with life and energy.

Alone on the mountain one day, Maggie stumbled across a cave hidden by thick vegetation. Strands of ivy cascaded down the entrance, forming a natural screen from the wind. Maggie used both her hands to part the vines, and stepped in. On adjusting her vision to the dim interior, a spacious cavern opened before her. Green lichen and moss covered the far wall, reminding her of green velvet curtains in a theatre. Outside, the wind whistled, and frogs croaked, but the interior was silent. Maggie thought of the time when Emma Calvé had taken her to the Gorges of the Tarn near her castle. The past came back in a wave of emotion. She shut her eyes and heard her patron sing once again. Exhilaration filled her soul.

Sitting on a rock, she contemplated her surroundings—an excellent venue for practice. A studio to perfect her craft. Maggie's normally sanguine nature triumphed, and she began to enjoy life once more. She re-gained hope for success—both in marriage and her career—and she looked forward to Giovanni's return.

Maggie stepped from the cave and lay on the grass, soaking up the sun. After a while, she made cat-like stretches and rose with a contented sigh, knowing that Giovanni would soon be back.

~ *Chapter 21* ~

Wedded Bliss

WEEKS OF ANXIETY PASSED BEFORE GIOVANNI returned at the end of the opera season and explained his absence in a mass of stumbling sentences. 'I'm so sorry... I was away longer than expected… I had to make arrangements for the Mass and funeral.'

Maggie threw her arms around him and burst out sobbing.

'*Ma Ma mia.*' He showered kisses upon her. 'It took some time before I could wind up my mother's affairs. I will never leave you on your own again, *cara mia*. We'll rent an apartment in Milan so we can be together during the opera season.'

She dried her tears. 'Could you afford two places, darling?'

'Yes, *cara mia*. My mother was glad to have me beside her at her deathbed. She left me the villa and some money.' He turned his face away, but not before his eyes began to mist. He steered the conversation towards other topics, describing, in glowing phrases, the stars he met. 'The maestro's jaw dropped when Ebe Stignani, the dramatic opera star, sang for the first time. She made her debut at *La Scala*. You'll do the same someday.'

The worm of jealousy crept into Maggie's heart. 'Will she be performing soon?'

'She's signed on to sing next year. By then we'll have our apartment at Milan, and you can come to the opera with me every night.'

'When am *I* likely to get a contract?'

171

His fingers curved under her chin. 'Please be patient, *cara mia*.'

Apart from polite inquiries, Maggie refrained from asking too many questions regarding his mother's death, realising he did not wish to speak of her at present.

For the next few months, Giovanni made up for the period he had spent away from her. Their conversation crackled like a bonfire.

'Now I'll devote myself entirely to you, *cara mia*. During the two years of mourning we won't be socialising, so I'll have more time with you. Where do you want to go? The higher altitudes are still covered by snow. How about learning to ski?'

'Wonderful!' All her doubts were dispersed by his mere presence.

'Then we'd better start straight away.'

After weeks of tumbling in the snow and going through the rudiments of skiing, he suggested that she savour the other delights Lombardy had to offer. 'Last year I promised to take you boating on the lakes,' he reminded her.

She beamed. 'Let's go.'

Within a few days they sported a suntan. 'This is like Australia. My father used to take us in his steamer on the Clarence River. It was such fun listening to him playing his harmonica.'

They drove along the Strada Francesca. 'To the north are plains where farmers produce wheat and maize,' Giovanni said. 'Towards the south, large farms grow forage for stock.'

Maggie gazed at the fields of grain, so much like Australia. 'I wish we were *always* together.'

'I need to work and put food on the table, *cara mia*.' He paused. 'Have you forgotten your career?'

'I don't neglect my singing practice, but you're more important to me than anything now, darling.'

'You haven't seen the true Lombardy yet. I'll take you along the River Adda before we return home.'

'Could we drop in and visit Giannina?'

'Where do you think I'm heading?' His voice held a suggestion of reproach.

She guessed he had wished to surprise her and was disappointed she had also thought of the same thing. They drove in silence. Maggie let the beauty of the countryside sink in. She leaned back on the seat and viewed the passing scenery through half-lidded eyes.

'Leonardo da Vinci used this landscape as the background to his Mona Lisa and other paintings,' Giovanni said, after a while.

Maggie slid her hand along his arm and gazed at the stands of alder, willow and poplar. They stopped at Pavia, only twenty miles from Milan. 'We'll have lunch here, then visit the church of San Pietro, where Saint Augustine is buried,' Giovanni said, getting out of the car.

After a short stop, they continued until they arrived at Giannina's villa. 'We'll just have a brief visit. Must take you for a walk on the mountains before I return to Milan.'

'Opera is our life, but do you have to talk about work, darling?'

'Yes, but you're coming with me this time.'

A surge of relief flooded her, and she reached out for his hand.

Giovanni rented an apartment in Milan during the opera season. Maggie often accompanied him to the opera house and watched the performances while he worked behind the scenes. When she heard Ebi Stignani sing at *La Scala,* she joined her legion of admirers, followed her career in the papers, and attended all her performances. However, they did not attend any parties, as he was still in mourning.

Giovanni took Maggie for auditions, hoping a producer would haul her out of her routine existence. She longed to play the lead role in an opera, but nothing turned up. With each offer of a supporting part, she put her hand to her forehead in despair. Giovanni was always there, however, assuring her she would soon be a star.

Maggie made the most of her singing practise and waited, confident she would be discovered sooner or later. Then in August 1927 at the Naples Arena, Maggie, now known as Margherita Grandi, performed in the stellar cast with the famed tenor, Nazzareo de Angelis, when he sang his valediction.

Dewy and optimistic, brimming with a cadenza of joy, she poured out her heart to Emma Calvé in a letter. The diva had completed her fifth tour of the United States, and now lived in her castle, raising sheep, training young singers, and entertaining elderly admirers. She did not take long to reply.

Maggie's hands trembled as she opened the letter. It read:

Dear Maggie,

So lovely to hear from you again. I knew you would do well in Italy.

I must tell you about my adventures in America. We travelled in a private train with the words 'Metropolitan Opera House of New York' emblazoned on the sides. Crowds would gather to watch us go by.

Three hundred cowboys greeted us at Houston station, Texas, with whoops and cries. Mr Grau, our manager, asked us to sing for them and Nellie Melba sang Home Sweet Home. By the time it was over, the audience was in tears.

Mr Grau then turned to me and said, 'Now Calvé, it's your turn to make them laugh.'

I sang a dashing Spanish air.

When we were leaving the station, the cowboys threw up their hats with whoops of joy, cracked their whips, and rode beside the train. I'll never forget the tornado of sound and movement. When young girls come to study at my castle I think of your time here. I'm currently writing my memoirs, so if I don't correspond more often, I'm sure you'll understand.

Your friend, Emma

Maggie showed the letter to Giovanni, then put it away among her treasures to read and re-read till it eventually fell apart.

Giovanni was always busy. 'It would never do if one of the props collapsed and killed someone. Too many accidents occur on stage. When Tosca throws herself down from the prison walls, I must ensure she lands safely behind the scenes and not end up breaking her neck.'

Giovanni's work entailed long hours and late nights, but Maggie realised he loved his job. One morning at breakfast, she asked, 'What's the most demanding thing in your profession?'

'Some singers are so fastidious. It is difficult to arrange everything to their satisfaction.'

'Do they annoy you, darling?'

'At times, they do get on my nerves.' He paused and sipped his coffee. 'Irene Mighini is a difficult person to work for. She quarrels with everyone and sometimes even continues her squabbles on stage.'

'Did she ever quarrel with you?'

'She spares no one the sharpness of her tongue, but I ignore her and try to keep out of her way.'

Maggie's bottom lip protruded into a pout. 'Despite her ill-humour, she's always in demand.'

'*And* she fails to honour her contracts,' Giovanni said.

'But why?'

'She lets the other party down if a higher offer turns up.' He kissed Maggie and sighed. 'If *only* they could hear you sing!'

'There are more singers here than sands on the seashore. I probably will never be an opera star in Italy.'

'Be patient, the time is not yet ripe. You must be prepared.to seize the opportunity when it arises.'

Maggie brushed the tears from her eyes.

'Are you unhappy, *cara mia*?'

Maggie thought of the times she had been all alone in Milan with Giannina Russ. 'Oh no, but I'd be miserable if I hadn't met you.'

He put both his hands on her shoulders. 'Know what you need?'

She bent her head sideways and lifted her eyebrows.

'A bambino would satisfy you.' He folded her in his arms.

She wrinkled her brows, having always thought a baby would mean the end of her career. *Have I left it too long to bear a child?*

The press continued to splash its pages with raving reviews of Mighini. The *Times* extolled her rich tones, saying it was similar to the American-Italian soprano, Rosa Ponselle's voice. The diva was doing well, not only in Italy but also in England. Consumed by envy, Maggie's thoughts were unable to focus on anything else. Why couldn't she get half a chance? She longed for leading roles, became fretful and could not contain her feelings. Her dissatisfaction grew. She pinched her lips together and, in her mind, she replayed the words in praise of Rosa Ponselle. Her throat closed. Her stomach hardened.

Then Maggie missed a period. When the doctor confirmed her suspicions, she broke the news to Giovanni. He drank a toast at the prospect of being a father.

Maggie's hands tingled with excitement. Her world spun. They were to have a child. She longed to give the good news to her parents. To share her joy with them. If only her mother was with her. She needed her more now than she ever did.

She held back. *I'll tell them after baby is born. They'll forgive me then. Forgive me for not marrying in church. For not confiding in them earlier.*

A new set of worries now plagued her. She had little inclination to sit down for a meal and gagged at the mere sight of food. Morning sickness kept her from eating until mid-day. She was in her mid-thirties and years of stress had aged her.

'Perhaps you should return to the villa,' Giovanni said. 'The fresh air and exercise will do you good, *cara mia.*'

Maggie recalled the early days of her marriage when she had spent a solitary Christmas and New Year. That must never happen again. She shook her head. 'I want to remain with you as long as I can, my love.'

~ *Chapter 22* ~

Motherhood

MAGGIE HUNG WHITE CURTAINS WITH PINK ROSES on the windows. The tiny cot had pink blankets and a little cupboard to hold clothing for the little one. They spared no expense. When everything was in readiness, Maggie continued her late nights with Giovanni, delighted to continue her lifestyle. She realised things would be different later, when the child within her grew and became more demanding. Barely three months after she conceived, Maggie had a miscarriage.

Giovanni caught his lip between his teeth and grasped Maggie's hands. 'Next time you listen to me, and don't overtax yourself.' He neither frowned nor reproached her, but she noted his disappointment. She could never forget the look on his face. Her chest ached. Her vision blurred.

Too late, she regretted the late nights and missed meals. *I've neglected to look after myself and the baby. If mother had been with me, it would not have happened. She'd have told me what to do and what to avoid. Why didn't we pay for my parents' passage to Italy? Why hadn't I thought of that? Selfishness! Yes, I'd been utterly and unforgivably selfish.* Maggie recalled that Italians were family-orientated. She blamed herself. Her grief increased. *How can I help alleviate Giovanni's pain for our loss?* She remembered Emma Calvé's depression following the loss of her child and gained new insight into what the diva had endured. *How much more tragic to carry a baby to term and then lose the precious one.*

Maggie and Giovanni had spent the last few months discussing the baby and adapting themselves to the necessary change in their lifestyles. Losing the baby meant more than just losing a child. She was no longer young. Would she ever be able to conceive again or carry a baby to full term? She lost her appetite but gave a quivery smile and tried to eat. *I must get strong again and give Giovanni a child.*

The following year Maggie became pregnant again. Delighted, she gave the joyful news to Giovanni amid sobs. This time, she returned to the villa, determined to keep healthy. She followed a strict regime and commenced her day with a brisk walk, avoiding rough roads and hilly terrain. She drank plenty of water, apple or carrot juice, kept a bowl of fruit beside her, and abstained from alcohol, except for a glass of wine at dinner. Maggie made sure she gave the baby everything necessary to grow strong and healthy. She could not face another miscarriage.

Giovanni fussed over her whenever he came home. 'Go to bed early. Keep yourself warm when you go out and tell Anna never to let the fire burn down.'

Although pleased with her progress for the first few months, as time passed, she grew heavier and suffered from constant backaches. Giovanni rubbed her aching back with balm and made an appointment to see the obstetrician.

'Your heels are too high,' the obstetrician admonished. 'Wear good walking shoes and keep up the walks.' Her morning sickness was not quite as severe as previously, but he was unsatisfied about other things. 'The space between your pelvic bones is too narrow. It's possible you may have to undergo a caesarean.'

Such an operation would weaken her abdominal muscles and prevent her from ever returning to the stage. She fell into a chair, laid her head on the table and wept. Then she got up, paced the room, and wrung her hands. *Please God, let everything be all right this time,* she prayed.

When the opera season opened in Milan and Giovanni left for work, Maggie sat by her piano and gazed out of the window, listening to the sound of his limousine until it died. She kept up her singing and her exercise, forgetting her worries during these sessions.

The days were long and weary without her husband or family. *If only Mother was here now, she would be able to advise me. Should I choose pink or blue wool?* She compromised by using both colours.

In the evenings, she placed a chair by the fire and knitted, anticipating the birth of their child. Her hands drifted to her belly. She thought of what was growing within and happiness rushed in. Her baby. Theirs…

Patricia was a dimply baby. Her tiny nose perched perfectly above her beautifully shaped mouth, which caressed the indent in her chin. Maggie wrapped the infant in a pink bunny rug and held her close. The infant drew upon all her reserves of strength until she felt totally drained of energy.

'It takes time to recover from a complicated birth,' the doctor warned. 'Strain on the nervous system, delicate tissues and internal organs, you know.'

Giovanni engaged a nanny named Maria, who proved to be a second mother to their child and gave her all the love and care she needed when Maggie was busy. While the toddler was under the supervision of her nurse, Maggie would saunter over to the cave and once again practise her singing. Slowly, by a strict regime of exercise on the mountains near their home, she regained her strength, but continued to lead a secluded life, devoting herself to her young child.

By the time the baby was able to walk, a telephone had been installed in their house. Giovanni made every effort to visit, but work commitments frequently kept him away. After his mother's death, he professed no desire for a grand wedding, and Maggie let things remain as they were. Their attendance at Mass dropped and, apart from their daughter's christening, they scarcely attended church except at Christmas and Easter. Living in Italy with an Italian husband, Maggie easily slipped into Italian customs. Whenever her conscience pricked her for neglecting Sunday Mass, Maggie recalled the Italian priest who had told her that God was everywhere and that she could always pray wherever she was.

Worried because the Church had not blessed her marriage, she had not written to her parents about Giovanni, but after the birth of her baby, she wrote, begging forgiveness for having kept the facts from them. Instead of being angry, her parents were delighted at the news. Bernard replied that he understood the importance of secrecy while Giovanni's mother was alive. Her first duty was now to her husband, he said. Catherine was ecstatic over the baby's photos. Letters of congratulation poured in from her sisters and aunts.

It was nearly as good as being home in Australia within the warmth of her family circle. Maggie longed for her parents, but Bernard and Catherine could not afford the trip to Europe. *Wish I had saved sufficient money to pay for their passage, and not squandered it on dresses. Madame Marchesi had spared no pains promoting Melba, her favourite protégé—provided her with letters of introduction to directors of opera houses and all her rich friends.*

I wasn't so fortunate. Emma had introduced me to the directors of the Opera Comique and Monte Carlo while in Paris, but I did not make a name like Nellie Melba, nor did I earn half as much as her. Giovanni offered to pay for my parents' trip, but I was reluctant to touch his savings, already diminished by death duties.

She thought of the hardships the Great War had wrought upon Italy. 'You should put away our nest egg. No one knows what the future will bring.'

~ Chapter 23 ~

La Scala

MAGGIE SETTLED DOWN IN HER NEW ROLE as mother. As a young girl, she had left her family to study in Europe. Now she made sure she would be with her child as much as possible. When Giovanni was away in Milan, she spent her days singing to Patricia and playing in the nursery or among the flowers in the garden. On his return home, they relaxed together with Patricia.

When the time came for the little girl to commence her schooling, she was enrolled in a local school run by nuns, and Maggie re-commenced serious singing practice.

On Maggie's fortieth birthday, Giovanni approached her with a broad smile. 'Here's a present for you.'

Maggie kissed him and took the gift, expecting to find a piece of jewellery in the envelope he handed her. She opened it and screamed in delight—a contract for the role of Aida at the *Teatro Carcano* in Milan. Maggie could hardly believe that her longed-for opportunity in Italy had at last arrived. She realised it would entail hours of hard work, but joyfully signed the contract. Could she face the crowds after an absence from the stage for a whole decade?

Maggie practised her singing for several hours daily, but frequently suffered from backaches and grew irritable when in pain. As the day of the long-awaited performance approached, she began to have misgivings. Her jaw tightened and her stomach muscles clenched as though they had tied themselves into knots. She needed to relax.

Before opening night, Giovanni gently massaged her neck and shoulders and slowly moved down her back. Intimate yearnings arose from his touch, and they made love.

The next evening, Maggie lingered beneath the glitter of the chandeliers, transported with joy. Her heart thumped and her breath came in short gasps. *This could be a new beginning. A restart of my career. I must not fail.*

While waiting in the wings, Maggie clutched Giovanni's hand to give herself courage. When her turn came, she stepped out and faced the audience. The violins introduced her theme. Maggie reflected on her own feeling about her homeland, and her emotionally charged voice surged through the theatre with *O Caeli Azzurri*. When the performance ended, spectators erupted into a thunderous applause. Men shouted, '*Brava*' and threw bouquets of flowers at her feet. Women waved white handkerchiefs.

The directors of the *Teatro Carcano* were so impressed by her performance they drew up a year's contract. A glow of confidence suffused Maggie's face as she signed the papers.

At breakfast the next morning, Giovanni looked from up the newspaper he had been reading. 'You've scored an overwhelming success and have received the highest accolades for the rich perfection of your voice and fine sense of drama.'

Maggie trembled with joy.

The following year, Maggie made her debut as Elena in *Mefistofele*. The opera touched on the familiar story of Faust and Marguarite. Although she was in only two scenes, she excelled in them. Giovanni showed her the reviews. 'You've received glowing reports in the papers for your dramatic presentation and vigour of voice. For the next two years, you'll appear at various Italian cities in Bioto's *Mefistofele* and Verdi's *Aida.* Here are the papers.'

Brimming with delight, she formed a steeple with her fingertips as she pored over them.

Despite her success, Maggie continued to suffer from nerves, often getting a sore throat on the day of a performance. Deep breathing exercises and a gargle with salt water fixed her troubles temporarily, but she dreaded the thought of being unable to hold a note before an audience.

While in Florence, Maggie had seen the audience hoot and jeer Giacomo Lauri-Volpi, a famous tenor, because his voice cracked on a high note. She winced and covered her face with her hands. *How can people be so cruel? Will that happen to me too, someday?*

At the Maggio Musicale in Florence, when Maggie met the singer Rosa Ponselle after the show, their talk drifted to Nellie Melba. 'I've been an ardent admirer of Melba since childhood,' Ponselle said. 'I even wanted to take her name. My dream was to be introduced to her. When I did meet her at Covent Garden, I was so disappointed.'

'Was she rude to you?' Maggie asked. It was not the first time someone had complained of Melba's manners.

'She was cold and curt.'

'I'm so sorry.'

Ponselle laughed. 'You're charming. Not at all like her.'

'Thank you. I've read the wonderful write-ups about you, Rosa. Critics have compared your singing to port wine and dark chocolate. I am delighted to have heard you tonight. You were magnificent.'

'It's been lovely meeting you. Good-bye. Call in anytime you're in the States.'

A few weeks later, Giovanni obtained a contract for Maggie with the *La Scala Company*. 'We'll be touring the Netherlands and Egypt with the *La Scala* chorus early in 1934. You'll be performing as Aida with John Brownlee, who is also from Australia.'

Thrilled to the core, Maggie's first thought was of their daughter. 'Patricia will be enchanted by the windmills in Holland and the pyramids in Egypt.'

Whenever they went overseas, the little girl always accompanied them with her nurse. During her free time, Maggie delighted in touring the city with Giovanni and Patricia, but she made sure the child was kept discreetly out of the way during rehearsals and social occasions.

Seven years earlier, Lisa Bruna Rasa had made her debut at *La Scala*. Her ovations had been endless, and she had signed a contract to sing the following year. By 1933, the star had risen to the top of Italy's operatic pinnacle. But the diva suffered from mental illness and acute depression, so she failed to appear for some scheduled performances.

Lisa's breakdowns proved to be a bonus for Maggie. On 11 May 1934, the diva was unable to perform as Elena in *Mefistofele* at *La Scala*, and Maggie replaced her, ready for the challenge. She had long waited to make her debut at *La Scala*, but her nerves were overwrought on the day of the performance. She couldn't sit. She paced the room. *Will I be booed by the audience?* Her head ached from the strain, but her voice carried her on a cloud of success and established her name as a dramatic soprano.

She obtained leading roles at opera houses in Italy, the most popular performances being *Tosca* and *Aida*. The following year brought Maggie further contracts. In October, she appeared at Venice's Palazzo Ducale in the Manzoni *Requiem*, and in 1936 she made a guest appearance at the Rome Opera House as Elena in *Mefistofele*.

Later in 1936, Maggie and Giovanni sailed in first class cabins to South America. 'We'll be in Rio for the carnival,' Maggie said. 'Isn't that wonderful?'

'Yes. It works out well. The ship's entertainment committee has requested you to perform for passengers during the voyage, and the fee has more than covered the cost of our passage.'

Rio de Janeiro crackled with joy, the boom of drums and the thundering of crowds. Maggie made guest appearances in the city and performed in *La morte di Frine* and *Tosca* in San Paulo, Brazil.

When Ebe Stignani appeared at the Carlo Felice as Eboli, Maggie completed the stellar ensemble. Maggie recalled the hurdles she had experienced when she had first arrived in Milan and praised God for her success.

In February 1938, when rumours of war floated around, Maggie appeared in *Othello* with Coriere Emiliano and Gaetano Vivani at Genoa. The applause at the first curtain call shook the theatre. Her heart pounded.

Maggie wrote home about her success.

One evening after their return from a season of opera, Giovanni hurried to her with a twinkle in his eyes. '*Cara mia*, how long has it been since you left England?'

'Twenty years. Why?' Maggie had been combing her hair before the mirror. She swivelled her chair around to face him.

He held a letter. 'The Glyndebourne Opera is holding its annual festival in June and July, and you've been invited to perform as Lady Macbeth in Verdi's *Macbeth*.'

She rose from her chair and hugged him. 'How wonderful. Will you come too?'

'Of course. Am I not always at your side?' His smile was as intimate as a kiss.

Maggie clasped her hands to her chest. *It would be wonderful to be back in England once more.*

Maggie left for England as excited as a young girl on her first date
The musical and artistic directors as well as the general manager
were exiles from Nazi Germany. When they first met the singers,
they said, 'We have selected the *best* singers for their respective
parts, *not* famous stars. Now, the onus is on you to prove your skills.'

Maggie's breathing came in quick gasps.

'What an opportunity to make your name in England.' Giovanni
slapped her on the back.

She flicked back her hair. 'I shall not let the audience down.'

The festival was held at a country estate in Sussex. The
Glyndebourne opera theatre catered to the upper class—a black-tie
affair with a pre-opera picnic on the lawn. The theatre seated an
audience of a thousand and was large enough to contain a symphony
orchestra. Guests enjoyed a delicious dinner in the garden during
the long interval, while the performing artists relaxed in their rooms.
Maggie found the bucolic surroundings calming.

Some people enjoy an emotional experience at an opera—others
favour a well-performed representation of character. Maggie gave
both to her audience and the opera house resounded with their cheers.

Delighted, she returned to her dressing room, and found a
round leather box inlaid with silk. Inside was an amethyst bracelet.
The stones shimmered beneath the lights. She lifted the bracelet
and laid it against her wrist. Her hand shook. *Who has sent me this?*
Maggie thought of the count who had attempted to seduce her at the
fancy dress party with Madame Calvé. She had come a long way
since then.

Among the floral tributes was a simple bouquet with a note
from her old admirer, Albert Longbottom. It brought tears to her
eyes. She hurried to the foyer.

Albert was grey at the temples and creases had formed on the
outer corner of his eyes. He smiled and stepped forward. 'Madame
Grandi, may I introduce you to my wife, Michelle?' He turned to
a lady beside him. Mrs Longbottom looked ten years younger than

her husband. Maggie was delighted for him, but surprised he spoke without the trace of a stammer.

'Michelle is a speech therapist,' Albert continued. 'After the war I found my impediment too much of an obstacle and went for therapy. I did not know I would find an ideal therapist as well as a wife.'

They shook hands.

'I'm delighted for the two of you.' Maggie said. 'Your husband has a heart of gold.'

Michelle smiled. 'Albert speaks highly of you. I'm so glad to meet you.'

'It's lovely meeting you,' Maggie said. 'And it's great to know of Albert's good fortune.'

While still in England, Maggie appeared in ten performances conducted by Fritz Busch, with tenor Francesco Valentino. Hailed as a new star of Italy and a true star of the Southern Cross, a coterie of admirers surrounded her after the performance.

Delighted by the way she had handled Verdi's most fearsome soprano role, critics gave her magnificent reviews. In *The Chesterian,* Edwin Evans, a London critic, wrote that Margherita Grandi had proved an intensely dramatic Lady Macbeth.

A review published in *Musical America* said,

'The Lady Macbeth of Margherita Grandi, a Tasmanian singer, was an extraordinarily powerful characterisation of the part— grim, persistent and terrifying, while her high notes rode over tragic effects. It was an interpretation that would have warmed the heart of Verdi himself. He had always wanted a great actress rather than a showy singer.'

Maggie sent a copy of the review to her parents, knowing it would give them joy and do the rounds among her friends and family. She leaned back in her chair with her hands behind her head, imagining their reactions to the news. *Now is the time to return to*

Australia—to tour the cities as Melba did. My family, my patrons and my country will be so proud of me.

The festival ended on 4 September, the day that Britain declared war. Once again, the storm clouds of conflict blighted Maggie's career. *Will war cut short my career again? At least I have Giovanni and Patricia now. I'm not alone.*

Maggie clutched her husband's hand. 'Together, we'll face whatever fate has in store for us.'

He gripped her hand in response. They returned to Italy, taking the ferry from Dover to Calais, and the train to Milan. Their intention was to return to their villa with the hope of seeing the war out in peaceful seclusion.

~ *Chapter 24* ~

Detention

ON THE WAY TO MILAN, MAGGIE AND GIOVANNI heard only talk of war. Although no one dared speak about the Fascists in public, everyone speculated on the future. Maggie strained to catch the fragments of conversation. 'Let them fight each other. We've just got over the last war. Italy should not get involved. All we need in life is wine, women, and music.'

'I'm sure Italy will join the Axis powers sooner or later,' she whispered to Giovanni.

He nodded, his voice low. 'Toscanini refused to conduct the Fascist anthem and has fled to the US.' He gripped her hand. 'We must listen to the wireless and find out what's happening.'

'At least we'll have each other.' She tried to be cheerful. 'I cannot bear the thought of separation. Bad enough being parted from my family during the last war.'

'Only death will ever part us, *cara mia*.' He squeezed her hand.

Maggie drew closer to him. 'Even then, I hope we'll be together for eternity.'

'Amen to that,' he said.

Dark thoughts squirmed like worms in Maggie's mind, as she imagined England invaded, Italy bombed, opera houses closing and her career at a standstill again.

Once back home, Maggie and Giovanni turned on the radio and listened to the news from England and Europe, their main concern being the impact of hostilities on opera. In Berlin, Siegfried sang of reforging his father's broken sword, and London broadcast Tonio declaring his love for the daughter of the regiment. At the time, Maggie and Giovanni thought both countries were broadcasting patriotic arias from opera to rally their citizens. Later, she discovered they were being used as coded messages to their network of spies.

For the next nine months, they lived on their estate. Giovanni's work schedule decreased, but they still managed to live comfortably on his salary and their farm produce. Patricia, now twelve, attended school at a convent in Bergamo.

In the earlier years of the war, the Fascist government lavished money on the arts. Mussolini, wanting to enhance Italy's image, had permitted the performance of non-Italian music and singers in Italy. Even though Mussolini was aware of De Sabata's heritage, he appointed the musician as Music Director at La Scala.

In 1940, Maggie starred as Maria in Richard Strauss's *Friedenstag* at Venice. She also featured in brief recitals at opera houses around the country. *This would not have happened without Giovanni who has given me his name.* She hated having to show respect to a regime she detested, by having to stand when the Fascist anthem *Giovinezza* played at the end of a performance. However, life continued uneventfully until June, when Mussolini declared war on Britain, and enemy aliens were interned.

On June 15, a police official and his constable knocked at their door with a warrant. 'The *signora* is to accompany me to a detention camp.'

A few weeks' ago, Maggie had been acclaimed as a rising star and now she was to be separated from her husband and daughter. She had never imagined anything so dreadful. Her shoulders tightened, her hands turned clammy, and she broke out in a cold sweat.

Giovanni's face reddened as he read the warrant. His chest heaved and his nostrils flared. 'She is my wife. Why are you taking her into custody?' His voice grew louder at each word, and he waved his arms in protest.

The policeman spread out his hands. 'The government states that your wife is an alien. She is to pack her suitcase and prepare for her journey to a prison camp. I'll return for her before noon tomorrow.'

'You can't do this. I'll see Mussolini himself, if need be,' Giovanni shouted.

Maggie hoped *Il Duce* would give her husband a favourable hearing because of his friendship with Dino Grandi.

'Your mother needs to visit my ailing aunt,' Giovanni said to Patricia, when the time approached for Maggie's departure. 'Enjoy the fine weather and take a walk on the mountains with Anna.'

The police arrived at the appointed hour. Maggie threw herself into Giovanni's arms, battling tears as she tried to put on a brave face. They kissed, and the floodgates broke. Great sobs shook her. The officer waited until the storm of weeping had passed, before conducting Maggie to a group of about a dozen women detainees who were waiting in a truck. The vehicle took them to the railway station where they were told to board the train.

'Where are you taking us?' Maggie asked.

The officer spread out his hands, palms upwards. *'Ecco il problema, signora.* I was ordered to escort you to a detention camp at Solofra.'

'Where's Solofra?'

'In Avellino province, 690 kilometres from Milan. It's a beautiful town in a plain surrounded by mountains.'

Stricken by the sudden turn of events, Maggie remained in a trance as the train rattled on. The countryside sped past, but she saw nothing until a church spire came into view at Solofra, and the officer crossed himself. 'That's the Church of Michael the Archangel.'

Maggie breathed a prayer, asking God for protection.

The engine drew up to the platform, wheezing and sighing. Clouds of steam arose, falling back like drops of tears. Maggie glanced out of the window. The station looked desolate and rundown. Even the sign hung at an angle, as though it had not been maintained for a long time. 'What a state the railways have sunk to,' Maggie exclaimed. 'Imagine what it will be like *after* the war.'

'The money for repairs has all been channelled toward building up our modern navy.' The officer straightened his shoulders and looked at the detainees. 'Please disembark. I will escort you to the waiting vehicles.'

When they did as requested, he said, 'Thank you, ladies. Now please line up in pairs and follow me.' Not once did he raise his voice or speak harshly. With a wave of his arm, he smiled and asked his prisoners to board the trucks, extending his hand to each as they climbed in and took a seat.

When all had boarded, he left the canvas flap of the truck open. Maggie sat facing the back. She considered trying to escape but squashed the thought. She would be caught escaping and given a harsher penalty. The day was hot, and the rank odour of perspiration spread in the crowded vehicle, adding to her discomfort.

A girl sitting next to Maggie, near the open flap, leaned out and vomited. Maggie rubbed the girl's back. She had brought along a few oranges, so she peeled one for the girl who mumbled her thanks.

Maggie trembled at the thought of being parted from her family, but she knew the nuns would take good care of Patricia. Giovanni would cope as he always had done. *The last war parted me from my family. This war has stolen my freedom, my husband and my child. Even if Giovanni is successful in gaining an audience with Mussolini, will I be released?* She opened her purse, took out a small vial of eau de cologne, tipped some drops on her handkerchief and held it to her nose. It brought some relief to her throbbing temples.

The truck followed the road leading to Solofro Centro. In the middle of the city, a blue and gold crest displayed the words *Citta di Solofra*. A crown stood beneath the letters. In the centre a face like the visage of the Greek god, Zeus, shone like the rays of the sun. She gazed at the beautiful crest and wished she had brought her paint and paintbrushes with her. It would have helped pass the time during her internment.

Maggie had expected a barbed wire encampment. A stone wall enclosed the camp, the gates were locked, and a sentry guarded the entrance, but no barbed wire surrounded the premises. A paved driveway led to a *castello*. Birds flitted among the cypress and sweet-chestnut trees, and Maggie glimpsed a small chapel among the trees. *Perhaps the estate has been requisitioned by the government.*

Maggie was pleasantly surprised to be greeted by the fragrance of lilacs. A guard directed most of the women to the servant's quarters downstairs. Another escorted Maggie to a sparsely furnished room. A wooden bed stood in the corner with a wardrobe and a locker against a wall. She suspected she was being given preferential treatment when she realised she had a room for herself. *Perhaps Giovanni had something to do with it.*

'Leave your suitcase here,' the guard directed, before he led her to the common room, now congested with inmates. Benches lined each wall and a wooden table stood in the centre, surrounded by stools. The place was devoid of curtains and any other furniture.

An officer stepped on the table. 'A set of rules have been pinned up in the hallway. Study it carefully. When a bell rings, gather here. At all other times you are free to wander in the grounds. Do not attempt to escape. If you do, you will be caught and handed over to the Nazis. Select a spokesperson among you and let me know if you wish to speak to the Commandant.' He sprang from the table and left them.

Everyone hurried to the hall to read the rules. Several copies were pinned on the walls. They were simple. Time to wake up each day, time for using the washroom, times for meals and for lights out.

Maggie met her fellow internees at mealtime. Her gaze swept over the prisoners. Fear hung on every face like a veil. Some paced the room with shuffling steps. Others hunched over, biting their nails. Maggie clenched her jaws. *War divides families, brings one's career to a halt and shatters dreams.* She recalled her early days at Milan. Meeting Giovanni had changed everything. Even now, he was placing himself in jeopardy by seeking favours from the Fascists.

The guards, captain and commandant were the only males on the premises. Like a salad in a bowl, the inmates included women from various lifestyles, including foreigners, Jews, gypsies and prostitutes. Catholics stood out with their gold chains and scapular medals.

Maggie had packed some books among her clothes. She kept to herself and read, but the words danced before her. Her fingernails bit into her palms. She moaned aloud. *How long will I be confined here?* She put away her book and wandered into the common room. The rain had kept most of the women indoors; many had brought along their knitting. Someone had a pack of cards, and a group had gathered, placing bets. Others chatted with each other to pass the time.

Maggie glanced around, wondering which group to join. A young girl in a flaming red dress with a low-cut neckline approached her. 'You look neither Jew nor gypsy. What are *you* here for?'

Maggie bristled at the girl's familiar tone. 'I have a British passport. Why have *you* been interned?'

'Because soldiers frequently visit me.'

'Why?'

'Don't play little Miss Innocent!'

'Oh. I wouldn't presume...'

The girl pouted her ruby-red lips. 'They tell us things at times, so we girls of the night are suspected of espionage.'

Maggie backed away, all the while keeping her smile fixed—not to offend the girl. 'Excuse me. I'm looking for someone.' Maggie singled out a tall, thin and fine-featured girl. Her shoulders were hunched, and tears streamed down her cheeks. She appeared to be about sixteen. Filled with sympathy, Maggie moved towards her. 'You make me think of my sister. She too, is blonde and beautiful.'

The girl wiped her tears and flashed a smile. 'I'm Teresa, from Poland.'

'I'm Margherita, from Australia,' Maggie reached out to shake her hand.

Teresa took Maggie's hand and held it. 'My real name is Czeslaw. I've read about your debut at Covent Garden.'

Maggie swallowed hard. 'Seems such a long time ago.' She wanted to weep but held back. *I must present a façade of joy even if my heart is breaking.* She felt it her duty to help this sixteen-year-old. 'What's been happening in Poland?'

'Jewish women are stripped naked and made to dance on the streets. Many are raped. The Nazis string up Jews, shove rubber hoses into their mouths and turn on a water faucet until their stomachs burst and their guts spill out.' Tears crept back into her eyes, and trembled on her long, curling lashes like dewdrops on leaves. 'My father is a doctor. One of his patients, an Orthodox Jew, came for treatment after the Nazis tore off his beard.' She attempted a smile. 'Perhaps my parents won't fare too badly. The Nazis *need* the services of doctors.'

Maggie's stomach lurched, and a sour taste rose in her mouth. Her brain could not process such atrocities. 'Why didn't your family leave Poland while there was still time?'

'My parents spoke about moving, but by the time they decided to go, it was too late.'

'How did you escape to Italy?'

'During music lessons at a convent, a messenger brought me money and clothes. He produced a letter from my father, asking the nuns to take care of me. After reading it, they would not let me return home, and kept me in their orphanage with other Jewish children until they managed to smuggle me out to Italy.'

'Are your parents still in Poland?'

'I don't know, but I wish they were safe with me. I often get a flashing image of my father in his white coat with his stethoscope around his neck.' She buried her face in her hands. Sobs shook her, belying her words. When her weeping subsided, she took a deep breath. 'If I had remained with the nuns, I'd have been safe. Life is comparatively normal for Jews in Italy. Restrictions and regulations are few, but I did not want to give up my religion or pretend to be a Catholic. I want to continue my music and perhaps be an opera singer. I had hoped that the conductor, Victor de Sabata, whose mother was a Jewess, would help me. I never managed to meet him, however. The Blackshirts, the *Camicie Nere*, were watching his house and reported my presence to the Italian police who brought me here.'

'I know how you feel, Teresa. I too am separated from my husband and daughter. We must pray for God's help. He alone can aid us. My husband is trying to secure my release, so I hope to return to my home in the mountains before Christmas.' Maggie thought back to her long decades of trying to make it as a singer— the sweat and hard work. She placed her hand on the girl's shoulder. 'Perhaps you'll have an opportunity to get in some singing practice while you're here.'

She was about to say more, but the dinner gong sounded, and they made their way to the canteen. The clock in the hallway showed that sixty minutes had passed while they had been speaking.

After her talk with Teresa, Maggie found herself more aware of her fellow sufferers. She watched them as they ate. At the long wooden table, a woman chewed her food with a faraway look in her eyes. *How does the poor thing feel? Is she resigned with her lot or is she contemplating the past?* Recalling how Emma Calvé had helped her at the beginning of her career, she resolved to help Teresa. *Perhaps I can coach her in singing. It will help us forget our misfortunes, if only for a few hours.*

Maggie consumed her food in silence. After the meal, as the rain had ceased, she invited Teresa for a walk beneath the sweet chestnut trees. She took a seat in the garden and asked her to sing. Teresa sang an emotional aria, which brought tears to her eyes. 'You sing well,' Maggie said, 'but you need to project your voice. When the war is over, I'll continue my career. Meanwhile, I'll be happy to give you voice lessons.'

Teresa clasped her hands as if in prayer. 'Thank you so much, Madame. My parents will be delighted for me.'

For herself, Maggie neither had the desire nor the inclination to practise her singing. A constriction rose in her throat as though a marble had lodged itself there, restricting her voice. Her mind returned to Jean de Reszke who had told her of the tumour that had brought on a pinging in Emma Calvé's voice. Her benefactor had feared cancer then, but fortunately it had been no more than a nodule caused by too much singing too early in life.

During the hot summer at Solofra detention camp, the trees provided a shady retreat, and walking furnished the only source of relaxation for Maggie. She was thankful to have a room for herself because the common room in the *castello* was crowded, and the hygiene deplorable. The odour of unwashed bodies filled the room. Seeing some of the women parting their hair and searching diligently for something, Maggie asked, 'Excuse me, what are you looking for?'

'Nits.'

Maggie returned to her room and combed her tresses several times, searching for head lice. She imagined her head itching from the bites, but she was more fortunate than the women who lived in the servants' quarters, as she had her own bedroom with an *en suite*.

Maggie kept her room clean and spotless. Despite this, bed bugs found their way into her bed, burrowing into her skin and bloating with her blood. She spent sleepless nights scratching.

Fortunately, relations between the camp commandant and inmates were friendly, and there were no beatings or solitary confinement. Each detainee practised her own religion, and all had free access to the little chapel among the trees. Archbishop Palatucci was in charge of foreigners. Arched eyebrows adorned his deep-set penetrating eyes, and his neatly brushed back hair matched a determined jawline. 'A priest always celebrates Mass on Sundays in the little chapel.'

Maggie read the sympathy in his face, and guessed he was hinting they should find solace in prayer. She often noticed him watching the Jewish prisoners, and never knew, until years later, that he had been scrutinising them to check who could pass as a non-Jew so he could obtain false passports for their escape.

The chapel soon became Maggie's only source of refuge, and once more drew her closer to God. The stained-glass windows depicting biblical scenes, reflected light—the light of hope. She drew strength especially from the one carrying the lost lamb. Maggie too felt lost without her family. In the chapel she regained her composure and realised that the avalanche of events would have swept her into the abyss of despair, but for her resource to prayer and faith in God. They enabled her to keep her hopes alive during that terrible time away from her husband and child.

On fine days, Maggie strolled beneath the old cypress pines and listened to the humming of bees and the songs of birds. She would sit still and enjoy the peace and tranquillity. The perfume of lilacs and wisteria took her back to Emma's estate in the Pyrenees. All too soon, however, worrying thoughts would steal into her mind.

Will I be home for Christmas? What's going to happen to me? To my family?

One day, a guard knocked at Maggie's door. 'The Commandant sends you his greetings and wishes you to join him for a meal in his private dining room.'

Maggie wore her cleanest and best dress for dinner and hurried to the Commandant's quarters. Her heartbeat was rapid as she thought of her home and family. *Will he give me some news of Giovanni?*

The table had been set for two. The silver cutlery shone, the wine glasses gleamed, and a vase of red and white roses served as a centrepiece. The Commandant stood and kissed her hand as though she was not his prisoner but a diva. 'I heard that you performed at Naples?'

'Yes. I've also sung in London, Venice and Milan.'

The Commandant steered away from politics and only spoke of music and opera.

Maggie enjoyed the meal, the pleasant atmosphere, and the conversation. It felt like old times with Giovanni. She'd missed him so much. After the meal he said, 'May I ask you for a favour, *Signora*? We're planning a concert for Christmas. Will you present us with a few arias?'

Maggie gazed at him, debating her reply. She did not wish to antagonise him in case she lost her privileges. 'My husband, Giovanni Grandi, is trying to obtain my release. I hope to spend Christmas with him, but if I'm still here, I'll be happy to oblige you.'

'Good luck.' He raised his glass. It sparkled in the light, and seemed to promise Maggie better times, telling her she would soon be free.

~ *Chapter 25* ~

The Rescue

JUST BEFORE CHRISTMAS, AFTER HAVING LIVED FOR nearly eight months in detention, the Camp Commandant sent for Maggie. Archbishop Palatucci was with him. The Archbishop handed Maggie a letter from her husband. 'A visiting priest delivered this to me. Read it.' Short and to the point, perhaps for fear it may be intercepted, the note simply stated:

I've seen Count Dino Grandi, the Minister for Justice. I'm coming to fetch you home. Be ready to leave. Yours forever, Giovanni.

Maggie covered her mouth with her hand, then reached out to the archbishop with trembling hands. 'Thank you, Your Grace.'

'May God be with you, my child,' he murmured. 'Remember to bear your sufferings patiently, and never fail to help others whenever you can.'

Maggie struggled to speak, to find the right words. She stumbled back a step and her knees buckled as she knelt to receive his blessing.

Within a few days, Giovanni arrived at the camp with a letter from Count Dino Grandi, authorising Maggie's release. The Commandant sent for Maggie. Giovanni was in his office, seated in a chair. She rushed forward to her husband and sobbed in his arms. He stroked her hair and dried her eyes when she lifted her tear-stained face.

'You are free to leave after you've signed these documents, *Signora,*' the Commandant said. 'You'll still be under surveillance and must report to the local authorities at specified times.' He handed the papers to Maggie, who took them with trembling hands.

Both Giovanni and Maggie thanked him and lost no time in driving back to Bergamo. On their return, the joy of being with Giovanni again overcame Maggie, despite all the restrictions. She realised that life was precarious and far more precious than her career, her husband, and her child.

They lived in their home in the mountains, but Patricia continued to board with the nuns at Bologna, and only returned to Bergamo during school holidays. Whenever an opportunity occurred, Giovanni worked as scenery director, returning to their mountain retreat when each contract expired.

In June 1940, not long after Mussolini had declared war on the Allies, Britain commenced bombing Milan. Maggie shuddered each time the sirens wailed.

'Don't worry, *cara mia,*' Giovanni said, 'They're only targeting industrial areas. Fortunately, we don't live anywhere near the iron and steel works or the warehouses. We're quite safe here.'

'We may be safe from bombing raids, but the occupying German forces have requisitioned farm produce for Germany. We'll starve!'

Maggie and Giovanni decided to take the southbound train to the Po valley, south of Milan, hoping to buy food, and sold their grand piano to raise money. Fortunately, Giovanni had many contacts, and he accepted the best offer. It broke his heart as it had been in the family for generations, but their source of income had dried up and there was nothing else they could do.

On the morning the new owners came to collect their purchase, Giovanni ran his hand over the ivory keys before playing a few chords. Then Maggie played the Steinway for the last time, rose, and stroked its polished surface. The movers were coming to take away her husband's heirloom. His gift to her. She began to hyperventilate.

He had been clenching and re-clenching his fists, but he extended his arms out to her and held her tight. The only sound she heard was the pounding in her ears and his heavy breathing. She clutched him.

Early the next day, sirens silenced the birds that were greeting the dawn. Giovanni and Maggie invariably ignored the raids, secure in the belief of their safety. This time, however, a solitary plane flew overhead, emitting a black trail of smoke. 'Look,' Giovanni said. 'It's circling. Must have been hit.'

'The plane is on fire!' Maggie recalled her experience of the bombing raids in London during the Great War, and panicked.

Giovanni grabbed her hand. 'A bomber! Run. Run. The pilot is trying to land and may ditch his bombs.'

They arrived at the cellar, gasping for breath. Mario, close behind, shut the door and sank to the floor. The roar of the plane grew closer, and the whining of a bomb sounded. Maggie trembled and placed her palms against her ears to deaden the sound. A loud explosion shook the house, showering them with clouds of dust and plaster.

Giovanni jumped to his feet in an instant. 'Stay here,' he ordered, and darted from the room.

Choking and coughing, Maggie stumbled after him. 'I'm coming. If anything happens, we'll die together.'

A strong stench of smoke and cordite led them to the little parlour. The spot where the piano had stood only yesterday was in shambles—the window had shattered, and shards of glass lay scattered like fractured ice. Part of the wall had crumbled. The rest of the walls were peppered by shrapnel holes.

'The pilot must have aimed for the grove of olive trees,' Giovanni said.

Maggie's heart leapt to her throat. *Only twenty-four hours ago the Steinway had stood here.* In her mind's eye, she imagined her beloved piano wrecked beneath the rubble, its ivory keys grinning at her like a pair of false teeth. Fear laid its clammy hand on her. She turned cold. 'Thank God we sold the piano yesterday.'

'A day earlier, *cara mia*, and you would have been sitting there, playing your piano.'

Speechless, they surveyed the mess. Everything was covered in dust. Dust and glass and shrapnel. The smell of sulphur saturated the air and stung her eyes. Maggie shuddered and recalled the disaster at Waterloo Station during the last war. Fortunately for them, this had not been an incendiary bomb, or the house would have caught fire.

Stunned and bewildered, the bombing left Maggie in a state of emotional turmoil. She picked up a splinter of glass. Even if she had survived the bomb, the shard could have blinded her or severed an artery. To have died would have been bad enough, but the thought of having her eyes or a limb sliced off shook her to the core. She thanked the Lord nothing worse had happened. They had come through alive.

Giovanni started to pick up the shards of glass. His action woke Maggie from her daze. She went to the broom cupboard and returned with a bin and a broom. Mario helped them gather the debris. When they had cleared the room as well as they could, they had a bath, taking care to comb their hair carefully to remove all the dust and tiny specks of glass trapped there. In time, they were able to remove all traces of the bomb, but the disaster tormented Maggie's memory, and she re-lived that day again and again. Her feelings fluctuated between fear and anxiety of further bombings, and elation at being miraculously saved. Her joy of being alive was mixed with a feeling that the worst was now over.

A few days later they took the train to the Po valley. The train passed a prisoner-of-war camp surrounded by barbed wire. Khaki-clad men laboured on a vegetable garden. 'Probably prisoners taken during the North African campaign,' Giovanni commented.

Maggie strained forward to get a better view. 'Wonder if some are Australians.'

'There'll be Australians among them,' he answered. 'I believe they fought well at Tobruk.'

'Perhaps my cousins are there,' she said with a shudder.

'Nothing we can do for them, *cara mia*. Thousands of Italians too are prisoners in North Africa.'

'I'm sure the Allies treat their prisoners well,' she assured him.

'They are more fortunate than those captured in Russia. I fear many will never return.'

She moved closer to him, seeking the security of his presence. 'I hate war. Living through the first one has been bad enough. This is far worse.'

A little later, their train pulled in at a siding and, within a few minutes, a military locomotive loaded with tanks, heading in a southerly direction, passed them. Steel-helmeted German soldiers stood at the front and rear of each wagon, rifles at the ready.

A passenger seated next to Maggie leaned over and spat out of the window. 'That's the re-named Herman Goring Panzer-Division, survivors of the North African campaign. They are heading for Naples.'

'Why Naples?' Maggie asked.

'They stop there for their Rest and Recreation Leave, then visit Pompeii, Sorrento and Capri. Pigs!'

Giovanni's brow creased. 'How do they treat the people?'

'The Nazis lured our boys to work in Germany, promising them good pay. Trainloads of young men departed for Germany but were treated no better than prisoners.'

Too prudent to join in such dangerous talk, Giovanni nodded in sympathy.

Their fellow passenger, once fired up, continued, 'On October 28, the anniversary of the March on Rome when the Fascists seized power, school children wore black shirts and marched with soldiers from the local barracks. At the end of the parade a priest blessed the flags.'

'Probably only done to appease them,' Maggie said. 'The Church does not sympathise with the Fascists.'

The man spread out his hands. 'If you say so, *Senora*. The Pope claimed that Fascism is the enemy of Communism, didn't he?'

Maggie fell silent, thinking of the ruthless Blackshirts—the *Camicie Nere*—who most people dreaded, although some had joined them merely to keep alive and to avoid being taken to Germany as slave labour.

The winter of 1941 was the coldest in living memory. In Bergamo, temperatures dropped to minus one degree centigrade and heating oil grew scarce. 'Now that the Greeks have launched a counter-offensive against us, Mussolini has imposed strict food rationing,' Giovanni said. 'We'll grow maize to supplement our diet and as fodder for the cattle. We'll also have to gather firewood from the forest to save our heating oil.'

Each evening, after a day's work on the estate, they gathered around the welcoming warmth of the fire to escape winter's wrath. Life was still tolerable despite the shortage of food, and they were together. Apart from the bombing of their home, the fierce battles had not yet reached their haven.

~ *Chapter 26* ~

The Resistance

1942 SLIPPED BY WITHOUT ANY FURTHER DISASTER. In April 1943, Maggie received an invitation to perform in Rome and the Teatro San Carlo in Naples. Clutching the invitation, she raced to the fields where Giovanni was working. The snow had cleared, and the frozen earth yielded more readily to the spade Giovanni held. He dropped it and looked up in dismay. 'What is it, *cara mia*?'

She waved the envelope. 'I've been invited to sing in Rome and Naples. It's not a lead role, but I'll be able to earn something, and we could buy more food.'

'Calm down.' Giovanni rubbed the soil off his hands on his trousers. 'What role have you been offered?'

'I'll be the Empress Ottavia in Monteverdi's *L'coronazione di Poppa*. It's only a minor role, but I'm grateful for small mercies.'

'Good. As soon as rehearsals commence, we can take the train to Rome and stay with friends.'

Maggie hugged herself with happiness.

Monteverdi's *L'coronazione di Poppa*, considered his finest opera, focuses on historical subjects rather than mythological characters. During rehearsals, her muscles tightened, and she found herself having to clear her throat frequently, but all went well on opening day.

Soon performances and lavish parties were a thing of the past. Within three months, British and U.S. Forces landed in Sicily, fighting broke out, and soon after, the Allies occupied Reggio in the toe of Italy.

Maggie stocked their cellar with sacks of flour for bread and pasta, and with beans, chickpeas, lentils, oil, sausages, bottles of wine and several rounds of cheese, hoping to tide them over until the war ended. Giovanni hid their provisions behind piles of firewood in case the Blackshirts searched the house again. Their car and wireless had already been confiscated. For Christmas, Maggie dipped into their stocks to lighten the atmosphere for Patricia, who returned during holidays.

One day in September, Giovanni burst out, 'The Allies have landed in Salerno.'

Maggie clasped her hands. 'Perhaps hostilities will soon be over. If only we can survive the next few weeks.'

A look of fear crossed Giovanni's face. 'The Germans still have sixteen divisions in Italy. Field Marshall Kesselring is in command of the South and Rommel in the North. You know how well Rommel fared in North Africa. They may yet crush any advance by American and British troops.'

For days, trucks rolled past, transporting German troops to the frontline. Not a day went by without the pounding of guns—a sound that grew closer as time passed. Maggie flinched and broke out in a cold sweat whenever the thunder of shellfire reached them. Before the month ended, Giovanni rushed home, flushed with news. 'King Victor Emmanuel has replaced Mussolini with Field Marshal Badgoglio, who has abolished the Fascist Regime and released all political prisoners. It's in the papers. Mussolini has been imprisoned and Italy is ready to end hostilities.'

Soon after, when Italy surrendered to the Allies, Maggie and Giovanni rejoiced. 'Italian Commandants have opened the gates of Allied prisoner-of-war camps. Some prisoners have fled north towards Switzerland. Others have gone south to Allied lines,' Giovanni said.

Mussolini did not remain incarcerated for long. On 12 September 1943, Nazi storm-troopers freed him in a daring raid and brought him to Lake Garda where he established an Italian Socialist Republic at Salo. Two Italian governments now controlled Italy. The Allies reached Naples in October but due to the early winter snow, rains and mud, their advance ground to a halt at the foot of Monte Cassino. The Benedictine Abbey there dominated the road to Rome and held a strategic position, so no advance was possible until the monastery was taken. Hope turned to fear.

'Will the Allies withdraw, and leave us to defend ourselves?' Giovanni asked a rhetorical question, not expecting a reply.

'I don't think they'll abandon us now that we're on their side.'

Partisans radioed details of the fighting at Cassino. When the news reached Giovanni, he chuckled. 'The Polish brigade at Cassino is using a bear to carry provisions and munitions up the mountain. I believe the animal escaped from a circus and a Polish soldier trained it to transport things for him.'

A surge of hope swept over Maggie, like a wave. 'It shows that God's on our side.' Then she broke out into Verdi's *Slave Chorus*—the song of liberty.

The Allies made three attempts to clear German troops from the hills around Monte Cassino but failed. Bogged down by mud and rain, they made little progress until the long winter came to an end, trees began to break into bud and purple and white crocuses bloomed on the hill slopes.

'I'm going to Rome,' Giovanni said. 'A friend over there has a wireless and tunes in to the BBC whenever possible. He passes on the news to us. I haven't heard from him for some time.'

'You're safer here. Surely you don't need to go.'

'I can't remain in suspense, *cara mia*. The news may tell what we need to do.'

'You know there is fighting at Monte Cassino. How will you get to Rome when the road is blocked?'

'Don't worry about that. There are ways of getting there. You don't need to know everything. The less you know, the better.'

Maggie guessed he was on some secret mission for the resistance. She assumed he had refrained from revealing more information in case the Nazis captured her and she talked under torture. She waved farewell with an aching heart.

The allies bombed Rome while Giovanni was away, leaving Maggie in an agony of suspense. Her thoughts flitted back to the time when they had rambled together among the Roman ruins. 'If only he was safe here with me,' she moaned, gnawing her nails in desperation.

Giovanni returned soon after the bombing of Rome. He held out his hands in a gesture of despair. 'Herbert Kappler, the SS chief in Rome, has rounded up the Jews and deported them to concentration camps. Thousands have fled to the Vatican and religious houses. The Pope is encouraging convents and monasteries to open their doors to the refugees.'

'The cloistered areas as well?'

'The nuns have placed *Off Limits* signs in German, forbidding entrance into the cloisters.'

'Thank God the Germans are respecting them.'

'Not all Germans are Nazis. Many are sympathetic. Cardinal Schuster is secretly working to save Jewish refugees. A government employee supplies blank identification cards and gives them to priests, who smuggle Jews into Switzerland.'

'Don't they realise what would happen if they're caught?'

'I'm sure they do, *cara mia*, but people rise to the occasion whenever there's a need. Peasants are hiding refugees and smuggling them into Switzerland. Others take them to safe houses, convents or monasteries. Jews are God's children too and should be protected. The nuns are sheltering hundreds at the Instituto Palazzolo in Milan. In case the Nazis search the orphanage, Jewish children attend Mass and learn to say the *Ave Maria* and the *Pater Noster*.'

'Not all Italians are sympathetic to the Jews.'

'That's true.'

'Surely the Jews are fighting back?'

'Yes. Many of them have joined the Italian underground movement. While I was in Rome, partisans laid bombs on Via Rasella and wiped out thirty-three German SS police.'

Maggie took a sharp breath, knowing the Nazis would retaliate.

Giovanni dropped his eyes. 'The Nazis dragged three hundred and thirty-five Jews to the catacombs of San Callisto on the Appian Way, shot them and sealed the caves with rocks.'

She gasped. 'This is horrible. I wish we could do something to help.'

He placed his hands on her shoulders and looked into her eyes. 'We must be prepared to take them in if they come knocking at our door.'

Maggie nodded. 'Of course, darling.' Her words were spontaneous, but the more she thought of it, the more her stomach churned. *What if the Nazis discovered them?* She prayed for strength, recalling Archbishop Palatucci's words, 'Never fail to help others whenever you can.'

By the winter of 1943, food was scarce, and Maggie thanked the Lord they had stocked their cellar. Even so, their supplies were running low. *What will happen when they ran out?* She envisaged them wasting away to skin and bone.

One morning early in December, the parish priest, Padre Antonio knocked at their door and asked how they were faring.

'Not too well.' Maggie pointed to a chair beside the fireplace. 'Giovanni's contract at *La Scala* hasn't been renewed, and food supplies are low. We've had to sell our piano.'

The priest gazed at the space where her piano used to be. The wall had since been repaired, but the bricks did not match the old ones and shrapnel scars remained on the walls and furniture.

'Mario told me about the bombing. The Lord has spared your lives.'

He sipped the ersatz coffee Maggie had served him and turned to Giovanni. 'We have extra mouths to feed. If American Hebrews did not smuggle money to us for their brethren here, I don't know how we'll survive.'

Maggie shifted uncomfortably in her seat. *Should she offer him a small bag of flour or dried peas?* She glanced at Giovanni, trying to signal her thoughts, but he was tugging at his shirt collar as if his feelings were choking him.

Padre Antonio studied the nearby hills. 'There are many ways one can help in these terrible times. You must be aware the Apennines and the Alps have become a refuge for Jews, escaped prisoners-of-war and anti-Fascists? Our disbanded soldiers have joined forces with the Resistance. Women carry messages for undercover groups, hide men in barns and warn them whenever the Nazis approach. Everyone is helping.' He heaved a deep sigh and turned to Giovanni and Maggie who sat on the shrapnel-torn settee. 'There are so many ways one can help.'

Giovanni's face was grim as he nodded. '*Si padre.* We'll not turn them away if they knock at our door.'

The priest rose and made the sign of the Cross. 'May God bless this house and all who live here. One never knows what will happen in the future.' He bid them farewell, leaving the pair with a grim sense of foreboding.

The days dragged on. When Patricia came home for Christmas, Maggie flew to her and held her close for several minutes before relinquishing her hold. 'I'll bake a cake for Christmas even if we have to starve afterwards. Today, we shall rejoice and be merry for tomorrow we may die,' she muttered, quoting the words of the bible, although they had been used in a different context.

She used some of their remaining flour and raisins to bake a cake.

Maggie's heart ached to see Patricia leave at the end of the festive season, but she knew their daughter would be safer with the nuns.

Late in January, Mario returned from a visit to his parents, bringing news from the grapevine. His eyes shone with excitement. 'The Allies have landed at Anzio.'

Maggie jumped for joy. 'That's so close to Rome.'

'Partisan activity has increased. Using hit-and-run tactics, they cut telephone wires and blow-up German vehicles. The Nazis are too scared to go out at nights. In the mornings, they search dwellings, burn the houses of anyone suspected of hiding Jews and partisans, and drag off able-bodied men for forced labour.'

Maggie bit her lip. *Any day now, the Germans may come for Giovanni.*

Maggie and Giovanni spent that night tossing in bed. Normally, he would be snoring long before she fell asleep. Now he lay on his back, staring at the ceiling. She snuggled up to him. 'Is something on your mind, dear?'

He rolled over to face her, reaching out in the darkness. 'The German swine have disbanded the Italian army and are force-marching all males between fifteen and fifty to build defences in the south or be dragged off to work in Germany.'

Her voice trembled. 'They'll come for you, Giovanni. What should we do?'

He traced a gentle line down her cheek. 'Men are fleeing to the mountains to avoid capture. Only the fascists in their black shirts and black boots are safe. Perhaps we should hide during the day.'

They lay in silence, thinking about the future.

For the next few days Maggie and Giovanni rose before dawn, consumed a hurried meal, and then scrambled through knee-high undergrowth and laboured up the heights. At twilight they returned, weary and footsore. Maggie's voice grew hoarse and painful. Haunted by fears of falling ill and losing her ability to sing, her thoughts continually wandered back to her attack of typhoid at the outset of her career.

After several days of toiling up the hills, being scratched by thorns and braving the exposure of inclement weather, Giovanni turned to her in concern. 'I think all this is too much for you, *cara mia*. You don't need to accompany me in the mornings. Women are not forced to work, so perhaps you should stay behind with Anna. Mario's father, Francesco, will help you during the day. He's almost seventy years old and won't be taken.'

When Giovanni persuaded Maggie to remain home, she clasped his hand and squeezed it. She saw the logic of his words and knew she could not have lasted much longer under the strain.

From then on, Francesco worked on the farm while Giovanni and Mario fled to the mountains each morning. In the evenings, they returned, too exhausted for anything but a warm bath and a hot meal. Giovanni always looked worn and haggard on his return. Too weary even to speak, he collapsed into bed and fell asleep. Maggie snuggled up to him, wondering how he spent his days.

One evening, while she painted the scratches on his arms and legs with iodine, he said, 'We met a group of partisans who are in contact with the Allies.'

Maggie nearly spilled the contents of the little bottle of iodine as she threw her arms around him in delight. They had been frantic for news of the fighting. It was far better to face the truth than to live in suspense.

Time passed. Unable to supplement the cellar stores, the last stocks of cheese and flour they had stored away the previous year dwindled to nothing. Their cheeks were sunken, and they tired easily. All too often Maggie's stomach rumbled with hunger.

One night, Giovanni returned home scratched and dishevelled. 'Wave after wave of planes have bombed the Benedictine Abbey at Monte Cassino. Nothing is left. Only ruins and rubble.'

Maggie choked with emotion, but there was nothing she could do. *A victory but at what a cost! So many lives lost and an ancient abbey destroyed.* Maggie looked out of her window. Trees and shrubs were covered in snow. The cold grew more intense every day. Hunger increased their sensitivity to the winter frosts.

$$\sim\;\textit{Chapter 27}\;\sim$$

Guerrilla Groups around Milan

THE ALLIES CONTROLLED MOST OF SOUTHERN ITALY by May 1944. Resistance groups fought alongside the Allies and became known as royalist forces. The Germans referred to them as rebels. One night, Francesco showed Maggie a leaflet dropped by German planes, warning residents not to harbour rebels and Jews, or aid Allied pilots shot down over Italy.

Maggie gazed long and hard at the leaflet. 'I long to help the Allies, but don't have the courage.'

The following week, Allied aircraft showered leaflets over villages, urging Resistance Forces to continue acts of sabotage. So, despite cruel retaliation by occupying powers, guerrilla activity increased. Giovanni often met members of the Osoppo Brigades, the communist Garibaldi and socialist Matteotti bands, all of whom operated on the foothills around Milan.

By early 1944, opera had all but ceased in Italy. 'Continue to practise your singing,' Giovanni said. 'You want to be ready as soon as *La Scala* re-opens.'

'I'll be too old to sing at a performance by the time peace returns,' Maggie said, making a show of indifference. The war was beginning to tell on her nerves. All she wanted was peace. Peace and plenty. Plenty of food. Plenty of quiet. Plenty of fun.

When the winter snows melted, Maggie hiked on the hills around their home.

Months passed.

In the early light of a summer morning, she ambled among alpine pasture, enjoying the fragrance of conifers as a fresh breeze rustled through the fir trees. She fought her way among alder thickets and rocky outcrops, climbing up stony paths towards the cave. The days were long now, and she imagined she heard the bluebells tinkle as she passed. The bright yellow rock roses gleamed like gold and bushes of red centaury covered large stretches of soil.

Maggie quickened her steps, hoping to spend some time away from the worries of war. Strands of ivy cascaded down, screening the entrance of the cave against the hot sun and ferocity of the wind. She parted the creepers, stepped into the interior, and blinked to adjust her eyes to the gloom. The earthen jug of wine, together with a little basket of fruit, nuts and biscuits were in a corner. She had asked Mario to bring them here so she could eat before returning home.

She sat on a rock to catch her breath. When her sight adjusted itself to the dark interior, an unfamiliar shape on the cave floor came into focus. She rose and crept forward. On closer inspection, she distinguished a man in peasant clothes. Stubble the colour of corn silk covered his chin.

He appeared to be in his early twenties and was fast asleep.

Maggie let out a cry of surprise, awakening the intruder, who jumped to his feet. '*Mi piace...*' He spoke in broken Italian, apologising for having helped himself to the contents of her basket.

'You're not Italian,' she said, in Italian. 'Who are you?'

No answer.

Maggie repeated the question in English.

'Thank God you speak English!'

'I'm Australian. What are you doing here?'

'I escaped from a prisoner-of-war camp.' He glanced at her empty basket. 'I was starving, so I tucked into your food and drank the wine.'

'You're most welcome.' She found it difficult to take her gaze off his pinched face and sunken eyes. 'I must get in touch with someone who can help you. My husband is not home, but I will ask our farmhand, Francesco. I'll be back as soon as possible. Stay hidden and be quiet. Don't go away.' She trembled, recalling the threatening leaflets dropped from German planes.

The young man placed a restraining hand upon her arm. 'How do I know I can trust you?'

Maggie put her hand over his and looked deep into his eyes. 'Because God brought you to this place. Neither of us are Italians, so we must stick together.'

'I don't want to get you into danger.'

She glanced at his blackened and torn fingernails; his scratched and bruised arms and was overcome by compassion. Then she parted the vines and raced downhill, arriving home panting.

Francesco was milking the cows. He turned around as she approached, a look of alarm in his eyes. 'The Germans have taken our prize cow. I couldn't stop them.'

'They spare no one these days, Francesco. Not even the Blackshirts.' Her heart pounded against her rib cage, and she hesitated for a few seconds, brushing the hair back from her forehead. 'Do you know anyone who can conduct a person to Switzerland?'

Francesco's eyes widened and the skin around his mouth puckered and wrinkled. 'Yes. Would you like to meet him?'

'As soon as possible, please.'

He nodded. 'I'll fetch him.'

Within an hour, he returned with an aged man. The old man's veins stood out like knotted rope on his neck and along the line of his jaw, but zest for life radiated from his eyes. 'This is Lucio,' Francesco said.

Lucio put out a gnarled and calloused hand. His firm grip told her of the strength remaining in his sinewy body. His hair was a mass of grey, his skin dark and toughened. He did not waste words. 'Where's he?'

'Over there.' Maggie pointed to the hills.

He nodded. 'I'll come along and check him out.'

She grabbed a blanket, a couple of candles, an empty bowl, some bread and salami, then poured hot soup into a flask and stumbled up the hill. Apart from her loud breathing, nothing broke the silence. The old man followed in the fading light. Leaping across rocks with the agility of a mountain goat, he soon overtook her.

When they entered the cave, he sized up the situation within seconds. 'He must remain here till dark. I'll bring along an airman who's been staying with us and lead them to a stretch of fence at the border where it's safe to crawl under.'

He spoke in Italian, and Maggie translated his message into English for the fugitive's benefit. She handed him the food and laid the candles and blanket beside him. He squeezed her arm in gratitude, before snatching the flask from her, took a mouthful of soup and gulped it down, before picking up the bread and salami.

He ate slowly after the initial gusto, making every mouthful count. Finally, he wiped his lips with the back of his hand. 'I'm Tommy. I used to drive buses in London.'

'I studied at the Royal College of Music in London and worked as a bus conductor there during the Great War. I loved the sense of humour and rhyming slang of Londoners. But tell me about yourself. How did you get here?'

'I escaped from a prison camp in September last year and joined the partisans. They were using a parachute as their tent. I stayed with them until June, then boarded a train to Milan, intending to escape into Switzerland. I saw some members of the Gestapo enter a carriage further back, so I jumped off as the engine slowed at a crossing and made my way to the hills.' Tommy reached into his pocket, took out a silk handkerchief and spread it out before her. On it was a large-scale map of the area. 'We use this if we're shot down.' He broke into a smile. 'The war will soon be over, and I'll be driving buses once again.'

Within an hour, Lucio returned, bringing more food, forged papers, and money—in case German patrols accosted them. A British aviator in peasant clothes accompanied him. Maggie struggled to hold back the sob in her voice as she shook hands and wished them the best of luck.

After that venture, she felt braver, and longed to help the Allies a bit more.

The roar of a low-flying plane startled Maggie that evening. In the distance, she heard a thump. *No explosion. An unexploded bomb?* Although frightened, she jumped to her feet and ran in the direction of the sound.

Francesco and Mario were already there, along with Giovanni— just returned from the hills.

'What is it? A bomb?' he asked.

Mario was grinning. 'No, *signor*. A parachute with provisions. A supply-drop for the partisans must have missed its target and fallen on our fields. We'll hide every trace of the air-drop before the Nazis get here in the morning.'

Giovanni helped Mario hide the food supplies in the cellar. It was a long night. Maggie ran a hot bath for her exhausted husband, who sank into it with a sigh. Glad to hear his expression of contentment,

Maggie fussed over him and, sponged the grime embedded in his knees. He stepped out, refreshed and ready for breakfast.

Before setting out for the mountains again, Giovanni held Maggie close, kissed her hair and whispered, 'You acted bravely yesterday, but take care.'

On 5 June 1944, when news of the Allied march into Rome reached them, Maggie grasped Giovanni. 'They should be here any moment now.'

'Yes, but the Nazis could vent their anger on us.'

Guerrilla forces continued to harass German troops as the rain and snow of winter brought communication to a halt.

A few months after the triumphal march into Rome by Allied forces, Lucio informed Maggie that both Tommy, the escaped prisoner, and the British aviator had reached the border. She sighed with relief.

Lucio scratched his head and looked at the ground. 'Would you be able to shelter a wounded airman? His plane was shot down in August last year, and he has been moving between hiding places for too long. He's exhausted and feverish from sleeping out in the cold and needs a warm bed. His mind is drifting. Can you help him?'

Maggie could not refuse. She knew Giovanni would be willing to take the risk.

Lucio soon returned, accompanied by two scruffy men holding the airman between them. The sick man had his arms around their shoulders and dragged his left leg as he walked. His waxen nose quivered. His golden hair, dank with perspiration from his fever, hung down over cheeks white as the bones showing beneath. Dark eye sockets held two blue pools. Emaciation showed, especially in the hands and face.

Maggie waved them in. To leave no traces of their visit, Lucio and the two men rubbed their feet on the doormat as if their lives depended upon it. She led them to her guest room, and they lay him on the bed, making him as comfortable as possible. If the Germans questioned her, she planned to say that the invalid was a visiting relative, who had contracted typhus. It would scare them off.

One of the men whispered. 'We've forged papers for him.'

She took the men to her kitchen and poured hot cocoa into three mugs. The provisions from the parachute-drop had descended like a gift from heaven when most needed. After they gulped it down, the spokesman smacked his lips. 'You're well provided?'

'A supply-drop obviously meant for your men landed in our fields a few weeks' ago. Take whatever you can carry.' She showed them her hidden store.

'Thank you. We're starving.' They filled their bags with packets of spaghetti, boxes of cheese and tins of corned beef.

'You'll need to fatten him up before we can conduct him to Switzerland,' the older man advised. 'Lucio will visit you. He'll come to deliver hay for your horses.'

The men backed towards the door. 'We must leave now. God bless you.'

Maggie's thoughts turned to Archbishop Giuseppe Palatucci's parting words to her in the prison camp. *Never fail to help others when you can.*

She would do all she could to aid the airman.

$$\sim \textit{Chapter 28} \sim$$

The Fight Continues

MAGGIE AND ANNA TOOK TURNS WATCHING THE FUGITIVE, spoon-feeding him with soup and hot cocoa. Within a few weeks his grey face had turned white with a tinge of pink, but his mind continued to wander among the stone cottages of an English hamlet. July crept by without any major change in him except that the colour returned to his cheeks. Still the fever persisted.

One day in August, the patient opened his eyes and looked wildly around the room. 'Where am I?'

'You're in safe hands, but you've been extremely ill.'

He rubbed his head. 'I recall being led to a house by two men—nothing more.'

'You've had a persistent fever for four weeks.'

'Have I been here for *that* long?' He broke into a most endearing smile. 'My name's Jack. So many people have helped me.' His voice grew stronger as he spoke.

Compassion swept over Maggie, and she smiled in encouragement. 'What else do you remember, Jack?'

'I was shot down over Milan. Some members of the Fire Brigade gave me first aid and organised a safe house. They warned me to stay away from the window and left.'

She looked at his sunken eyes. 'How did you manage by yourself in Milan?'

'Someone brought food and dressed my wound every day until my leg healed.'

'You must have been healthy.'

Jack nodded. 'Fighting fit.' He paused. 'Each morning, the sound of Mussolini's Blackshirts marching along the road filtered through to me. I had to get away before they discovered me. I took the passports and clothes my benefactors had given me and slipped downstairs one day. I'm fluent in Italian, having studied it back home.'

'Why didn't you wait for your partisan friends?'

'I hadn't the heart to endanger my contacts any longer. Besides, planes had been strafing Milan heavily at the time, and I didn't want to be hit again. I found my way to the mountains but ran across a German patrol. I lay low for a while since the city clothes I wore were not right for the countryside.'

'Did you ask the farmers for help?'

'I did. A farmer gave me clothes and hid me, but not wanting to endanger them any further, I left. By then, winter had set in and the wind bit into me like a sharp knife. I feared I'd lose my footing when forcing my way through the tall bracken. Finally, I lost my way in the hills.'

'That must have been when you developed a fever and things went awry. Eat something and go back to sleep. Don't tire yourself talking.'

After drinking a steaming bowl of broth, Jack fell asleep.

Within a few weeks, he could take short walks around the estate and help Francesco with his chores. Jack often spoke of his home. He loved opera and joined Maggie in the stables when she sang. Filled with pride as though she stood before an entire hall of devoted fans, her voice resonated within the stable walls. Her heart beat fast, as his adoring eyes settled upon her.

At times, Lucio came by to drop a bale of hay and check on the airman's progress. When he thought Jack strong enough, he arranged to escort him to the border.

Maggie had grown attached to the tall young man and his charming smile. She prayed for his safety, but knew she would miss his quiet confidence, his gentleness, and his charm.

As the momentum of war gathered force, the partisans brought in more survivors from crashed aircraft. British planes made secret airdrops of food, guns, munitions and radios for Resistance fighters, but many of them were shot down. The airmen wore identity discs and carried foreign currency. Whenever possible, guerrillas would retrieve the aircrew and spirit them away before the Germans arrived.

In retaliation, the Gestapo parachuted their own men down in English or American parachutes. They spoke perfect English when picked up, so partisans put the pseudo-aircrew through escape routes. The Nazis then rounded up the partisans.

Despite this, survivors continued harassing the Germans, sending vital information such as the location of enemy troops, airfields, and storage dumps to the Allies. Resistance workers lived with death as their constant companion. Most had a life expectancy of a mere three months. To avoid a domino-collapse if captured, they were given only the codename of their immediate contacts.

A string of escapees came and went through the estate. Some staggered in, supported by a man on either side. Others were brought to her on makeshift stretchers, covered with dust. Blood-stained blankets concealed their broken bones and bleeding wounds. Maggie tended wounded airmen and guerrilla fighters whenever she could. Anna helped nurse the wounded, many of whom were her friends and relatives. A village doctor came in at nights to set their bones and give them a shot of morphine, but he could not stay long.

One day, as Maggie bent over a casualty who had just been brought in, Anna said, 'He's bleeding to death, but we have no more room to hide him, *Senora*. He was shot while attempting to rescue Allied air crew.'

Maggie cut his shirt open and gazed at the wound. 'Fortunately, the bullet has gone right through.'

The victim was no more than sixteen and appeared pale and faint from loss of blood. Anna grabbed a clean rag and helped staunch the life blood. 'We call it the wine of youth,' she sobbed.

Maggie placed powdered sulphur on his wound and bandaged the boy's arm. 'Go to sleep now. The doctor will be here soon,' she murmured, not sure whether he could hear. When he had dozed off, Maggie turned to Anna. 'Remember the time they brought in an escaped prisoner-of-war? I'd gagged at the sight and smell of the green pus. I hope we managed to save his arm, but I think gangrene had already set in. This boy's wound is fresh, and the doctor should be here tonight. I think he'll be alright.'

'I hope so, *Senora*. I don't get the stench of rotten cheese like we did from the last young man.'

Maggie nodded. She seldom discovered the fate of those she helped.

One morning, Francesco brought in Peter, an American pilot, who had escaped unharmed from the crash. His body filled the doorway and exuded an aura of vitality. He stood tall and straight like a towering spruce, and wore a woollen jacket, with overalls tucked into knee-high boots. He extended his hand and Maggie grasped it. She beckoned him towards the fire.

Sufficiently warmed, he removed his jacket. Golden hairs covered his forearms. Maggie's pulse quickened, remembering the time she had been thrilled at the sight of Giovanni's glossy body hair. Her heart hammered against her ribs. A sudden desire that had remained dormant during the past year arose within her, and she felt young again. An extraordinary feeling—almost of magnetism seemed to pass between them. *Am I losing control of my senses? Is it possible for a mere stranger to arouse me? I love Giovanni, but every evening he returns too exhausted for anything.* Maggie's chin quivered and her chest tightened. She raised her left hand and covered her mouth.

She wanted to keep Peter with her for the duration of the war, but she gave him the choice of joining the resistance or returning to carry on the fight. 'Would you like to join the resistance fighters or return to your friends?'

'I'm keen to return and bomb the Nazis to hell,' Peter replied.

Weeks passed. Peter helped in the farm and waited impatiently for a guide to the border.

Anna rushed in one day. 'A new German officer is making a house-to-house search in the village. He'll be at my place within a few hours.'

Fear clutched at Maggie's throat. *We'll be caught and tortured. Thank God our daughter is with the nuns.* She had no time to send word to Francesco. His cottage was probably being searched already. Peter was still at her house and in immediate danger of being caught.

'Anna, I'll explain to Peter the route he should follow. Our partisan friends will catch up with him and escort him to the border.' She turned to Peter. 'I'll take you as far as I can. May God be with you the rest of the way.'

He smiled a crooked smile. 'I've been through worse situations, lady. Don't worry.' Laughter tumbled from his throat as he held his head high.

Maggie wiped her hands on her apron in a futile effort to remove the cold sweat that had broken out. She knew the consequence of being caught aiding an airman—interrogations, torture, and gouged eyes, followed by death, but Archbishop Palatucci's words, *'Help others whenever you can,'* kept ringing in her ears.

She placed a bundle of food in his pack and grabbed his arm. 'Come now. There's not a moment to lose.'

Normally Maggie used the longer and easier route, but today she took the shorter and more direct one. Her knees hurt with the constant stumbling over the rocky terrain. She wished she were ten years younger. She scrambled up the mountains towards the cave, speaking little, sensing that the time was fraught with danger. Clouds wheeled drunkenly across the sky. She struggled on, her breath coming in quick, short gasps.

Peter reached out a hand. 'Let me help.'

She clasped it. As soon as her fingers touched the warmth of his outreached hand, she felt safe. She clutched it but tripped. His firm grip kept her from falling on her face. He pulled her upright and held her to his chest. 'Did you hurt yourself?'

A thrill ran through her body. She wanted to remain in his arms.

Peter released her gently and they continued towards the cave. When they arrived, Peter crushed her in his arms. 'Thank you. I've escaped from the Nazis so far. Don't worry. Your underground system is excellent.'

His fingers were strong and warm against her skin, sending delicious shivers down her body. Strength surged into her, filling her with desire. She huddled there, her heart throbbing, and remained in his embrace, enjoying his youth. His strength. Letting it flow through her. Strengthening her.

Finally, she drew away. 'Goodbye. Keep going as fast as you can and lie low if the pursuers get too close. The partisans will show you the safest route into Switzerland. There are still a few hours left before curfew. Hurry, and pray to God the Nazis have no tracker dogs.' She gazed at his disappearing figure as he set out in the eerie darkness. Even though they had never kissed, she was overcome with longing for him. Longing for his merest touch. Longing for his strength. Longing for his youth.

He looked briefly over his shoulder, then plodded up the hill until out of sight, the granite slopes towering above him like a fortress.

Puffing and panting from the climb, Maggie entered the cave and sat on a rock. The walls faded in and out of focus. A few minutes passed before she could regain her composure. Nervous as a deer sensing danger, she unscrewed the bottle of wine and took a sip, praying that God would protect Peter. He meant more to her than any of the others she had helped. After a few moments, guilt stole over her. *How can I have such feelings when my husband is in danger?*

As she rose to leave, voices sounded in the distance. Arrows of thought pierced her brain. *The Germans must have completed their search of the village and discovered my absence from home. Now they are looking for me.* She inhaled a deep breath, did a few warmup exercises, and broke into Tosca's fiery aria—*Il tuo sangue o il mio amore volea*—telling how she killed the villain Scarpia. Maggie's voice rang out. She knew her strains would reach Peter and he'd take it as a warning.

Soldiers drifted in silently. Even their jackboots made no sound. Maggie continued her aria; her singing echoing over the hills. When she stopped, a loud clapping broke out, followed by silence. The lieutenant in charge jerked his head towards the entrance and the soldiers left, their boots crunching over the gravel.

Tall and handsome, the officer's uniform fitted sleekly to his slim, unbelted waist.

He clicked his heels. 'What are you doing here so late in the day?'

Her feet were anchored to the floor as if her blood had settled down there, sealing her to the spot. She had always been the consummate actress, immersed in each character she played. Now she called upon all her acting ability to remain calm and show no fear. 'Practising. This is my studio. My private studio.'

'Do you come here often? Your maid told me you had gone for a walk.' His voice was devoid of malice, almost apologetic.

She summoned up her most seductive smile. 'On fine days, I stop here to sing. You've heard of Margherita Grandi, of course.'

His face softened. 'I'm an ardent admirer of yours. I heard you sing in April last year.' He took a step towards her, moving with grace and agility. 'I'm arranging a concert for my men. Will you perform for us?'

Maggie noticed his powerful shoulders. She did not answer him directly. 'The sun is setting, and I like to be home before dark.' She placed her hands upon her hips and threw back her head. 'I'd invite you to dinner, but food is scarce.' Maggie's manner was both flirtish and challenging—the only way she could avert suspicion from herself.

'Don't worry about that. I will bring something. What time should I call?'

'Would ten suit you?'

'Thank you. I'll be there.' He appeared to study her. 'I must let you go before curfew commences.'

As soon as Maggie arrived home, she sent Francesco to meet Giovanni when he came down from the hills.

The lieutenant appeared promptly at ten o'clock. A truck full of armed soldiers followed his staff car. Once they had alighted, the men spread out among the trees in strategic positions to guard their commanding officer in case of a surprise attack.

Two men, carrying steaming dishes of food and freshly baked bread, followed him into the villa. After laying them on the tables, they clicked their heels and saluted, then left to join the others and form a perimeter around the precincts.

Maggie hoped that none of her friends from the Resistance would visit her. If they did, they'd meet with a fiery reception from the Nazis. Despite the fear hanging over her, she passed the evening talking about music and opera, and indulged in the delicious food. As she expected, her guest requested her to sing a few arias for him. She obliged.

God, please let Peter get through to Allied lines. I am doing this for a good cause. I'm not consorting with the enemy.

Giovanni, always a good father and loving husband, insisted she no longer endanger their lives—especially the life of their only child. 'Summary executions, ransacking and retaliations against civilians are not uncommon practises.'

Maggie was unable to aid Allied airmen after this. Her frayed nerves could not continue the work, as she would break one way or the other. One cold February morning, she shivered on her way to the barn. The wind penetrated her shawl and her breath rose in little clouds of mist. She found Francesco; his shoulders slumped as he milked the cows. He looked up with a face contorted in misery. She had never seen him in such distress. 'What's wrong, Francesco?'

'The entire command of the Ossopo division has been wiped out.' He used the back of his hands to wipe his tears.

'The Nazis?'

'No. It was the communists from the Garibaldi division.'

'Why? Why? Weren't they all fighting the common enemy?'

'The men were under Yugoslav command and our Osoppo boys wouldn't accept Tito's authority.'

'What happened?'

'A hundred communists approached the Ossopo hideout, pretending to have been disbanded. When they drew closer, they gunned our boys down. Only one escaped to bring the news.'

Blood drained from her face. Her tongue clung to the roof of her mouth and the bitter taste of fear arose. She thought of the partisans who had brought dozens of ailing men to her, and her heart bled for them. It was cruel to die so close to the end of the war. She could hardly wait for Giovanni to return from the hills and sob out the story to him. When she imparted the news, he grasped her in his arms and swore. She had never heard him swear before.

They stayed up late, pondering their next move, but there was nothing they could do. After a restless night, Giovanni and Mario fled to the mountains before the break of dawn. The next morning, with tears in her eyes, Maggie attended Mass for the slain. In his eulogy, the priest mourned the loss of the partisans who had been martyred by communists just when the Germans were being routed.

Sobs rose to Maggie's throat.

After Mass, Padre Antonio stood at the Church entrance. He was talking to some of his parishioners but turned towards Maggie as she was about to pass. 'Wait a few minutes. I must speak to you. Wait in my office. I'll be there *un poco*.'

Maggie's heart pounded. What worse news did the priest have? She hurried to his office. It was locked. She waited outside, shivering with cold and fear.

Padre Antonio arrived shortly afterwards. He unlocked the door, waved towards a seat, and sat at his desk before speaking. Then he leaned forward and whispered. 'Hitler has ordered Field Marshal Kesselring to annihilate the guerrillas and destroy everything before they leave.'

Maggie gasped and half-rose, but he motioned her to be seated. 'The SS contacted the archbishop and promised not to carry out a scorched-earth policy if we grant them safe conduct back to Germany.'

He looked away and continued speaking. 'Partisans refuse to negotiate with the enemy. They will mine the roads and blow-up retreating Germans. Keep off the roads. Remain indoors.'

Maggie clasped her hands. 'Thank you, Padre. I'll tell Giovanni not to go to the mountains any longer.'

In the last week of April, factory-workers at Milan subdued their German overseers. Meanwhile, partisan forces poured into the city, taking control of the radio station and police headquarters. Giovanni and Mario watched German trucks driving away.

On April 27, the US 1st Armoured Division entered Milan and two days later, Mussolini and his mistress, Clara Petacci, were executed by partisans who strung up their bodies in the Piazzale Loreto.

A feeling of euphoria overwhelmed Maggie. Instead of the pounding of artillery, she heard the thudding of her own heart. She would hug Giovanni for no apparent reason.

By early May, Churchill declared that hostilities were at an end.

When the radio announced the welcome news, Maggie burst into Verdi's *Slave Chorus*. Giovanni joined in. They took the train and left for the convent where Patricia boarded, smothered her with kisses, and brought her home in a delirium of joy.

~ *Chapter 29* ~

Victory

VE DAY BROUGHT AN END TO AN ERA. The sound of music and firearms echoed in the streets, as partisans let off their rifles in the air and people danced in Milan's Cathedral Square. Bergamo feted too, though on a much smaller scale.

A bright future rose before Maggie, who lived across two continents where several major issues converged—her career, her family in Italy, and her family back in Australia. She wrote to her parents, hoping that, safely ensconced at Hobart, they were in the best of health.

Weeks later, she received a letter from Aunt Polly, informing her that both her parents had died in 1942. Maggie climbed the stairs, breathless and distraught, clutching the missive that had pierced her heart. The bitter gall of remorse for not being near them when they had passed away weighed her down. She moved around in a daze, remaining remote and abstracted like a dog gazing too long into a fire. Unlike Siegfried who forged the broken pieces of his sword together in Wagner's opera, she would never be able to restore her parents to life or see them again.

She paced the corridors of her mind and recalled all they had done for her—their words and gestures. Death, the inevitable end of everything, confronted her with irresistible force. *I would have been near them in their last days if I'd not gone to Milan but returned to Australia after my time with Calvé.*

Maggie wept on Giovanni's shoulder. 'One of my sisters should've written telling me of their illness.'

He put his arms around her. 'Think of what Italy was undergoing in 1942 and in 1943. It wasn't possible to have been at their bedside even if a letter succeeded in coming through.'

'We should have sent for them when my luck turned,' Maggie sobbed.

Giovanni drew Maggie to him and stroked her hair. '*Cara mia.* You cannot blame yourself for not being with them when they passed away. Besides, I don't think they'd have been better off here during the war.'

'You're right,' she said.

At nights, she lay in bed with Giovanni, but his touch aroused no feelings. When she looked back on the sensations Peter had stirred, she buried her face on her husband's chest and blushed with shame. *Disaster dodges my footsteps. There is nothing left for me.*

Maggie tried on one of her evening dresses. It hung like a nightgown. She tore it off and flung it on the floor, then collapsed on her bed, clutching her hair. Minutes passed. A gentle knock sounded on her door but, utterly exhausted, she did not move. For the last few years, all her energy had been expended on escaped prisoners-of-war and injured airmen. She had no reserves left.

The door opened and Patricia stepped in. *How young and fresh she looks. A mirror image of myself in my youth. If only I can start afresh.*

A look of concern clouded Patricia's face. 'Are you all right, Mama?'

Maggie opened her arms, and her daughter flew into them.

'I dreamed of the time we'd be together again. The nuns encouraged me to keep up my piano practice and I sang the songs you taught me… We're together now but I never hear you sing.'

'Your grandma and grandpa are dead, and I wasn't with them when they died. How can I ever forgive myself or sing again?'

'You can't do anything about what has passed, Mama. You still have us. Cheer up! We *need* you.'

'I'm so glad you escaped all the horrors of war, child. Glad you're too young to know anything about guilt and remorse.'

'The nuns always taught us to trust in the Lord.'

'Yes, darling. I was taught by nuns too. Time is a great healer. I'll get over this shortly.'

Giovanni applied for his old position at La Scala. He urged Maggie to keep up her singing practise, but she remained in a state of inertia. She knew she could not have coped without her husband and daughter, but the black dog of depression grimly hung on. A month later, Maggie's sister Kitty wrote. Four years her junior, she had been endowed with a lovely voice but had chosen love and marriage rather than a singing career.

Dearest Maggie,

We've been so anxious about you. Wonderful to know you're safe and sound. Still on rations here, but conditions in Europe must be far worse. I know you're trying to pick up the pieces but it's time to look ahead.

I think of you especially when I read about Marjorie Lawrence in the papers. She's also from Australia. I'm sure you've heard of her. She had polio in 1941. Despite her disability, she has continued to perform in a wheelchair. Your friend, Sir Thomas, referred to her as the world's greatest living dramatic soprano. Always remember that the voice is given to us by God, and we should not bury our talents.

Your affectionate sister,
Kitty.

PS Love from all of us down under. Aunt Polly has already given you the news, so I won't repeat them. No need to rake up old wounds.

Maggie read and re-read the letter. *My parents and, in particular my father, had always wished me to be a star. I will not fail them. Time to stop feeling sorry for myself.* She recalled that her colleagues had suffered far more than she had. Emma Calvé had died in unoccupied Southern France, on 6 January 1942, at a clinic at Montpellier. Just before the surrender of Italy, the prima donna Irene Minghini had lost her life in a bombing attack by the Allies. Ebe Stignani too had suffered when German officers occupied her villa and confiscated her grand piano. *At least I was able to sell my piano and I still have my husband and daughter.*

That night, when Maggie nestled against Giovanni, anxiety and guilt ebbed away and warmth flowed into her heart. She had continually developed her voice, realising that her lungs, vocal cords and abdominal muscles would not be as strong as formerly. I'll use singing as an escape from sorrow. *My career can serve as a balm to suffering.*

Soon after Kitty's letter, Maggie made a comeback, performing in Verdi's *Requiem* in 1945 at the *Teatro Lirico*. It now served as a temporary home of *La Scala*. The famed opera house stood scarred—a stark reminder of the war. Maggie bore the scars of hardship too, but just as the edifice would be rebuilt, she too would rise from the ashes like the proverbial phoenix. She sang the thunderbolt explosions of the *Dies Irae* and the hushed prayer of *Libera* with passion, imagining herself at her parents' funeral.

Riding on a wave of newfound excellence and pride, she drove herself unremittingly. July found her at Rome in *La Gioconda*, joining the firmament of stars—Ebe Stignani and Beniamino

Gigli. The following month, she opened Verona's post-war season with *Aida*. The curtains were clouds, and the rays of light, haloes. The flute was the murmur of fountains and the warbling of birds. The soothing melodies cast off her sorrows, and she vibrated with joy as the bows of the violin were drawn over her nerves like a healing wand.

The theatre rang with cheers. *How wonderful to be back in harness again. I miss Patricia, but I have devoted myself solely to her during her babyhood and early years. She must continue her education. She must choose which path she wishes to follow. Will she be an opera star or follow Kitty's footsteps? I tried to juggle both career and marriage. I have no regrets for my choice… but if only I was with my parents when they died.*

In 1947, Maggie joined the Glyndebourne Opera at the first Edinburgh International Festival. It included classical music and international theatre production. Giovanni had resigned from his position at *La Scala* and become her business manager. They boarded the apple-green *Flying Scotsman* to Edinburgh, leaving battle-scarred London behind them. The train passed through York and the spectacular scenery rushed past. Soon, the Lowlands emerged.

Edinburgh Castle towered above sheer cliffs and stared down at them as they approached the city. A smile played around Giovanni's lips as he gazed upwards at the magnificent edifice. His cheekbones stood out. Below them were depressions like saucers. 'We'll have a great time here, *cara mia*,' he said, a gleam in his eyes.

Maggie's heart ached for him, but she caught his enthusiasm.

Crowds milled around the station platform, stifling Maggie with the odour of unwashed bodies, but the island of flowers outside Edinburgh Station wafted a clean, fresh perfume. Maggie and Giovanni followed the porter and joined the queue for a taxi. *La*

Scala and many other theatres had been razed to the ground after the war, so the entertainment world converged upon the unscarred city of Edinburgh. Unlike the war-torn cities of Italy and London with their crumpled buildings and huge craters, a magical aura surrounded the Scottish capital.

Maggie scrutinised the crowds. 'Our Glyndebourne group has to squeeze in at the King's theatre. I wonder how the others are coping.'

'The receptionist said that all accommodation is fully booked,' Giovanni replied. 'Latecomers have had to stay at places further out.'

Someone from the crowd waved at them, and Giovanni lifted his hat in acknowledgment.

'I never expected to find so many famous stars in just one area,' Maggie said.

Giovanni jerked his head towards two actors. 'There go Trevor Howard and Alec Guinness.'

Maggie glanced at the programme she held. 'They'll be performing in *The Taming of the Shrew* and *Richard II* with London's Old Vic Theatre Company. Must not miss the performance. I adore Shakespeare.'

'Of course, *cara mia*. Another passion we share.'

A little later, Margot Fonteyn passed them, tripping lightly on the pavement. Maggie squeezed Giovanni's arm. 'Fonteyn is performing *The Sleeping Beauty* in Sadler's Wells ballet. Must get a couple of tickets for the show.'

'Thought you'd say that. Anywhere else you'd like to go?'

'Cannot miss a thing.' She was as eager as a young child visiting a fair. And for the first time in a long while, her heart dared to soar again.

A spirit of gaiety prevailed. The government still rationed petrol and food, but gone were the days of semi-starvation and fear. Baskets of geraniums hung from lampposts; tramcars rattled along with tiny Union Jacks trailing from their electric arms. Crowds filled the streets and gardens. The famous floral clock of forget-me-nots spelled out the names of Tchaikovsky and Beethoven and ticked away for all to admire.

Helmeted policemen wearing snowy white gloves, directed crowds to keep moving. To the north lay the new town. The Princes Street Gardens separated the two towns. A road known as the Royal Mile, connected the Castle Rock to Holyrood Palace.

Maggie glanced up at the ramparts silhouetted against a star-studded sky. 'It's a shame the flood-lights were banned at the last moment. The castle would have looked so wonderful with all the lights on.'

'Government officials think it's wasteful because there's still a shortage of coal and not enough electricity,' Giovanni said, spreading out his arms.

In an ecstasy of excitement, Maggie burst out, 'I'll never forget today, darling.'

He dropped a kiss on her lips. 'Just wait until the festival commences tomorrow.'

In the following weeks, Maggie had a heavy schedule. On Sunday 24, the Edinburgh Festival made a rousing start with *L'Ochestre Colonne* of Paris playing the English and French National Anthems. Maggie starred as Lady Macbeth with Valentino in the Ebert production of *Macbeth*. She stepped out on stage and scanned the faces of dignitaries in the front row. Giovanni, a few rows further back, smiled at her.

Now is my chance to enchant the audience. Maggie thought of all those who had helped her in her career and imbued with their spirit and enthusiasm, she sang as she had never done before.

She excelled as the tragic queen in *Macbeth*, and the audience of nearly three thousand gave a resounding response. A flood of joy engulfed her. She kept a souvenir programme of the First

International Festival of Music and Drama and put it away with her reviews. Then she posted one to her daughter and to each of her aunts and her three sisters in Australia. She had finally made an impression on England.

'The press has portrayed you as leaping fearlessly into the top register, your domination of ensembles complete. They also say that your voice rode effortlessly over orchestra and chorus.' Giovanni waved the newspaper at her.

Maggie licked her lips and thanked the Lord for helping her come thus far.

At dinner the following evening, Maggie picked up a copy of the *Manchester Evening News*. After perusing the reviews of *Macbeth*, she read out some snippets to Giovanni as he sipped his cup of coffee. 'This lady says the city is a mixture of Rome and Manchester, seasoned with a drop of Paris and a dash of Budapest.'

He slapped his thigh and laughed. 'Sounds like an appetising dish.'

'Accommodation is a major problem and private houses have offered visitors a spare bed or a sofa,' she continued. 'Last night's performance filled Usher Hall. At the end, the entire audience applauded for about five minutes, stamping their feet and crying for more.'

'The conductor, Paul Paray, was remarkable,' Giovanni said.' I admired his vitality and swift changes of mood. You'd scarcely believe they'd flown to Paris from Rio de Janeiro only five days ago.'

Maggie placed a hand to her chest. 'It would have been such a long and tiring trip to Edinburgh.'

The Edinburgh Festival was a smashing success. In the afternoons, kilted soldiers marched down from the castle to dance reels. For five hours each evening, the British Broadcasting Corporation broadcast the festival live.

After the festival, the BBC insisted on recording Maggie's sleepwalking scene, but by then she was tired and stressed. 'What do you think I should do?' she asked Giovanni. 'I'm utterly exhausted.

The privations of war and my heavy schedule haven't done much for my health, and age is against me.'

She had been working relentlessly and was now fifty-six. Maggie picked up a newspaper cutting in which her drooping eyelids and haughty looks had been accentuated. 'Look at me. My face seems to be much longer than before.'

'But, *cara mia*, the BBC only wishes to record your *voice.*'

She tossed her head. 'The muscles of my larynx tighten up when I'm stressed and I'm not always able to take certain notes.'

He swung her around to face him and gazed into her eyes. 'Explain the situation to Sir Thomas. Rosa Ponsella, too, had problems. I clearly remember her trouble with high Cs, but everyone still loved her.'

'Sir Thomas is aware of my condition.'

'Then, that settles things.'

Maggie tried to calm down, but at the back of her mind a warning voice whispered that this was only the beginning of the end.

~ Chapter 30 ~

The Cross and the Crown

MAGGIE FOLLOWED HER HUSBAND'S ADVICE and told Sir Thomas Beecham about her problem of not managing certain notes when stressed. He listened intently, then lightly touched her shoulder. 'Don't worry. I'll get the staff to phone Dorothy Dobson to fill in a few notes for you.'

Dobson was a twenty-six-year-old soprano who had just given birth, and unable to resume her singing career at this stage, she was willing to earn some easy money.

On the day of the recording, Maggie's voice resonated with the sleepwalking scene, but remained silent for the last three notes, as arranged. Dobson trilled them—F, A flat and top D flat. She received five guineas and agreed never to speak of the arrangement.

'Thank you, Sir Thomas, for being so understanding,' Maggie said after the singer left.

'It's all right. You need to relax. You've been through a tough time.'

Maggie never imagined the anguish those three little notes were to cause her. Dorothy Dobson kept her word and said nothing, but one of the musicians whispered it to a friend who sold the news to the *Daily Express*.

Eight months later, in the first week of October 1948, the whole of London came to know of the substitution. The scandal soon crossed the Atlantic and raised a storm of protest. Newspapers questioned whether a ghost had stood in the wings and sung the same F, A flat and top D flat for her at the Edinburgh Festival.

A reviewer wrote, 'From now on, I shall have the gravest suspicions when sopranos sing their top notes.'

At first, Maggie was merely indignant and complained to Giovanni. 'Rosa Ponselle has always been praised for the richness and depth of her voice, but the rich darkness only seems to have bolstered her name.'

'True,' he agreed. 'Ponsella transposed the high Cs down to a B in *Norma*. In *La Traviata*, she had her *Sempre Libra* all reduced by a whole tone because she couldn't manage the high Cs.'

'It's not fair. The press has ruined my hard-earned reputation. Yet it praises Ponsella and compares her singing to port wine and dark chocolate. The critics never crucify her.'

Journalists hounded Maggie with phone calls until she finally declared she could take no more. A singer needed firm muscles, strong lungs and abundant energy but Maggie's vocal cords were taut like a strained bow. Eyes swollen from weeping, she retired to bed and refused to leave it. It was all too much for her. She no longer felt strong enough to withstand the tide of events. She had been through a stormy life. Now, she could no longer put up with this deluge. She looked away from Giovanni, the shadow of a haggard smile on her face.

He handed her a glass of chianti. 'Come, *cara mia*. We'll return to Milan.'

Italy welcomed Maggie back. She sang Verdi's *Requiem* at the Palazzo Ducale in Genoa and her drooping spirits revived. But the British press would not leave her alone and kept the phones hot. Unable to tolerate their biting sarcasm and taunting barbs, Maggie refused to answer their calls.

Giovanni picked up the receiver. 'My wife is indisposed.' When the phone kept ringing, he took it off the hook.

The Dorothy Dobson incident left Maggie arrogant and aggressive—a cover-up for her anxiety. When the British press asked to speak to her, she faced them like a caged tigress. Fully recovered from the onslaught of their barbed arrows, Maggie clutched the phone and tilted her head back.

She inhaled a deep breath before answering. 'I assure you I can *sing* a D flat, but I am sometimes under such emotion that it's a help if someone sings it for me.' She slammed the receiver down.

'I'm taking you back to face the Londoners, *cara mia,*' Giovanni said. 'You must return and redeem your good name.'

She gritted her teeth, determined to go down fighting. 'Yes, I will not end my career like an injured beast licking its wounds in a cave.'

Once back in London, Maggie consulted a specialist about her changed looks. 'Due to facial muscle hyperactivity and respiratory hyper-function, it is common for the mandible, maxilla and face to lengthen in professional singers,' he said. 'The tone of most menopausal singers also darkens and settles in a lower placement as they mature.'

Knowing there was nothing she could do about her appearance, Maggie concentrated on her singing. With her husband beside her as designer and stage director, she performed to a capacity audience at the Cambridge Theatre in London. Violins shrilled and cornets trumpeted. Maggie's voice trilled out—strong and vibrant. Cool and rippling.

After she had taken her bows, Giovanni rushed into his wife's dressing room and grabbed her hand. 'Come quickly. The Queen wishes to meet you.'

Maggie turned bright red, followed him in a trance, and gave a deep curtsey to the Queen, who complimented her on her performance. After Her Majesty had left, Maggie clutched Giovanni and sank into a chair, dizzy with joy. Never had she dreamed of this. Never had her heart pounded so painfully. Never had she felt so exalted.

Her Majesty's endorsement erased all the damage to Maggie's reputation. When news of the royal visit to Margherita Grandi got around, critics praised Maggie for her solo, *Visi D'Arti*, and described her singing as rich and flexible. Maggie formed her hands into a steeple and faced reporters, oozing with newfound energy and cheerfulness. She spoke in a steady, low-pitched voice.

Soon after, she appeared regularly for the new London Opera Company at the Stoll and Cambridge Theatres in London and played Donna Anna in Mozart's *Don Giovanni*. Ever since *Don Giovanni's* world première in the 18th century, opera companies have found it tricky to cast the piece's main female protagonist, Donna Anna, and Maggie was thrilled at having been given the opportunity to tackle the role. Mozart expresses the different sides of her character in two vastly different arias: the first extremely dramatic and the second ending in a fiendish coloratura. Only a dramatic soprano who is also able to sing with the lightness and flexibility of a bel canto singer, can do justice to both the drama and the vocal gymnastics. Thanks to Madame Marchesi's coaching, she was capable of both.

In *Don Giovanni*, Mozart wrote three important soprano roles—Donna Anna, Donna Elvira and Zerlina—and each must sound distinct from the other two. Donna Anna's tessitura is extremely high. She sings between D and F at the top of the stave all night. Maggie excelled herself.

When Maggie took the leading role in *Tosca* with its pieces of iconic music, she faced her audience with blazing eyes. *Tosca's* score is full of musical motifs that represent different characters and ideas, and Maggie sang the famous soprano aria *Vissi d'arte* with verve.

Her triumph was such that two years after the First Edinburgh Festival, Maggie performed in the next festival as Amelia in Verdi's *Un Ballo in Maschera,* a masterpiece of musical drama with relatively short arias. Unlike Verdi's other operas, it contains humour, both light-hearted and sardonic, in a tragic context. Verdi used a real-life event to intensify the emotional impact of his music and achieved the perfect marriage between the characters' melodies and the meaning of their words in the duet, *Teco io sto*, sung by Gustav and Amelia. Maggie sang with passion and intensity and her rich soprano voice soared in her role as Amelia.

'This time, the castle, now flood-lit at nights, looks even grander than in 1947,' Maggie said that night, as she lay contently in Giovanni's arms.

In October 1949, Maggie finally made her debut at Covent Garden, creating the role of Diana in Bliss's *Olympians*. She lingered on with Giovanni after the celebratory dinner was over. 'I had so longed to make my debut here,' she recalled.

'Now you've done it.' He raised her right hand to his lips.

She wiped the tears from her eyes. 'Thanks to you.'

'And your perseverance.'

In the beginning, Giovanni's love had intoxicated her, and she had thought of nothing else. Now he was also her manager and mentor and husband and lover.

Maggie followed up her success with five performances of Verdi's *Il Trovatore*, a masterpiece of romance and complexity. Her appearance at Glyndebourne provoked extraordinary reviews. Critics billed her as incomparable.

'She is magnificently voiced,' the *Sunday Times* wrote. 'It was thrilling to hear those notes rolling out with such power and freedom.'

Maggie had sought this acclaim ever since her graduation from the London College of Music, and the accolades soothed her battered and worn-out soul like balm. She walked with fluid movements and experienced a feeling of weightlessness—the joy of being truly fulfilled. Basking in her triumph, she thanked the Lord.

Maggie made her stage farewell in Puccini's *Tosca* at Covent Garden on 19 November 1951. A rolling thunder of applause exploded as the exhilarating finale of *Tosca* ended. She took her bows before gliding off to the seclusion of her dressing room; her face flushed, and her forehead wet with beads of perspiration. She sipped a glass of wine to still her racing heart.

These precious moments away from the crowds were her own. She reclined on the settee for the last time and the whole of her life came flooding back. Now past her fifty-ninth birthday, the beauty of her youth was overtaken by her maturity, and an army of creases forged their way across her features.

Like Nellie Melba before her, she had negotiated the reefs of criticism from the press but had risen undaunted. Her ultimate triumph had come later than anticipated, but she had skilfully manoeuvred her little barque through the stormy sea of life.

A soprano who possessed a powerful voice and a temperament to match, she was an impressive singer, concerned with raw emotions rather than conventionally sweet sounds. Misfortune had blotted the pages of her life. She had survived two world wars.

She had struggled against adversity, but she had learned how to combine love, marriage, and career. She had reclaimed so many lost years and had continued to perform even beyond her prime.

Despite all obstacles, Maggie had arrived just short of the pinnacle and attained her dream. Maggie concluded her career as a queen of tragedy, and departed as Tosca, leaving behind an adoring audience. Margherita Grandi was not a meteor that left no trace in the sky. She was a star. A star—bright and constant. A star that shone, not only in Europe, but in the whole of the northern hemisphere.

~ Author's Bio ~

Hazel Barker fled from Mandalay, Burma, before the Junta stopped her bid for freedom. She sought refuge in Perth, where her studies at the University of Western Australia gave her a new lease of life.

She met Colin within a few years after her arrival in Australia. They married after a whirlwind romance and moved to Canberra where they lived for fifteen years before finally making a home in the Redlands.

Writing takes up most of her retired life with stories that stimulate readers. Stories of suffering under the Japanese regime in World War II. Stories of life under the Burmese Junta. Stories stranger than fiction, but always full of hope, not despair.

Hazel Barker writes memoirs and historical fiction. Her short story *Hunger* was published in the 2013 Redlitzer Anthology, by the Redland City Council Libraries. It was the beginning of her writing career. She has won awards along this journey, both at home and abroad.

For more information look up:
http://hazelmbarker.wordpress.com

**Hazel's books are available from Amazon
and other online bookstores.**

www.ingramcontent.com/pod-product-compliance
Lightning Source LLC
Chambersburg PA
CBHW070623170726
48291CB00003B/854